GARMENT
OF PRAISE

GARMENT
OF PRAISE

AN AMISH ROMANCE

NEW DIRECTIONS
BOOK THREE

LINDA BYLER

New York, New York

GARMENT OF PRAISE

Good Books books may be purchased in bulk at special discounts for sales promotion, corporate gifts, fund-raising, or educational purposes. Special editions can also be created to specifications. For details, contact the Special Sales Department, Good Books, 307 West 36th Street, 11th Floor, New York, NY 10018 or info@skyhorsepublishing.com.

Good Books is an imprint of Skyhorse Publishing, Inc.®, a Delaware corporation.

Visit our website at www.goodbooks.com.
Please follow our publisher Tony Lyons on Instagram @tonylyonsisuncertain.

10 9 8 7 6 5 4 3 2 1

Library of Congress Cataloging-in-Publication Data

Names: Byler, Linda, author.
Title: Garment of praise / Linda Byler.
Description: New York, New York : Good Books, 2024. | Series: New directions ; book 3 | Summary: "The final book in the New Directions series delves into the complexities of a blended Amish family"-- Provided by publisher.
Identifiers: LCCN 2023041723 (print) | LCCN 2023041724 (ebook) | ISBN 9781680999068 (paperback) | ISBN 9781680999129 (epub)
Subjects: LCGFT: Christian fiction. | Novels.
Classification: LCC PS3602.Y53 G37 2024 (print) | LCC PS3602.Y53 (ebook) | DDC 813/.6--dc23/eng/20230929
LC record available at https://lccn.loc.gov/2023041723
LC ebook record available at https://lccn.loc.gov/2023041724
Print ISBN: 978-1-68099-906-8
eBook ISBN: 978-1-68099-912-9

Cover design by Godfredson Design

Printed in the United States of America

GARMENT
OF PRAISE

CHAPTER 1

TITUS MILLER SURVEYED THE SCENE BEFORE HIM, TUGGED AT HIS work gloves, and wished he were anywhere but here. He lifted his Carhartt beanie, ran a hand through his thick, wavy hair, and wondered again how his father could reasonably justify the felling of these magnificent trees.

Chainsaws whined, the sound of destruction and death to a haven for birds and small creatures, the depletion of life-giving, earth-saving oxygen.

The mountain stretched beyond the logging area, untouched, amazing in its height and beauty, the sky above it a brilliant blue with scudding white clouds hurrying before the stiff gale.

He'd given in to his father's pleading to learn the trade, to accompany him to the foot of the Bighorn Mountains and areas beyond, some of them a hundred or more miles away from the small Amish settlement in the rural areas of Wyoming.

He'd worked on local ranches, suffered through his father's marriage to Susan Lapp from Pennsylvania, taken life lessons from his teacher, Darlene Yoder, and had no interest in social gatherings or girls. At almost twenty years of age, he'd finally agreed to take part in his father's logging business, and here he was, reeling from the onslaught of negative emotion yet again.

It was the trees, the natural beauty of them, that put a lump in his throat, made him feel like screaming at his father to stop. Stop the madness. But he knew there would always be a demand for lumber, the building, the construction of new homes, garages, pole sheds, and so many numerous uses all across the United States.

And so he climbed into the skidder, the huge piece of equipment that was indispensable to every logging project. Skidding the logs meant dragging or hauling them from the cutting area to the landing, an area filled with cut trees. As he worked the controls, steered the giant wheels in the general direction of the whining saws, he swallowed his resentment yet again, leaving a sour taste in his mouth.

He watched his father make an expert undercut in the side of the tree that was to fall to the ground, then swing his massive chainsaw to the opposite side to begin the job of felling it. His thick shoulders heaved, his coat torn at the seams from hours of cutting. His massive hands gripped the saw as if it were a spoon or a fork. His feet were planted in just the right position, his thick legs all the support he needed.

Titus knew the tree would crash to earth in the exact spot his father wanted, before his employee, Jason Luhrs, would begin the work of sawing limbs, preparing it for Titus to haul away.

Over and over, his father had explained forestry to him, trying to get Titus to see the beauty of taking out the mature trees, leaving the saplings, replanting, sowing grass to eliminate erosion, but he remained obstinate in his own opinion. He could butter him up all he wanted, he was still destroying natural habitat for owls and ravens, songbirds, chipmunks, and squirrels. Every creature of the forest he knew would be misplaced, driven out of their home by man's greed for lumber.

And so his days were spent, performing his duties well on the outside, resentment eating away on the inside.

SUSAN SIGHED AS she turned the chicken in the cast iron pan. Too dark. Isaac would notice. Well, nothing to be done about that now.

It was too hot in the house, as usual. That woodstove in the basement was way too big, and burned like a roaring monster all winter long, and that was all there was to it. She'd fussed about it for a few years now, but Isaac turned a deaf ear every time she mentioned it.

She lifted the chicken—the burnt pieces irritating her—and plopped it on a foil-lined pan, shoved it into the oven, banging the door to make herself feel better. Then she moved to the window above the sink, snapped the lock and wound the lever furiously, basking in the cold air of early winter.

The Bighorn Mountains in the background gave her the usual sense of peace, the momentary pause she so badly needed.

Her eyes took in the snow-tipped peaks, the lines creating dark and light, the ridges cascading vertically along the mountains' sides. She felt the presence of a higher power, the Creator who had designed all things, including her love for Isaac, and the willingness to join him in Wyoming, to be a mother of his two children, and to have children with him.

On some days, none of it was easy.

Titus was the one who could wreck her days as thoroughly as a fast-moving tornado, leaving everything she had ever built in shambles.

She'd tried everything, including taking his side as a protection against the strong will of his father, keeping the logging at bay.

She didn't admonish or wheedle, never tried to force him to change, always staying low key, without ruffling feathers. But lately, she picked up an even greater resentment from him, a disapproval of everything she said or did. She felt she was walking a narrow path along the side of a steep cliff, desperately watching every step she made in order to clear up his bad attitude.

She jumped when she heard the mudroom door open. Lost in her reverie, she'd failed to hear the throbbing of a diesel engine, heralding her husband's return. A cry from the bedroom, then a distinct wail.

Thayer.

At two years old, he was old enough to climb off his youth bed and make his way out to the kitchen, but he preferred the luxury of having his mother come to him, hugging and kissing, showering him with her love. It was so easy, this natural biological love for the children you had borne yourself, flesh of your flesh, and all that.

There is a special place in every mother's heart for her children. No greater truth had ever been instilled in her own heart, but this truth often served the purpose of filling her uncomfortably with guilt for the irritation she felt toward Titus.

Thayer was sitting up in the middle of his little bed, his dark hair matted, a distinct odor giving away the fact he was soaking wet, as was the clean bedding she'd put on yesterday.

She reached for him, smoothed his hair, and kissed his cheek, carrying him by his armpits to the bathroom, quietly telling him he'd need a change of clean clothes. Should have taken him before his nap, but it was too late now.

"Hey!"

Isaac, yelling from the kitchen.

"In here," she called.

A shadow filled the door.

"Hey, little man!"

She drew up the suspenders, tucked his shirttail into the elastic waistband, and got up from her knees. She gave him a small shove in the direction of his father and turned to take the wet clothing to the wringer washer in the mudroom, without meeting Isaac's eyes. She didn't feel like greeting that overabundance of enthusiasm shining from him, that level of clear-eyed happiness and overflow of the great outdoors, the invigoration of fresh air and hard work. Did he even care that she was stuck in this overheated house with the little ones all day?

She heard footsteps behind her as she walked through the kitchen, but made no move to start a conversation. Titus was slouched in a chair, his face impassive, his blond hair tousled.

"Hey, Titus," she managed.

"Hey."

"How was your day?" Isaac asked her in his booming, much too loud voice carrying over from his day of logging.

"Good. A day at home with the children."

"That's good," he remarked, watching her face.

Good. Yes. Everything is always good. It's the way we live, our lives, skimming the froth over the top and thinking it's great, afraid to dig deeper and see the true bitterness of the bottom of the glass.

"Supper ready?"

"Not for another hour. Sorry. I was trying to finish Kayla's dress."

"It's okay. I need to spend time in the barn anyway. You coming, Titus?"

They shrugged back into their coats and went back outside.

"Mom?"

Kayla stood in the doorway, a petite little girl of four, her brown hair neatly braided, her large green eyes opened wide, her eyebrows lifted.

"Thayer is getting my Play-Doh."

Susan hurried to remedy the situation, shaking her head when Kayla told her he had some in his mouth.

"Thayer, no. Do not eat this. No. It's not good for you."

Thayer's face scrunched into a grimace, and howls of indignation erupted, setting Susan's teeth on edge. Burnt chicken, wet bedding, Play-Doh ingested, time for supper and no potatoes peeled.

Oh, motherhood, where is thy joy? she thought. Someone should have warned her the minute she even thought of coming to Wyoming, thousands of miles from her family, to a man she most certainly had not known well enough to marry.

She set Thayer on his high chair, scattered a few Cheerios on the tray, filled a sippy cup with apple juice, and turned to peel potatoes. If they didn't eat so much, she'd have a break sometimes, but you'd think they hadn't eaten for a week when they came home from work.

The mudroom door opened again, and Sharon walked in, her face red with exertion, her breath coming in gasps.

"Whew! Glad to be home. That wind!"

"It's too far on your bike, Sharon. I wish you'd let Lucille drive you home."

"No, Mom. I love biking."

"I know you do."

Susan turned to look at her twelve-year-old, a happy, energetic girl who would soon have her thirteenth birthday, loving school and her friends, having spent time with her best friend Rhoda after school. She was the opposite of Titus, her carefree nature a blessing for a step-mother. She loved her as if she were her own, which she was, though she hadn't birthed her. She and Titus were both her own and had been since she married their father, and yet it was so much easier to feel it with Sharon.

"Mom, Rhoda's Mom made chocolate cupcakes with cream cheese icing in the middle. Like, down in. On top, there was chocolate icing with tiny little chocolate chips. The best thing ever. Hey there, little Thayer honey. Hi! Give me a Cheerio. Come on. Just one."

Thayer shook his head, his mouth wide open, saying, "No, no. Mine."

Susan put the potatoes on to boil, smoothed a hand over her apron, and smiled at Sharon.

"They sound good. What else did you have?"

"Just them. We were working on turkeys for Teacher Darlene. They're made from paper plates, but we're using real turkey feathers. You have to come visit school, so you can see how neat they are."

"I bet."

"Where's Dad?"

"He's in the barn."

Which was where Sharon would be as soon as possible, Susan thought, as she ran hot water over a Zip-loc bag of frozen corn.

She watched her race to the barn, throw the door open, and disappear, leaving Susan alone with her thoughts. As she made gravy and shredded cabbage for coleslaw, she thought she might need to call Kate, her sister who was married to Levi Yoder now, the only man Susan had thought she could ever love. Well, that certainly hadn't worked out well, and most of the time she was relieved. God surely did work in mysterious ways, and Kate was designed to be a true helpmeet to a man who had been unfaithful to Susan. She felt as if she could use a large dose of Kate's sweetness, her absolute devotion to Levi.

Isaac was a good husband and father, just an absent one, and one who became easily self-absorbed, talking only of himself and his logging enterprise.

When they all clattered through the door again, Susan was dishing out the buttery mashed potatoes, pouring gravy, the kitchen warm and inviting.

"How come that window's open?" Isaac asked.

"Guess why."

Her tone was more disgruntled than she meant it to be, so she quickly looked at Isaac and smiled. He met her eyes and raised his eyebrows, then burst out laughing.

"Don't put so much wood on the fire," he shouted.

She swallowed a surly comeback.

She watched the men pile on the mashed potatoes, dump copious amounts of gravy. Titus's plate was running over, so he drew a finger through his potatoes to keep the gravy from spilling, then licked it off. Susan opened her mouth, then closed it, thought of walking the slippery path along the cliffside. She glanced at Isaac, saw he hadn't noticed.

"Mm, crispy chicken," Sharon trilled.

"Very crispy," Isaac mumbled around a mouthful of potato.

"You say one word about this supper and I'm getting out the cast iron frying pan, and it won't be to fry more chicken, either," she said, her voice rising slightly.

Isaac, good natured as always, threw back his head, opened his mouth, and guffawed. Titus's mouth twitched. Susan glared as Sharon's laugh mingled with her father's.

"Sorry, my dear. It's delicious. Just a little darker than normal," Isaac said, wiping his eyes with his napkin.

"Yeah, well, that's what happens when you marry a girl from Pennsylvania. I have to learn how to make an apron for Kayla. Nothing went right. They're not like ours at all. I ruined one and the second one doesn't look promising."

Titus busied himself removing the skin from his chicken. He leveled a look at her and told her he was sorry they were such a burden.

"You're not, Titus. I was just saying."

The snort was accompanied by flashing eyes, a taunt, a look that sent her sliding down into her chair only a bit.

"You wish you'd never met us," he finished.

"Titus, that's enough."

Sharon looked at her plate, choked on her chicken, picked up her water glass, and took a swallow.

The remainder of the meal was stiff, with only the scraping of utensils, the polite remarks about the weather. After the dishes were done and the children bathed and put to bed, Susan swept the kitchen and enjoyed a long, hot bath, a few drops of lavender oil and a eucalyptus candle burning on the ledge. She fully expected Isaac to be snoring in his favorite chair, but was surprised to see him awake, sitting on the couch as if ready to flee at a moment's notice.

"You're awake."

More a question than a statement.

"You're worrying me, Susan."

Straight to the point, as always.

She sighed, sat beside him. Keeping her distance, her arms wrapped around herself. This was the part about marriage she had not been quite able to comprehend, even now. The stuff that wedged its way between them. Metaphorical trash. Neglect, bad table manners, resentment, caring only for oneself and not for the other, control, all these stupid niggling little things that turned into a mountain, making it hard to be open and honest and vulnerable to each other. It was far easier to go to bed, turn your back, to hang onto whatever wrong had been done at the time, than to bring it out in the open and risk appearing foolish and needy.

"I can't see why."

"You didn't like me today when I got home from work."

"Yes I did."

"Huh-uh. You wouldn't even look at me."

"But . . ."

"Tell me."

"It's too stupid."

"Nothing is stupid if it comes between us."

"You're just so away all the time. And when you're home you don't notice me or anything. You don't talk. It's the kids, supper, the horses, and asleep on your chair."

"You don't want to hear what I have to say."

"But you have nothing to say. Nothing except trees, trucks, skidders, and chainsaws. The occasional raccoon."

He chuckled.

"Come here."

"No."

"Susan, I apologize, okay? Men just aren't worth much, right?"

"You said it."

"I know I tend to be selfish, and I forget the sacrifice you made coming out here, away from family. And yes, I do not appreciate that the way I should. So, if you have a bad day, I'm probably the last person on earth you want to see coming through that door."

"That's not true."

"It was tonight."

She knew he was right. All day, she'd been collecting hard feelings like pieces of trash, placing them conveniently in a self-made barrier so that when he came home, she could not see clearly over the pile of self-pity and ill feelings harbored in her subconscious. In her mind, she blamed Isaac and all the western *ordnung* (rules) for the disastrous apron. Even the burnt chicken was a direct result of living in Wyoming, somehow. Now she thought of Isaac—loud, happy, fulfilled by a day's work—coming home to a sniveling wife thoroughly exhausted by her day of accumulating a hefty barricade of useless garbage.

Slowly, the moisture collected in the corners of her eyes as the full realization mushroomed in her mind. It wasn't Isaac at all, but her own simmering thoughts, the cauldron of self-pity that had been kept on the back burner until she chose to light the fire of selfishness beneath it.

She bent her head, picked at a loose thread on her robe.

"Why don't you greet me with the same glad look I used to get?" Isaac asked gently.

"Sometimes I'm mad at you, blaming you for certain things."

"I know that. And I'm asking how I can make it better."

She did not know how to answer. What was it that lacked in their union? Where had the excitement, the thrill of his love, actually gone?

"You could start by caring about me. Do you even know what I do in a day? Do you care if I freeze my fingers hanging out your laundry? Your shorts?"

She didn't want to laugh, but an explosive sound emerged from her mouth, which she tried to stifle with her hand. He reached over to take it away, and she burst out laughing, becoming quite hysterical.

"I hang your big shorts on the line in the freezing, never-ending Wyoming winter air, and I want to go back home and let my mother do the washing. And I pity myself stuck away on Piney Road in a big, beautiful log house that I should appreciate and I don't."

She was crying now, her nose swollen and colored, her mouth loose and wobbling.

"I had two babies and my stomach feels like bread dough and Titus hates me most of the time. I have to live with the ghosts of his hatred and disapproval, and you don't even notice. Or else you stick up for him instead of me, as if I'm the one to blame."

The spigot had opened now, and there was no stopping. She brought out every piece of trash and together, they examined it, piece by piece.

Ashamed of her pettiness, her wallowing in self-inflicted martyr-dom, her words dwindled to nothing, afraid to face the denial in his eyes.

The flapper on the draft of the woodstove made a metallic jingling sound as they sat in silence, the wind moaning around the corners of the hose. Titus's feet hit the floor upstairs as he got out of bed to close the window, which he usually left cracked open a few inches.

Susan could only follow the pattern of the braided rug in front of the couch, listen to the clock's ticking, and wait for the outburst from

Isaac she knew she deserved. She waited when he got up from the couch and walked over to the triple windows that looked out over the front yard and the driveway. For a long time, he stood, his back to her as he gazed into the dark night.

When he turned, his voice was broken with emotion.

"Tell me, Susan, do you ever regret your decision to take me as your husband?"

"No. Not that part. No, of course not. I just wish I could know the really hard parts would be . . . more bearable."

"What are the hard parts?"

"Living so far away from my family and being a stepmother to Titus."

"Is it so very hard?"

"Titus is, yes. Living here is only sometimes, when other circumstances get me down and any other tiny thing sends me straight over the edge. But Titus. . . He hates me, Isaac."

"Not hate. That is a very strong word. He resents you, taking the place of his mother, but . . ."

"No, Isaac. He lives to make my life miserable. He's jealous to the point he'd do just about anything to come between us. You know this is true."

"Ach, Susan. I want to tell you this isn't true, but I know it is. But he doesn't like me, either. I don't know what it is. At work, he doesn't speak to me, simply drives the skidder around, hooking and unhooking chains on the logs, ignoring everyone. Jase says he needs a good whop up along the head."

"I don't know what he needs," Susan said in a quiet, miserable voice.

"I'm sorry."

"It's not your fault, Isaac. I don't think it's anyone's. He's simply a child who is smart, who loved his natural mother, was devastated by her death, and has no intentions of accepting a substitute. Maybe we both don't realize how very hard his life has been, accepting the death of his mother, and then me, the unwelcome imposter."

"But he has to learn to give in to life's hurdles. We can't smooth every bump in the road for him. He has to do the work himself."

"Isaac, have you ever considered counseling for him?"

"No. I wouldn't know where to send him."

He sat down beside her, and she lay her head on his shoulder. He put an arm around her and drew her close, then bent to kiss her forehead.

"I'm glad you married me, though I'm sorry it's so hard." he said. "I have no idea what I could possibly have done without you. When I think back to the times when I was alone with the children, it was incredibly hard. And I know I failed Titus many times. But like you said, he is old enough now that he needs to do some of the work himself. Prayer goes a long way, and I know I lack in that area."

Susan put both arms around his waist and marveled again at the solid bulk of him.

"We have to work on our relationship with each other, and with Titus."

"Pray about it and leave it to God. He can do what we can't, which is take away the bitterness and create a clean heart."

And so they prayed together, side by side. Kneeling on the braided rug by the couch, tender prayers of mercy, asking for guidance and love for Titus, who by all appearances needed divine intervention.

UPSTAIRS, TITUS HEARD the low murmur of voices, figured they were discussing him again. Well, they should. His father gave him no reason to stay, and at twenty-one he'd be gone, free to carve out the perfect niche for himself. He'd find a job on one of the big spreads in Montana, ride the range, and live the way he wanted.

That was the thing he hated most about being Amish. You were placed in the same stupid notch your father chewed out of life, his being the murder of trees. Titus had no intention of turning into a logger, or marrying an Amish girl. Every one of them was the same— silly, simpering, mocking him in their sly way. He couldn't stand any of them.

Well, maybe that Trisha, or her sister Millie. They were good riders, the best riders he'd ever seen. But he was sure they'd never look at someone like him, so there was no use sticking around. Another nine months and his twenty-first birthday would be here, and then his dad and Susan would have no reason to sit in the living room planning his future, figuring out the best way to convert him into their righteous little lives.

It was only the memory of his late mother that placed question marks around his way of thinking. He knew his attitude would pain her, and that made his heart tighten up. But what was he to do?

I want to be too wild, Mom.

CHAPTER 2

Titus watched Isaac wolf down two ham and cheese sandwiches, perched on a log like some oversized hawk, even his nose reminding him of the curved bill of a red-tailed. Always in a hurry, as if the next dollar would run away if he didn't get back to work. Titus felt a need to sit on the ground and lean back against the log, cross his hands over his stomach, and close his eyes, a blissful smile on his lips, to see how irritated his father would become.

Things had started off well enough in the morning, with Isaac saying Susan was sleeping in, they'd been up late, so they'd stop at Cross Point for a breakfast sandwich and to buy their lunch. He had a happy smile and a soft look on his face, which meant something had gone right between the two of them.

It was when they entered the small grocery that he felt the sour feeling starting in his chest, like heartburn. Isaac's voice boomed, bouncing off the walls and ceiling as his smile spread across his face, greeting everyone with the same ebullience.

"Hey, how's it going here, Jen? My wife wouldn't get up this morning, so you guys have to take pity on me."

"Oh, come on!" the friendly Jen replied, all woolly white hair and gigantic apron-covered bosom.

"No, no. I told her she should rest and we'd get breakfast out. Hey there, Harry! What's up?"

He slapped shoulders, bumped fists, teased and carried on, thoroughly wrapping Titus in the cloying nonrecognition he owned when he was with his father.

"Whaddya want, Ty? Bacon or sausage?"

Ty? So now he was Ty. Whatever.

"I'll get it," he muttered.

He thought a look of pity crossed Jen's face, but he couldn't be sure. She was always nice to him, never missed saying good morning, asking him how he was, and wishing him a good day. But then, she was nice to everyone, so he wasn't special or anything.

Susan had quit trying that smarmy stuff a few years back, since she recognized the fact he knew she was just doing her duty, trying to win him over, which was sickening. He didn't like her, and he tried to portray the obvious, but she kept trying. She didn't like him either, if she was perfectly honest, which she never was, gushing on about how good he looked, or how his lunchbox was always clean.

Her words weren't genuine, like his real mother's words. No one could ever take the place of a real mother. Ever. He should write a book telling all stepmothers to calm down and get real. They didn't belong, and the only reason they were there was on account of the squishy romance between adults. How could a man forget his first wife and allow someone like Susan to live with him? How could he even pretend everything was okay?

It wasn't.

When they got to the logging site, Titus looked around. The landing was almost full. They'd better get some trucks out here today or he'd hardly know where to go with the logs. He looked at Isaac. As if his father knew what Titus was thinking, he looked back at him and told him the trucks were due in an hour or so.

Titus nodded.

"You want to load?"

"I can."

"Good. You can run the skidder."

A thrill raced up his legs. His heart began a faster rhythm.

He wanted to ask his father if he thought he could do it, but he was already stomping off, chainsaw swinging from his powerful arm.

Loading logs on a truck was a learned skill, and he felt he hadn't done it often enough for Isaac to handle it quite this casually.

He was plain scared, scared of the impatient truck drivers, scared of his own inability to do the job properly.

He looked anxiously at his father, a small figure halfway up the slope, where the next stand of birch and oak trees awaited their fate. The grinding whine of shifting gears brought his attention to the loader, the job at hand. All he could do was to stay focused and hope for the best.

He saw a mud-splattered Peterbilt coming down the logging road, the driver hitting the jake brakes with ease, throttling down to make the turn, the driver a hulk in a plaid shirt, the white hair and beard recognizable. Pete Monns. The worst.

The truck ground to a halt and the engine idled as the door was flung open. The behemoth in plaid limped up to him.

"Where you want me?"

Titus pointed to the first pile, the one they'd need to get out of the way before tackling the rest.

"You loading?"

"Yeah."

No words, only a grimace, a shake of the shaggy head. Skin like cottage cheese, all the facial hair making him appear goatish.

Titus walked away, climbed into the loader, started it up, and felt his heart sinking. He was fairly new at this. He'd never impressed his father before, that was sure. Why was he trusting Titus with this job now?

Pete certainly wasn't impressed either.

Suddenly a hot tide of raw anger swept over him. He ground his teeth, swore under his breath, resolved to show this grizzled old man what he could do. He was going on twenty-one, sick of walking in his loud father's shadow as the skinny, blond, timid son.

He adjusted the seat, wiped dust from the window with a wad of paper towels, set his mouth in a straight line, and touched the controls for reassurance. He shoved one lever and stomped on the gas pedal, determined to let Pete know he was no pansy.

As each log was grasped by the massive iron jaws, the long beam extending and retracting, Titus felt a surge of adrenaline, his fingers flying across levers, touching lightly, then with a more secure grip.

He fell into a rhythm, almost like playing a musical instrument, one log picked up and placed gently on the truck bed, then another.

Pete went to the truck cab and retuned with a can of soda. He propped an elbow on a pile of logs, one leg over the other, the toe of his boot stuck in the sawdust.

Titus felt a new confidence building up in him.

When Pete held up a hand, Titus climbed down and ran—yes, ran—over to the truck bed and dragged chains, climbing up as agile as a monkey, securing the load in record time. And then he stood by the truck, suddenly unsure, with no help or input from the old truck driver.

He might have done it all wrong, he thought uncomfortably.

Pete came from around the cab, wiping his mouth.

He looked Titus square in the eye, nodded his head. "Not bad, kid. You keep that up, you'll be as good as Isaac."

Titus blinked. A wide grin broke out.

"Thanks."

"You got the makings of your old man, sure enough."

All that afternoon, he loaded trucks, talked to drivers, and felt as if he owned the business. He could not have imagined it was possible to feel like this. It was pure exhilaration.

The whine of Isaac's chainsaw cut into the thrill of his accomplishment, bringing him back to earth, the bitter realization of ruining the pristine beauty of the western mountain area.

Eventually, he talked to Pete about it, after the old man gave him the respect he had fully earned. Pete assured him it wasn't new, these feelings of destroying the trees, but there would always be a demand for lumber. And if more young trees were planted and grass sown to save the hillsides, it was a good thing. Look at the recent wildfires. Too much old growth.

Titus stood with one elbow propped on logs, his beanie pulled low, talking with Pete as two adults, and he felt like a million dollars. Pete told him again he took after his father. He said he had never in all his days seen anything like his father. He cut three trees in the time most men cut one.

He tilted his head, shook the Pepsi can to drain the last drop, then pointed a finger in the general direction of the whining saw.

"He's by far the best. But those kinda guys often die in the woods. Eventually, he'll have an accident."

A thread of fear ran through Titus. Would he? What would be left if his father died in the woods, the way Pete predicted?

There was Susan, but what could she do?

He shook it off, nodded, told Pete he'd already been smacked in the face, titanium plates holding his cheekbones in place.

"Yeah, I seen it. The guy's crazy."

From that day forward, Titus felt a new energy. The praise he'd received from the hardest person to please on the team had left a clear mark, and he no longer felt the same sense of despair about logging. He still battled the inevitable unworthiness, walking into a store or talking to truck drivers with his father, but the wish to leave, to disobey, to hurt Susan slowly dissolved, replaced by the urge to impress, to become a true forester, to learn everything he could about how forests were managed.

Isaac noticed. He told Susan about Titus's new drive with tears in his crinkly blue eyes, and together they decided it was best to keep quiet. Titus was not the type of person who wanted to be fussed over, so they let it go, allowing him to open up about the unexpected turn of events when he was ready.

They were relaxing in the living room on a Saturday evening when Titus came down the stairs in his stocking feet, a shirt thrown over his T-shirt, unbuttoned, his blond hair tousled. Susan noticed he was putting on weight, his trousers were snug, his arms thickening. He stood almost as tall as Isaac.

"Hey Dad."

"Hey what?"

Titus held out a copy of the most recent logging periodical.

"Could you send for these?" He pointed to two hardcover books.

"Sure."

"Thanks. And, uh, you think you'll be going to Dan Miller's to the singing tomorrow night?"

"We hadn't planned on it. But we'll go if you want. Right, Susan?" She nodded, looked up from her book, and smiled.

"Okay."

And he went back up the stairs.

Isaac raised his eyebrows at Susan, and she shook her head, but thought about the two of them kneeling on the braided rug, the amazing power of prayer. This was only a beginning, she told herself, only a small step in the right direction. But still, the change in Titus was undeniable.

She thought about how each child was different. Sharon needed affection, happiness, joking and laughing, where sullen Titus resisted all overtures, his resentment redirecting every compliment, every display of companionship as an assault to his privacy. He lived to protect his inner feelings with a wall built solidly out of memories of his mother, his real mother. His father had often been impatient with his mother when she was sick, frustrated with her lack of good housekeeping. His mother knew she was inadequate. Now a tender pity for his mother rose in Titus whenever he opened the door to their house and a slow rage toward Susan filled him. She was pretty, shapely, a good manager, housework flying beneath her capable hands, easily winning the admiration his mother had never been able to secure.

All of this Susan knew. Isaac shared every moment of his past with her and Susan was insightful enough to understand Titus's feelings. Eventually, though, she came to the conclusion she had to be herself and let Titus sort out his own feelings. But it was extremely dishearten-ing and the constant weight of it had aged her, really.

She came to realize there was no quick fix, no easy way of being a stepmother, so you lived your life and let the chips fall where they may.

She was certainly grateful for Titus's apparent change of heart, but if everything went south, she would be prepared. Titus was complex, hard to understand, so she wouldn't be surprised if this was temporary.

THEY ALL DRESSED in their Sunday best, Susan fussing with Sharon's cape, red-faced and much too warm as usual. She braided Kayla's hair while Thayer got into the snack drawer, upending a bag of stick pretzels all over the kitchen door.

Titus took his own horse and buggy, a high-stepping Friesian-Standardbred mix named Champion, while Isaac hitched shaggy old Clopper to the family surrey, and they were off. The wheels screeched on frozen snow, but the roads were plowed, white banks of the fluffy stuff stretching away on each side. The wind had blown the snow off the fir trees, so a line of dark green stood out in stark relief, the jagged tips creating an interesting effect.

The moon was full, astonishing in its beauty, especially when they came to the high plateau, the prairie stretching for miles in front of them, the untouched countryside like a new earth.

The children chattered, wedged in the back seat wrapped in heavy coats and bonnets, a woolen blanket tucked around them. Sharon was excited to go to a hymn singing, old enough to realize this was the ultimate social setting for the "rumschpringa," a term no longer used much in the small Wyoming settlement. It implied the loosely con-trolled sowing of wild oats in times past, an area in the life of the Amish church many parents wanted to improve on.

So they were called "die youngie," or "the youth," which seemed to imply a different level of respect.

Susan greeted all her church friends with eager handshakes, hand-ing Thayer to the oldest member, Abe Sullivan's Anna. She was round and jiggly with eyeglasses held together with strips of duct tape. She had apple cheeks and a shock of unruly snow-white hair.

She began her usual tirade immediately after taking off the child's outerwear, saying old people like herself had no business being out late in the evening like this. But after a week at home in the snow, Abe got on her nerves so badly she had to get out of the house and a singing was the best place for her to be, remembering why she'd married him in the first place.

Everyone had a good laugh, cups of coffee were supplied, and Susan settled in, already experiencing the lightheartedness that came from being with other women.

Suvilla was a stand-in for her own mother, someone she could always turn to for help, and Susan watched as Thayer was passed to her welcoming arms. She thought how blessed she was to be a part of this group of loving women.

"Winters get so long," Roy Edna sighed, always negative.

"Oh, put a quilt in frame. Buy a couple puzzles. Bake something," Suvilla chirped.

"That all gets old."

"We should get together more often," Susan said. "Have a hen party once every two, three weeks. Once a month?"

"What would we do?"

"Talk. Eat. Do stuff. Switch recipes. Patterns."

"Go to Florida," Edna said, sour as a lemon.

"What for? So many Amish down there it simply drives me bananas."

"Have you ever been there?"

And so they conversed, everyone enjoying the easy camaraderie between women of the church. They all filed into the living room and sat quietly as the youth were seated around a long table with German songbooks scattered along the length of it. The young men were seated on one side, the girls on the other, shyly keeping their eyes on the words of the hymns as the singing began.

Susan felt an elbow poke her side.

"Titus is here?" one of the ladies whispered.

Susan nodded, smiling proudly. It all seemed so good and proper, Titus being a part of the youth group, even if he still didn't attend regularly. There was hope he would turn out to be a normal youth, interested in normal activities his culture chose for him. Susan had pondered this after Titus had asked to go to the Sunday evening hymn singing. A young person had his path before him, cut out quite clearly and without confusion. You reached the age of sixteen, attended youth activities, sought a member of the opposite sex, married, raised a brood of children, made a living, grew old, and died, having never questioned the possibility of significant change. It was a simple and well-ordered life, free of disturbing questions that so often led to dissatisfaction.

Yes, yes, this she could see. Titus was finally showing the fruits of an obedient spirit, acknowledging a willingness to learn the logging trade. They would be patient with him when he had days of disliking the work, or Isaac, or anyone who came into proximity.

She opened her hymnbook and sang from the bottom of her heart, feeling richly blessed, delivered from fear of Titus's rebellion by the power of a prayer united with her husband.

When Titus looked up, he could see Susan watching him, so he quickly averted his eyes, vowing not to look at Trisha or Millie one more time. The last thing he wanted was Susan meddling into his affairs where girls were concerned.

These two were far different from any other girls he'd ever met—not that he'd met very many in his life. He was aware of them at church, tall, curly-haired, tanned and freckled, with lively blue eyes missing out on nothing, interested mainly in the horses and the great outdoors, he knew.

They hunted, trapped, fished, rode horses, and now were the talk of the community, learning to ski. His father had heard Roy Yoder talk of this, both girls learning the technique from an English friend, and no good could come of it. As talented as they were in riding, they could be competitive barrel racers and even more, but with skirts and head coverings, both knew their limits. Ski suits, paying to get on lifts, all of it strongly *verboten* (forbidden).

Sitting at the singing table, boredom came off of the two girls like steam. Yawning, fidgeting, looking out the window, watching the clock, they were clearly putting in their time being obedient, just waiting till it was over and they could both go home to bed. Titus was fascinated, noticing how completely uninterested they seemed in boys.

He'd gone to school with them, the best ball players ever. He cringed, remembering the rodeo Darlene had attempted, his refusal to take part in it, Millie and Trisha begging him to stay.

What childishness.

They both probably remembered him as the chief troublemaker in school, if they gave him a thought at all. Well, they certainly didn't care about anyone else either.

But he did.

A new restlessness had taken hold of him, a wondering about life.

For a month or more, he'd come to see logging in a different light, and with the praise coming from the grizzled old truck driver, Pete, he felt as if he might not always be a small, weak shadow of his loud, confident father. He'd become good with the loader, his fingers moving with an accustomed rhythm across the levers, expertly picking up logs and placing them on waiting trucks.

He started to feel a certain peace in the idea of following in his father's footsteps. Maybe he could even do things better than his father if he kept studying the magazines and books. He had read some articles about sustainable forest management that intrigued him.

When the cookies, cheese, and bologna platters were served and cups of coffee poured, he sat back against the wall and crossed his arms, watching the silly antics of a group of young men vying for Trisha's attention. She was clearly not interested, ignoring them in a polite manner, her eyes averted.

Finally, Millie got up and left the table, with Trisha quickly following.

Titus watched them. They were quick, graceful, reminding him of movie stars or dancers. He wondered if his thoughts were improper, but my, they were both simply the most attractive girls he'd ever seen. He had a sincere wish to talk to them but had no idea how to go about it.

How did a young man let a girl know he found her attractive?

He wished he had directions, a book to read on these matters. Not that he hadn't read enough silly, stupid romance books. Susan devoured them like candy, but they weren't real life. It was always an extremely attractive guy meeting a beautiful girl, marrying, and living happily ever after in a pink bubble of unreality.

Lester Yoder stuck an elbow in his ribs.

"Go with me to church in the next district over on Sunday."

"Why would I do that?"

"Oh, because. They have a bunch of pretty girls over there."

He laughed, his face reddening.

Titus couldn't imagine any of them coming close to Trisha or Millie. Not even close.

Suddenly he realized that the restlessness in his spirit would no longer have a question mark attached to it. He knew for whom he was longing. And the most surprising part was the misery accompanying the rock solid conviction that Trisha was the one. Millie was her copy, but there was something about Trisha that spoke to him—the way she was quiet inside of herself, quiet and relaxed and kind.

That was it, she was kind.

He sat back, listened to Lester and Duane, and watched the doorway for Trisha's return. He knew he was a perfectly incapable young man, without confidence, without good looks, and completely devoid of charm. With that kind of self-awareness, he gave up hope, relaxed, and decided the whole thing wouldn't be worth it. She'd turn him down anyway.

Trisha went to the bathroom with her sister, looked in the mirror, and tried smoothing her hair, but it sprang up into the same curly mess it always was.

"Titus is here," she said calmly.

"Yeah."

"He's, like, grown up or something."

"I think his blond hair is so cool, even though it's not really my thing. I like the tall, dark guys."

"I know you do, Millie. But we're too young. We both have way too much to do, and you know it."

"It's okay to look."

"Sure, but everyone is so childish. Why do boys act so stupid at the singing table? We're not school kids anymore."

Millie was waiting at the door, getting impatient. "Come on. You know you can't do anything about that hair, and it doesn't matter anyway. Didn't you just say we're too young to worry about boys?"

TITUS WAS WATCHING the doorway when they reappeared, a lightning bolt stabbing through him when she looked directly into his eyes for a moment, a moment of incredible wonder.

Just as quickly, the connection was broken, but he felt as if his heart might never slow down again, slowly draining his vitality. He put a hand on his knee, to see if the joint was still normal, the way both of them turned into a substance like jelly.

He felt sick to his stomach.

Outside, the cold bit through his woolen coat and frosted his nose and mouth. His horse would not stand still or lower his head to slide the bit easily into his mouth. Duane came over to see if he had a problem, which he clearly did.

"Don't drive him enough," he remarked.

"I know."

"You need to come to the singing more often. Your horse needs the miles on him."

He was only listening with half an ear and his eyes kept searching the kaleidoscope of LED buggy lights through the dark of night. He scanned the snow-covered landscape and darkly clad figures hurrying through the cold. Did Trisha drive her own team? She had no brothers to take her to the singing. Or did she go with a young man who was a regular? Maybe she was already dating someone.

His mood lifted when he saw both girls lead a small, compact horse from the barn, lift the shafts of a buggy, easily hitch up in a matter of seconds, and move off seamlessly. He stood in the glare of his own headlights and watched them go, an unexplained gladness warming him, knowing they did have their own team.

He added bravery to her list of positive assets.

Wild animals, questionable characters riding around lonely roads, the horse slipping and falling . . . who knew what might happen? And then it occurred to him that if they took their own team, it was clear they didn't want to be asked by any young man to be taken home, meaning they were independent and not interested in guys at all.

He hardly remembered getting into his buggy, but somehow he was going down the road, following them a short distance before they put on their turn signals and made a right turn on Brush Road.

CHAPTER 3

Wहen winter's grip tightened, the temperature falling well below zero, Isaac told Titus it was time for the midwinter break. Chainsaws froze up, equipment slid, engines stalled. Frostbite was never far away.

Titus had already discovered the frozen bodies of rabbits and martens, the beautiful creatures whose homes had been wrecked by skidders and the whining teeth of the chainsaws. He struggled all over again with the sense of being the most destructive person in the state of Wyoming, the bitterness of upending the lives of innocent creatures, of slicing off the balanced growth of mature trees.

So when his father suggested a week off, he didn't object. He slept in a few mornings, made his own breakfast when Susan had already left for some event or other. He cleaned and oiled his rifles, sharpened his hunting knife, thought of Darlene. He shook his head, chuckled to himself, thinking of her scrambling up steep inclines. She had the best eyesight in the world. A crack shot.

She'd taught him all there was to learn about hunting, or most of it. She'd tried to instill basic knowledge of living a clean life, of trying to like his stepmother at a time when he was struggling. He should be more appreciative of her, pay her a visit. But it would be awkward, not having hunted with her in such a long time. What did a youth have to share with a middle-aged teacher?

Sharon said Darlene seemed quite unhappy this winter, acting as if the kids all got on her nerves.

He should go for a sled ride, hitch the Haflinger to the small cutter.

He put away his rifle, stored the cleaning supplies, went to the kitchen and poured a glass of milk, found a handful of monster cookies and ate them standing at the sink. Wiping his mouth with the back of his hand, he let himself out, coughing as the frigid air hit the back of his throat.

He found his father in the barn, in his shirtsleeves, mucking stalls, going at a frenetic pace, sweat beaded on his upper lip. He barely glanced at Titus, just went on shoveling furiously.

"Need help?"

Isaac straightened, drew a hand across his forehead.

"Do you have other plans?"

"I was going to hitch Harry to the cutter. Maybe go see Darlene after supper."

"No lights on the sleigh."

"I can rig something up."

"I could use another pitchfork, yeah," Isaac said, pushing his beanie up.

Titus turned, brought him another one. "Here you go."

Not used to Titus joking about anything, he took it seriously until Titus grinned, "Here. Here's your pitchfork."

They both laughed. Titus shucked his coat, grabbed the pitchfork, and began forking manure in the next box stall over, determined to show his father he could keep up. Which he couldn't do, of course, his father finishing every stall long before he did.

Titus stopped to catch his breath, caught his father's eye. He grinned.

"You're crazy," he said dryly.

"Just showing off. I can't keep that pace up all afternoon. I'll fizzle out here after a bit."

Isaac watched Titus walk back to his work, aware of the gradual change happening in him. There had been plenty of times when he would have stalked off, angry about one thing or another, times when he could do nothing right, so this easy joking around was refreshing. Could it be he was actually beginning to peel away the first layer of bitterness?

They spread clean shavings, brought the horses in from the cold, fed them grain and hay, then stood in the middle of the clean barn to bask in a job well done.

"Harry shod?" Titus asked.

"I think he's good. Raymond was here a few weeks ago."

"I don't want him to slip and fall."

"I wouldn't take him out after dark. Anything could happen on these roads. The low places are a sheet of ice."

"We'll be okay."

Isaac shrugged. "Whatever. But don't go running races."

Supper consisted of a questionable ham stew, the carrots under-cooked and the ham scarce. That was the way of things when Susan spent a day with her friends. She came home late and slapped some last-minute dish on the table. But her face was flushed and she was smiling and laughing about the news that circulated among the women, relating small anecdotes, clearly entertained by Roy Edna's antics.

Titus listened with half an ear, until he heard Louise Mast's name being mentioned. Trisha's family. He stopped chewing when he heard Susan say how Louise worried about those girls driving home from the singing on Sunday night. It wasn't the wild animals as much as the local hooligans, the young ranch hands who were bored on a Sunday evening, out riding around looking for trouble.

Isaac was buttering a roll and reached for the apple butter before showing he'd heard.

"I don't know why those two girls are allowed to do that. Don't they have brothers? Well, I guess not. Abes' just have those two."

"She had all kinds of complications, I think. Likely lucky to have two. But no, she said last Sunday night there was a pickup following them almost the entire length of Brush Road, and you know how iso-lated that road is."

Titus looked up sharply.

Susan went on, "Trisha made her horse go faster and faster, but nothing made a difference. They simply stayed about a car's length behind, until they turned off onto Parkset Road. It was miles. I guess they were both shook up pretty badly. Roy Edna told Louise flat out what she thought of allowing those girls to drive by themselves."

"A lot of girls wouldn't do it," Isaac observed.

To keep his feelings to himself, Titus made no comment, but thought if he had the courage to approach them, he'd mention a warning.

But probably wouldn't.

"Sharon, want to ride with me to Darlene's?" Titus asked, turning to watch her cut Kayla's bread.

"Sure. May I, Mom?"

Susan frowned. "Seriously, Titus. It's much too cold."

"No. I want to go. Please, can I?" asked Sharon.

Susan looked at Isaac. "Help, Dad."

"Does she own a face covering?"

"Yes. Of course. I have two. I'll bundle up."

In the end, she was allowed to go, but not without Susan's misgivings. It was cold, it was dark, too many miles to Darlene's house, and hadn't they just heard of the pickup following Abe Mast's Trisha?

"Titus is a man," Sharon said forcefully.

"He is? I didn't know that," Isaac joked.

THE NIGHT WAS crystal clear, the cold crippling. The stars were like pinpricks of shattered ice, the surface of the ground as glossy as a mirror. Stone quiet.

The only sounds were iron hooves on packed snow. Splintered ice. Steel runners making a soft hissing noise.

Sharon huddled beneath layers of wool and fur. Titus's mittened hands felt the bitter cold. Fir trees spiked into the night sky. There was not a sound of life from any creature or night owl.

Behind them, two headlights illuminated the road ahead, the flare from behind them clearly revealing every stump, rock, and pile of brush.

Titus had no mirror to gauge the distance between them, so he stayed to the side of the narrow road as much as possible, giving the truck room to pass. He couldn't help but feel relieved when the vehicle slowly went around him, the occupants of the truck presenting a lifted hand in greeting.

He didn't recognize the driver, the truck, or the passenger, but then, he didn't know everyone either.

It was almost too cold to be out in an open cutter. He should have stayed home, or else taken the buggy. His hands felt like ice.

He quickly unhitched, stabled Harry, and together they raced to the welcoming rectangles of yellow light from Darlene's small house. They knocked and let themselves in, grinning at her uplifted hands and gasp of recognition.

"Oh, you blessed little souls!" she screeched. "Come on in, for Pete's sake! What an honor. Indeed."

Titus felt honored, uplifted, knowing she was genuinely glad to see both of them. But especially him. She searched his face, touched his arm, asked dozens of questions, her eyes moistening when he spoke of logging with his father.

Oh, she'd thought about him. She'd so often wondered why they no longer went hunting together. Of course she knew his priorities would change as he got older, but still, she missed those days of traipsing through the woods together.

He was almost twenty-one years old now. Last she knew, he'd been having some issues with his stepmother and didn't much like his father.

Darlene made hot cocoa, her own rich concoction of baking chocolate and chocolate chips, brown sugar, vanilla, and heavy cream.

It was delicious, the hard pretzels and yellow cheddar a perfect side. They talked, Sharon's giggles punctuating the lively conversation. She became sad, though, hearing of Darlene's plans of retiring, returning to her ailing parents.

"It's not all my parents' health. Living out here, a woman alone, takes the life out of you eventually. It's a tough, hardscrabble kind of life, and somehow I just don't have the heart for it anymore. When school is over, we'll have a good picnic, and I'll be gone."

"That makes me sad," Sharon said quietly.

"I would like to tell you it makes me sad, Sharon, but it doesn't really. You know, there's a time and place for everything and everyone, and my time to go home is in spring. My parents need me."

Titus nodded soberly, already feeling a sense of loss. She was a fixture in the community, a welcome face in church, a great source of support for them all.

He looked up when a rumbling laugh started somewhere in her chest. She leaned back in her chair before her eyes gave away the fact that she was bursting to tell them something.

"Well, I wasn't going to tell you or anyone else, but since Sharon seems to be pretty downhearted, I'll tell you. Just throw caution to the wind and let the cat out of the bag. You can tell your parents, but don't breathe a word to anyone else."

Oh boy, Titus thought. *Still treats me like a kid, but whatever.*

"I got this letter from an old friend whose wife passed away about a year ago. A Dr. Dan Stutzman from Holmes County, Ohio. Eight children, all married, ten years older than I am, maybe more than that. He wants to start a friendship, but I'm sure . . ."

Here she lifted a hand, waggled a finger back and forth, opened her mouth and laughed like a hyena.

"He wants to marry me, and I certainly was never going to do that, ever. Not ever. But I remember him well, and he is a very nice, kind, and patient man. I would do well to be in his care as I age.

"These years in Wyoming have taught me well, taught me, in fact, that everyone has their limits. I love this country, love it beyond anything I expected. But it's a hard life. Chopping ice for the horse, watching grasshoppers consume my garden, the threat of wildfires, the loneliness—it has kind of worn at me like water on river rocks. So, I prayed, and placed my trust in the Good Lord, and here comes the letter. The only man I know I would even consider."

"Hm," Titus said, a flood of unnamed emotion taking away his speech.

"You could come live with us if you're lonely," Sharon reasoned. "Remember how often you used to be at our house, before Titus started acting like a grownup?"

"Oh, we all have growing up to do before we're a hundred years old," Darlene quipped, then laughed uproariously at her own joke.

Her house smelled of boiling cornmeal, that rich smell of roasted corn bubbling in thick blups of sound that made his mouth water for fried mush. He wondered if she ate fried mush every single morning. Given her size, he wouldn't be surprised. She was an amazing person, though, and her size certainly didn't hold her back from climbing mountains, maneuvering difficult terrain at a surprising rate of speed.

She told them both how much she would miss everyone, but especially them. Close to her heart, that's what they were. Even when Titus had been so angry, she had understood him. He had a reason to feel that way.

He was embarrassed to feel quick tears rising to the surface. She saw this and laid a hand on his arm.

"Titus, I want you to know I have prayed. You were always on my mind, and I can tell that you have found a measure of peace, which makes it so much easier to go back home and make a life for myself. God is always faithful to hear our prayers, in spite of what we might think."

Titus nodded, could not speak for the unhandy lump in his throat.

The cold increased as the night went on, so Titus felt they should leave before their parents worried. Darlene hugged them both and wished them a safe journey. She offered to help them hitch up, but Titus kindly told her to stay in where it was warm.

Titus led the shivering Harry from the barn, hitched him to the cutter with fingers already fumbling from the cold. Darlene at the window waving with both arms, calling her goodbyes into the night, as they moved down the short driveway and out to the road.

They did not speak at all, the cold a numbing master.

Sharon slid completely beneath the heavy blankets and Titus felt the ache in his forehead, the only uncovered area exposed to the freezing temperatures. He drove with one hand, pulled on his face scarf, but there wasn't much he could do to remedy the situation.

He noticed a vehicle behind them. He pulled gently on the right rein, allowing them to pass. The silence of the night was broken by the thrumming of a diesel engine, the sound he knew.

A loud popping revving noise, an impatient stepping on the gas, drawing back, only to speed up, uncomfortably close now. Titus felt irritation, no real fear, willing them to pass.

Harry ran with a bit of increased speed, his ears flicking now, hearing the sound of the engine. Running uphill, his speed slowed. The vehicle slowed, shifting gears, stepping on the accelerator, falling back only to creep up behind them, uncomfortably close again.

And still Titus felt no real fear. He'd spent years on a neighboring ranch. He knew the jokes kids played, the pranks bordering on dangerous. You had to go along with it, show you were a good sport, and they'd let you alone.

He saw his chance. On top of the incline there was a wide shoulder, a bit of leeway to get off the road, perhaps a place where snowplows had taken a break. He swerved to the right, brought Harry to a stop.

The truck stopped behind them. Titus waited.

There was no reason for this. He turned, took on the glare of headlights, thought, *Come on. This is not the night for this kind of nonsense.*

The engine idled. With the illumination of the headlights, there were no visible features on the hatted driver. Titus shifted the reins, made a wide arc with his arm, the signal for him to pass and leave them alone.

Now he was getting angry.

Nothing. So Titus shook the reins, chirruped, and Harry moved on. When Sharon's worried face appeared, he told her to get back down. They'd soon be home. The pickup truck behind them followed, sometimes making loud impatient noises, sometimes falling back, but always there. Until the lights of the homestead came into view. This seemed to be the signal the driver needed, to watch him drive off the road and up the winding drive.

The pickup roared past, fishtailed, slowed, then roared again. Titus ignored it and drove straight to the barn. He tumbled out of the sleigh, grateful for the warmth he knew would be inside.

Sharon stood shivering in the forebay, waiting till he'd taken off the harness, rubbed Harry down, fed and watered him, her teeth chattering. She asked no questions, her large eyes watching every move he made. He grabbed her hand, and together they hurried to the warmth and welcome of the house, enormous against the white backdrop, a thick plume of smoke curling from the stone chimney, yellow rectangles of light creating reflections on the snow.

They burst into the mudroom. A glad cry from Susan, who appeared immediately, wrapped in her heavy robe, her eyes large with concern.

"Oh, Sharon! My goodness, girl. It is much too cold out there for anyone to be on the road. Aren't you frozen?"

"Pretty cold, yes," Susan chattered.

"Titus, how could you drive?"

He lifted a hand, fingers red with the cold.

She made cups of peppermint tea, sugared, with milk, and a saucepan of Cream of Wheat. Isaac appeared in the doorway of the bedroom, then came out to the kitchen and put a heavy hand on Titus's shoulder.

"You're braver than I'd be," he said seriously.

Titus shrugged. "It was worth the cold."

He told Darlene's story, grinning. Sharon chimed in, eager to tell her parents the best part. Darlene had a boyfriend, sort of.

Susan gasped, her eyes large, then shrieked, a soft sound of surprise.

Isaac helped himself to tea, lifted the lid on the pot of cereal.

He grinned, sat opposite Titus and shook his head.

"She must really trust you two, and that's a huge honor, so be sure to keep it to yourselves. That woman has a heart of gold, and I wish them the best. Wonder if we'll be invited to the wedding."

"Surely," Susan said, smiling.

The evening was filled with warmth, a certain soft glow of togetherness, a budding promise of what was possible as a family. Isaac watched Titus, the softening of his features, the lack of tension around his mouth, and thought how God was reaching down to touch them all.

"Mom, there was a truck following us. They kept revving the engine," Sharon said, reaching for her cup of tea.

Isaac looked at her, a piercing gaze.

"What?"

"Someone playing a joke, I guess," Titus answered. "I wasn't afraid, really. Just an uncomfortable feeling. Knowing they had ample space to pass and wouldn't."

"Titus, this is serious. They could have been dangerous."

"Nah, I doubt it. Likely a couple of ranch hands out to relieve the boredom of winter. I know how they can be. I worked with them."

But when they lay in bed, Susan asked Isaac if perhaps it wasn't worse than Titus made it sound.

For a long moment, Isaac didn't say anything, then said he guessed time would tell, but Titus had definitely done the right thing, showing no fear.

He had never met unsavory characters here in Wyoming, but he supposed they could be anywhere.

Susan drew close to her husband, felt the strength of his solid form, and told him how glad she was she was married to him, how safe she felt at night, knowing he was there for her.

No one had to be up early, with the men taking the week off. At breakfast, they planned a trip to Sheridan, all of them together. Titus needed new shirts if he was going to start attending the hymn singings, Susan needed boots for school, the pantry needed to be replenished, and they'd all treat themselves to a good meal at the steakhouse.

Isaac called a driver, who was available at ten, which left Susan scurrying to dress the little ones, get the car seat, pack her large leather bag. Sharon did not have to go to school that day, taking one of the three absences she was allowed.

Excitement ran high. A trip to town, especially with all members of the family, was rare.

Titus appeared, looking very nice, and Susan smiled appreciatively, but said nothing.

"Whoo!" Isaac called out, eyebrows raised.

No reply from Titus, no indication he'd heard a word.

In town, the snow was partially removed, enough to allow parked cars, with piles molded along empty streets, a film of gray covering them, peppered with bits of stone and debris. Storefronts looked inviting, shops with brilliant posters touting percentages off, sales, rebates, lowest price in town. But even the "lowest prices" weren't that low, Titus thought, the transportation of goods to the west adding to the wholesale price.

Kayla and Thayer were wide-eyed, quiet, the world around them an unaccustomed scene. They gazed at the bright lights, endless color, objects new and strange, folks wearing unusual clothing, ink portraits on arms. Thayer wanted a toy skid loader, which was an exorbitant price, but Isaac said, "Go ahead and get it." Kayla stood by the children's clothes and looked and looked, her eyes like shining stars, but she shook her head when asked if she wanted something.

"No, Mom, I have pajamas. No, I have woolly socks."

Titus went off by himself to a men's clothing shop and was shown to a display of bright flannel plaids and Western shirts with fancy snap closures and elaborate stitching.

"No, I'm looking for dress shirts," he told the beaming proprietor.

He came out with three pricey items, but they seemed like good quality. Why did he think of Trisha as he paid? He walked out with his chest expanded, breathing in the cold air deeply, a spring in his step.

He laughed and smiled, carried Thayer, offered to take Susan's heavy leather bag. He joked with Isaac, bantering in a friendly way.

Sharon found black leather boots with fur lining and a rim of fur along the top. They were almost too fancy, but Susan said her skirt would fall over the luxurious fur. Sharon clutched the plastic bag containing the box of boots and would not allow anyone to touch it.

Warm socks were purchased for them all, and red mittens for Thayer, who lifted his face and howled, clapping his hands.

Isaac went to the gun shop, the hardware store. The van filled up with his purchases, bags and boxes stowed under the seats between them.

They stopped at a steakhouse for dinner. Titus noticed the smiles on elderly people's faces as they followed the waitress to their table. He knew his family stuck out with their Amish clothes and hairstyles, but today he didn't mind.

The meal was served after a long wait of sipping on soda, drinking coffee, children hungry and impatient, playing dangerously with straws and tipping drinks.

Susan ate chicken breast on a salad, while Isaac and Titus tore into their steaks, the baked potato and coleslaw merely an unnecessary distraction.

They all had chocolate pie for dessert.

Isaac's table manners were horrendous, though, which Susan gently remedied, saying he had butter in his beard, a speck of cabbage on his chin. "Use your napkin," she chided gently.

Driving home, the sun setting across the snowy western landscape, the vast and unspoiled beauty of their state was like a crowning blessing, the homestead warm and welcoming. After the bustle of town, it was a haven of quiet, a way of life cherished and appreciated.

Titus couldn't understand his own change of heart; he just knew where he had been angry, suspicious of Susan, and unaccepting of his own father, he now felt peaceful, content.

Nothing was perfect. He'd have his moments. But somehow, the loss of his mother was fading, dimming into the muddled past. Was life like that? As years went by, was there a reprieve in pain and anger, like a discovered nook, a welcome spring found in a dry landscape? Did God have anything to do with it?

He thought maybe so.

He unwrapped his new shirts and tried them on. The mirror sent back his reflection, and he wondered how much physical attraction had to do with love.

How did one go about getting to know a girl from school who would only remember him as a tyrant, a bully? He felt the first pang of regret for his past.

He folded his shirts and wished he'd not spent all that money for something that, in the end, would make no difference at all.

CHAPTER 4

SUNDAY AFTERNOON GRAY CLOUDS ROLLED IN FROM THE EAST, casting a yellow glow, a weird otherworldly cast that set Isaac's teeth on edge. He went out to the patio and set the snow shovel firmly against the north wall. He lifted his face, saw the brilliant sun dog in the west, and felt a keen sense of portent.

Whatever, he muttered.

He was used to winter storms, the ordinary lowering of clouds, maybe six or twelve inches of snow, followed by winds sending great clouds of loose snow ahead of its power. The sun would melt it gently across the top, the beauty of it absolutely breathtaking.

But this crackle in the air sent the hairs on his forearms into a bristling, electrical brush. He had a severe sinus headache and the children's fuss wasn't helping. A cup of tea did nothing to ease the misery, so this low-pressure system must be a humdinger.

UPSTAIRS, TITUS TRIED on the pale blue shirt, decided he looked washed out, and switched to the navy blue, which gave him the appearance of a police officer, or a minister gone to visit the sick on a Sunday afternoon. He flung that shirt on the bed and tried the deep beige, which was definitely not the right color with his pale blond hair. He wished he could return every one of those stupid-looking shirts and get a refund.

In the end, he wore the navy blue with the metallic snap buttons, which he supposed gave it a bit of class. He pulled on his vest and went downstairs.

Sharon looked up from her work with colored pencils, arched one eyebrow, and said, "Ooh."

He grinned, waved a hand in dismissal.

Susan cast an appreciative smile, but said nothing, knowing it was best. Isaac came in from the patio, swinging his shoulders back and forth, rubbing his palms. All he said was, "Titus, you sure?"

There he went, questioning him and his choices again.

"Sure about what?"

"Going to the singing tonight. I don't like the atmosphere."

"Did you call the weather?" Titus asked.

"No."

"Well, then."

"The weatherman is not always correct, and I can tell you, my hair is standing on end. I saw the bank of clouds moving in. Brassy. The air is strange."

Titus shrugged into his coat, adjusted his best stacking cap.

"I'm taking Kernel."

"I don't know, Titus. I really wish you'd stay home."

"Not tonight, Dad."

"Don't take the cutter, though. Case it gets bad."

"I'm not that dumb. Froze my britches off the other night."

"Mine too," Sharon giggled, adoration for her older brother shining from her eyes.

"See you guys."

"See you!"

"Careful now, Titus."

KERNEL WAS A magnificent cross, part Friesian, part Saddlebred, a high-stepping glossy black with flowing mane and tail. He wasn't much for speed, but looked amazing, especially if you were trying to impress a certain someone.

He felt good, the reins between his fingers held the way Isaac had taught him, windows cleaned, buggy blanket shaken out and aired, the thick carpeting on the floor creating a coziness. He couldn't imagine the feeling of having someone like Trisha beside him, talking, relaxed.

He hoped this would be possible someday, but first he had to leap the most difficult hurdle of his life, and that was asking her. He had to be patient, take his time, get to know her.

He had never said as much as "Hi" to her.

The thought of approaching her sent shivers of fear down his back. Real fear, the kind he felt in the woods when he knew daylight was losing out and a mountain lion had been sighted in the surrounding area.

Best not to think about it too much.

He enjoyed the drive, watching the sway of the glossy back, the lift of the heavy mane, and imagined he was quite a sight, traveling on a level road.

When the light dimmed behind him and turned gray in his window, his eyes scanned the skies ahead. That was strange, the way the darkness was like a giant hand, wiping out the light behind him. Or was it only an illusion? He did notice the sickly yellow cast to the air around him, as if the sun had become weary and was only giving off a portion of light.

He slid open a door, leaned out for an overhead view. He sniffed, could tell the temperature was dropping. Above him the clouds looked like fish scales, layered in unruly shadow and swells. When he drew back and closed the door, chills raced up his spine, putting the hair on the back of his neck on edge.

He was glad to drive up to the barn at Lester's place, the buggies already parked in rows along the fence. They were serving homemade pizza tonight, so there was sure to be a crowd of youth.

Lester came to help him unhitch. He was a short, stocky youth of around Titus's age, his wavy brown hair tucked beneath the brim of his hat.

"Hey there, Titus."

"Hey, yourself."

"Driving the Cadillac tonight, are we?"

Titus laughed and his eyes twinkled around Kernel's head.

"He is an expensive horse, yeah."

"I have to drive Robin, the stocky, longhaired little mare. I think she was a reject at the killer pen, but she gets me where I want to go. My Dad isn't a logger like yours."

"Yeah, well. Sometimes I wish mine wasn't."

Lester nodded. Together, they walked to the house, a simple two-story Lester's parents had bought.

Leroy Yoder, Lester's father, was also short, with the stocky build of a blacksmith. He was an accomplished farrier who had ruined his back with years of painful bending over to care for horses' hooves. Eventually, he'd had surgery for a slipped disc, but it was a dismal failure and left him unable to do the work he loved.

He'd started a leather business making hilts, saddlebags, wallets, and other western paraphernalia, but he could hardly support his family on it. Lester's mother baked bread, rolls, and pies to sell to loyal customers, but it was a known fact they would need help from time to time. Regardless of their status in the community, Lester had always been a good friend to Titus in school, through the bad times, and now.

In the crude basement, battery lamps illuminated unpainted walls and a sagging ping-pong table held up by blocks of wood. A cornhole game was the main attraction at the far side, where four young men were arguing about the score. A card table in another corner was occupied by four girls, but he noticed Trisha's absence immediately. He hoped she was upstairs.

The pizza was served at six, so when Leroy Yoder called the boys to supper, they adjusted collars and ran a quick comb through their hair before making their way up the stairs. Titus was the last one in the group, so he closed the basement door behind him and turned, searching for her.

She was there.

His mouth turned dry and he felt the color drain from his face. He knew the navy blue shirt was all wrong. He felt bald and wished he hadn't allowed Susan to give him a haircut. When he thought his breathing alone would serve the purpose of strangling him, taking his life quickly and efficiently, she looked at him directly, her eyes staying on his for a moment. Was that actually a quick hint of a smile, or was he losing his mind on account of his impaired oxygen supply?

How did anyone ever ask a girl and live?

He needed to read a few instructions somewhere. Or ask someone.

He stood in line. Somehow, he stayed upright. She was wearing the color of windflower, not blue or gray or lavender, but some heavenly color in between. Her eyes were large and dark, her skin tanned and freckled. Her nose was so small, her lips the mouth of an angel.

He froze when Trisha handed him a slice of pizza on a paper plate. "Hello, Titus."

Her voice was low, soft, the way he remembered it in school. He opened his mouth to say "hi" or "hello" or "Hey, Trisha," but nothing came out. To meet her eyes and smile would be like seeing God—you just couldn't do that and live, the Bible said. So he nodded, averted his eyes, and spent a few moments in self-hatred and misery.

Someone should have warned him about this. He had no idea things would get this bad. People got married. They dated. How?

He bent his head and kept his eyes on his pizza. Finally, he lifted it to his mouth and took a bite and found it delicious, now that the initial shock of meeting Trisha was gone. He finished his pizza, drank his root beer, and sat by himself, unsure of the next move. He wished Lester would come over to sit with him, but he looked fully occupied talking to the girls, Trisha among them.

Boy, he made it look easy enough.

He got to his feet, stood uncertainly. Then he decided to have more pizza, which seemed like the proper thing, and went back to his corner to consume it.

When Duane came over, he was relieved to strike up a conversation, appearing normal, if anyone cared to notice.

This thing of going to social gatherings was exhausting. He was going to devise another plan somehow. Yes, he wanted to see Trisha, of this he was sure. But did all the rest of the youth have to be a part of it?

How did one maneuver through this?

Duane was talking, but Titus had not heard a word he said.

"Hey Titus, you want to?"

"What?"

"Challenge the cornhole players?"

He looked at who was playing, a foursome. Trisha, another girl he did not know, and the two boys from church who had moved in not too long ago.

"Oh, I don't know. I'm not that good. Better at ping-pong. Sharon and I play."

"Your sister?"

Titus nodded.

The thing was, he had no idea how he would manage to focus if Trisha played on the opposite team. The whole idea made him weak all over. On the other hand, it was a way he could hope to get to know her.

He berated himself again, remembering their times in school. She had been the best baseball player, the best rider, and they'd tossed playful insults, congratulations, smiles like confetti, free and easy. His anger, his swagger, the power over the loneliness and heartache had lifted him out of this crippling shyness, insecurity, whatever it was. Plus, he didn't know back then, how hard a person could fall in love.

Was it love? He sure didn't know what else it could possibly be. He wanted Trisha. He wanted her the way a young man does, to love her as his girlfriend, to take her home every Sunday evening, and eventually marry her and spend his whole blessed life with this beautiful girl. If he could have her, he would not ask for anything more.

He thought of his father and Susan. She was a pretty, younger woman when he asked her to stay, and he sure wasn't much to look at. How had he ever accomplished it with those plates in his face and all that unkempt hair all over the place? But then, his dad had enough nerve, enough self-confidence and swagger, for three men.

Titus thought he must have taken after his mother, Naomi. So small and quiet, allowing Isaac to go ahead with whatever he chose. Followed him to Wyoming, even though her heart was breaking.

Shy. She was shy. That was the word. Well, he'd never been shy in his life till now.

"Come on, Titus. You used to be good at this."

Taking a deep breath, he nodded. "Alright."

The game was close, but the girls lost, which was a relief. He wouldn't have to play against them. Titus picked up the corn bags, chose a side, and began to throw.

He loved competition, usually. Soon he was focused, lost in the game, and he really was good at it. He placed his body in the exact position for the best leverage. He won with Duane, easily. Immediately, Trisha was there, saying, "Our turn."

He saw only a blur of heavenly colors, then her face, looking across the space of the game, smiling. Challenging. He could not meet her eyes, but he thought maybe he smiled.

He felt sickly.

Titus thought the girls wouldn't be that good at cornhole, but was surprised to find he had to try his best, Duane yelling and hopping up and down like a schoolboy. Trisha was all grim focus, competitive, determined to beat everyone, exactly the way she'd been in school. And Titus found this empowering. Her competitiveness fueled his own, but both of them were mature enough to keep it good-natured and playful. Soon he was laughing, even shouting here and there when a beanbag narrowly missed its target.

He met Trisha's laughing eyes, briefly. He was warmed by her presence, found she wasn't like God, only a girl who was very human, even got kind of mad when things didn't go her way.

And, if possible, he fell even harder.

Oh, she was lovely, animated, so sweet and alive and endearing. There were no words.

Afterward, he was sorry she wasn't seated close to him at the singing table, which meant the evening was basically over for him.

He agonized about asking if she felt safe driving home. He had an uneasy feeling about the pickup truck following him, could still picture the front, the headlights' glare, the shape of two men wearing hoods up over their heads. He was okay with it for himself, no need to jump to conclusions, but two girls alone might prove a different story.

He'd gone over the route, mentally traveling the country roads, deciding how he could follow them from a distance, ensuring their safe arrival.

The hymn singing was lost on him. He was unable to concentrate, barely able to sing. If only he were a courageous person, throwing out ideas and suggestions without sounding weak or anxious. If only he could channel his father, yelling, slapping people on the shoulder, loud, confident, sure of who he was, acting as if everyone approved of him.

He tried to watch the girls, carefully aware of their hitching up the well-trained horse. He left at the same time, holding his horse back so they wouldn't know they were being followed. He would drive miles out of his way, seeing them arrive safely. He had to.

His horse wanted to run, lifted his head, arched his neck, swung his feet the way he did when he became impatient, but Titus drew back on the reins steadily. He watched every passing vehicle, of which were only a few, but each set of headlights was a warning, his heartbeats returning to normal after they'd passed and moved out of sight.

He knew Bushkill Road, knew the long stretch of wild, overgrown forest, also knew it was the road they would follow. His shoulders ached, his arms tired of holding Kernel back, but he'd be ashamed beyond redemption if Trisha knew he was following her.

The horse fought the bit, resisted turning on Bushkill Road, knew the way home was straight ahead. The girls' horse moved steadily, with no great amount of speed, but the kind of horse who moved along with great strides, covering miles with no effort.

There was an oncoming set of headlights, the road on either side a blackened grove of trees and brush, the night seemingly without a pinprick of light.

Slowly the vehicle approached, then passed the team ahead of him.

He breathed easier, lifted a hand in answer to the one in the window.

He lost sight of them and urged Kernel forward before noticing another set of headlights in the mirror.

Let it be okay.

And it was, the vehicle passing slowly, well on the opposite side of the road, another lifted hand. He berated himself for his foolishness, driving at least five or six miles out of his way, and was glad to see Abe Mast's ranch building come into focus, shadowy dark shapes in a sea of starlit, snow-covered fields.

He watched the turn signal, the horse plodding steadily.

He couldn't pass now—they'd see him and might recognize Kernel, especially after Millie had cast an appreciative eye in his direction. So he found a wide space, slowed, turned, and went in the opposite direction, thoroughly ashamed, telling himself he would never do that again.

THAT WHOLE WEEK, he watched his father and tried to imitate all his ways, wanting the courage he had. He was like a lovable pirate, full of swashbuckling charisma. All his father needed was a wooden leg, a black eye patch, and a ship.

As usual, as they entered the country store, faces lit up at his father's approach. Forearms were whacked, shoulders clapped, and Titus felt overlooked like a small, obedient puppy who just got in the way.

"You sure it's a good idea, Isaac?" a grizzled old man said, grimacing after a hot swallow of coffee.

"What?"

His father turned, his eyebrows raised.

"Ice. My weather channel says ice. A warm current of air will bring rain, colder temperatures will turn it to ice. You best take a day off."

"Nah. What's a little bit of ice? Our equipment will go through anything."

"You're crazy. Never seen a logger like you in all my life," said an observer perched on an old barstool.

"Gets in your blood. Nothing like it, being in the woods." Isaac laughed. He turned, "Hey, Titus. Whaddaya want?"

"I'll get it," Titus muttered, wishing he'd quit treating him like a six-year-old.

Back in the truck, he unwrapped his sausage, egg, and cheese sandwich, drank his chocolate milk, and started in on his orange juice.

His mood lifted as he thought about the day ahead. Today he'd learn how to de-limb trees the way his father did, a dance with the running chainsaw.

An enormous leather belt around his waist would hold at least fifty pounds of hatchets and iron wedges and mallets, all hanging on leather loops. How many times had he watched his dad carry his Stihl chainsaw as easily as an empty bucket? Walking on top of a log, bending left, then right, whacking branches, all the while keeping his balance. One slip of the saw, or his feet, would have disastrous results, but his focus and expertise kept him safe.

His chainsaw wasn't the murderous monster most people would think it was. It was merely a tool. Sure, it was heavy and capable of doing great harm, but eventually it became a part of you, like an extra limb you never even thought about, Titus supposed.

The lowering sky was menacing, the wind picking up. Spruce trees whipped unexpectedly.

Isaac got out of the truck, lifted his face to the sky, watched the swaying branches. The hillside was steep, the logging road cut by the skidder wheels, Douglas fir and Englemann spruce thick as the hair on a dog's back. It would be dangerous work.

The Bighorns loomed in the background, snow covered, rising to the sky like a great jagged lizard, owning the landscape, holding sway over wind and precipitation. The clouds above churned, interchanging shades of gray and black, threaded with white and off-white, a display of powerful winds and falling ice.

"Dat!" Titus called, pointing to the sky above the mountains.

"What about it?" he yelled back.

Feeling foolish now, Titus turned away. Jason had his back turned, getting into his coveralls, so there was that. At least he'd been saved from the humiliation of having the driver see his fear.

Chainsaws whined and trees shivered, toppled, crashed on the snowy slope, the inner life of the tree exposed, the beauty of its growth revealed.

Branches were stripped, chains clanked as they were attached, the skidder roaring to make the grade. Titus was lost in the moment, the skidder working the controls, careful to avoid the steepest sections.

It was the bits of ice hurling from the sky that caught his attention. He frowned.

He wished he could talk to his father about his misgivings, but after their exchange earlier, he didn't want to seem cowardly. Driving the skidder in snow was one thing, a layer of fresh ice quite another.

He looked to the right. His father was red-faced, his mouth wide open, arms waving wildly as he made motions to drive up, up farther. Logs scattered like oversized toothpicks. The slope ahead would be too steep in the snow. To obey his father meant risking his life, he knew, but to appear cowardly was not an option, either. He'd worked hard to win his respect, to carve out a notch where he felt he belonged. Today he would prove his mettle.

He lifted a hand, thumbs up.

I got this, Dat, he whispered. And he gunned the engine.

Ice pinged against the windshield. He held steady to the wheel, turned slightly to the left when he felt the pull of gravity on his right. The massive wheels dug in, the tracks flattening everything in its path. Branches, loose snow, frozen clumps of soil, rocks—everything was navigable. Black smoke billowed as he climbed steadily, found his positions slowly, the risk of sliding sideways always a possibility.

He saw Isaac's face below, purple with the force of his yells, arms spinning like pistons. The skidder was in the wrong position. Titus raised his shoulders, hands up, a question.

What am I doing wrong?

He stopped the machine. The door was yanked open his father appeared, pushed him over, and got in the driver's seat. Titus climbed down into the snow, but not out of earshot of his father's words.

"You can't slow down like that. You have to keep moving until you're ready to go downhill. You can't run this thing scared."

He revved the engine, turned on a dime, did in less than a minute what Titus could not manage in fifteen.

He yelled at Titus, "You are never going to get this right if you're chicken. You'll get yourself hurt, is what's going to happen. Man up, Titus."

And then he was gone, down over the side.

Titus was seething in anger, embarrassment. A mixture of hurt feelings and the desire to punch his dad in the face all took up space in his chest.

The image of a small, motherless boy, his father absent, took his breath away. A lump formed in his throat, a powerful buildup of past torment.

His mother was gone, buried in cold soil. He could still hear the meaningless niceties: "Oh, you poor children." Women from the community streamed through their doors, but no one loved them the way a mother had loved. How could they?

He'd tried to crawl into his father's arms and feel the same love, the same sense of cozy comfort, the belonging so absolute a sigh would escape his lips before a blissful drowsiness would take over. But his father simply wasn't there for large chunks of his years. He was working, making money, sleeping, rising early, leaving the house, working late at night, the only solace some housekeeper or another. No one who could come close to memories of a real mother.

And now, here in the wild, icy forest, he felt the same. Alone.

How long could a person hang on to these past hurts?

He guessed it was up to him. Anger was a crutch, but after a while you realized the handicap, knew it got you nowhere. In spite of his quick evaluation of the implosion in his chest, he yanked at chains, red-faced, tears close to the surface. He stood in the whirl of ice and hard bits of snow, picked a splinter out of his thumb with the point of his pocketknife, and clutched at a new resolve.

He'd get this right. He'd man up without hating his father. And maybe he'd learn to have courage without the backbreaking burden of past inability. That courage could include certain unthinkable questions asked to one certain girl who took his speech simply by walking on the same earth.

The rest of the day he did his best, doing what Isaac required, the fear pushed aside by sheer force of will. As the ice continued, the trips up and down the treacherous slope became less invasive to his courage. As he turned the skidder, he became aware of a newfound trust in himself.

He grinned, turned the wheel as furiously as Isaac, saw the front hood turn, felt the shifting of massive wheels, and felt indoctrinated. When he saw his father's thumbs-up, he knew his new determination was working.

CHAPTER 5

Spring brought merciful warmth, coupled with bitter winds swooping off the snowy tips of the Bighorn Mountains. Snow melted under the gentle rays of the sun, then froze over at night, creating an unbelievably difficult surface for man or machine. So they took a break from work, eliminating the frustration of accomplishing very little in a day's time.

There was no rest or relaxation at home, though, the way Susan was stripping beds, taking down curtains, and stuffing it all into the washing machine, the whole house reeking of liquid detergent and some unappetizing cleaner she used on walls and flooring. Titus's own room was in disarray, dresser drawers yanked open, piles of clothing set aside, and a rag swung around the inside. Windows were pushed open, washed, dried, and closed while curtains flapped hysterically in the stiff Wyoming gale.

Thayer got into his tackle box, embedded a fishhook in his thumb, and yelled and screeched and carried on. Susan was yelling for Sharon to get her father and Kayla was watching, all big eyes and tender sympathy. Titus looked and knew it would either be a snip of the curved scissors, blood everywhere, or a trip to the doctor in town, a distance of twenty-nine miles, more or less.

Isaac thought it wasn't worth such a fuss at all. He gave Thayer a dropper full of Tylenol, waited a while, then cut the jagged edge of the hook and pulled gently while Thayer opened his mouth and yelled for all he was worth.

Kayla began to cry. Isaac kept steady pressure on the hook and extracted it with no harm done except for the flow of blood and Thayer's screams. Plenty of ointment, a large Band-Aid, and a soft blanket on Susan's lap soon remedied the situation, and Thayer fell asleep with his thumb in his mouth. Susan went straight back to her housecleaning while Isaac watched after her.

"Looks like we're on our own, Titus," Isaac said, heading to the kitchen and opening the refrigerator door. Titus hid a smile, thinking there was one person who made his father feel inferior, unsure. His wife.

Isaac straightened, clutching a package of cheese, then rummaged in the snack drawer for crackers. Frustrated, he yelled, "Susan!"

"Don't be loud, Isaac. What?"

"There are no Ritz crackers."

"Eat something else. What do you expect living in Wyoming? It's not like there's a Walmart on Pioneer Road."

Isaac shook his head and looked at Titus. "I tell you. When you get married, everything is your fault. Everything."

"Huh," was all Titus said, but a warmth spread through his chest as he thought that no matter how powerful a person appeared to be, they had weaknesses somewhere. Susan was a strong personality, capable of holding her own with Isaac, that was sure. Here he was, hoping for a burger, some chili, maybe, and couldn't find Ritz crackers, and she blamed it on him.

He didn't mean to laugh, but a snort escaped him and Isaac looked up from opening a bag of stick pretzels.

"What's so funny?"

"Oh, just thinking how Susan handles you pretty good."

"Just wait."

Isaac sat crunching pretzels, throwing whole slabs of cheese into his maw, then frowned.

"You know, Titus, this just doesn't cut it. Let's hitch up one of the horses and go down to the corner grocery. The horses need exercise, every one of them. Winter makes them restless, and the pasture is still plenty wet."

"What do you want there? Ritz crackers?"

"No. They make huge subs. Pizza. Burgers."

THE STORE WAS merely a room built on to an old, prefabricated house, but there was a sign and a small parking area with a tree to tie the horse. It was warm, smelling of used cooking oil and fried meat, the walls painted a cheerful yellow with white trim. There was a small counter with a marbled top, a few barstools, two booths, and a pinball machine, country music wailing from a speaker in the corner.

The owner was sitting at a booth, knitting needles flashing as she worked on a hat. She had leathery skin with vertical grooves, all wrinkles and smiles of welcome.

"There ya are, Isaac Miller. How are you? I got fresh elkburger today. Ralph shot a nice doe back at the barn this week. Not much meat to her, but makes good burger. Forget your boy's name there."

"Titus."

"That's right. How's the missus?"

"Housecleaning. We're here for lunch."

"Want fries with your burgers? Anything on?"

"Everything," Isaac said with a grin, winning her with his smile.

They each had a cold soda, a greasy burger on a toasted roll, dripping with mayonnaise and ketchup, onions sliding onto the tabletop, fries burning their mouths. Then they sat back, expanding with good will. Full stomachs, comfortable burps, shared smiles.

"Much better than pretzels," Isaac said.

"Can't log in this smear, now can you?" the owner called from the coffee maker, filling two cups.

"Not this week."

The bell above the door tinkled. Titus swallowed, felt the color drain from his face. Trisha. Windblown, her scarf was pushed back, falling around her lovely throat. Her coat was unbuttoned, revealing a red dress.

"Hello there, Trisha," the owner called, carrying both coffee cups in one hand.

"Hi, Cindy. Oh."

She stopped, looked at Isaac and Titus, smiled.

"Hello," she said, a bit shy now.

"Hey, Trisha! How's it going? Good to see you. How's Pap?"

"Good. Dad's cleaning stalls."

"Oh boy."

All this time, Titus was silent, wishing the floor would open with great compassion and swallow him whole. Like Jonah in the belly of the whale.

She moved away. Titus poured cream in his coffee, his face tuning an uncomfortable hue. He wished he weren't in dirty everyday denims, his hair the uncontrolled mop only a snug beanie can produce. His shoes were caked with mud.

Trisha made her purchases, paid for them, and carried the box to the door, waving a hand.

"See you."

She was gorgeous, like a model. How could a young girl have a face like that, in winter? Tanned, freckled, her hair in natural curls. She'd ridden her bike, that was why she looked as fresh as a spring morning.

Misery overtook him.

Isaac slurped his coffee, eyed the whiteboard on the wall.

"Apple pie. Wonder if it's any good."

So he hadn't noticed a thing. It was amazing the way a locomotive of feelings could rumble through him and his dad hadn't thought anything of it.

TRISHA PEDALED HOME, trying to keep her mind on the beauty around her, small flowers emerging from tangled brown grass, water trickling from rocks, cutting grooves in the mud by the side of the road.

Spring was doing its best to make an appearance, but the cold north wind kept it from its full glory. The warmth created a liquid gold in her veins, her nostrils dilated at the rich scent of wet earth, decayed grass, and new growth pushing up underneath. A longing, almost a sadness, kept her from the burst of joy she would normally experience at the first rays of warm sunshine in April.

These days, she hardly understood her own moods, going from gray to pops of yellow and orange and back again. Everything made her cry, the sight of a new foal struggling to stand on spindly legs, her mother's butterscotch pie, the fact she'd gained five pounds, Millie's new nest of kittens.

And there he had been, sitting in that booth, his blond hair tousled, just gorgeous in faded, smudged denim. He was an extremely good-looking young man, and she wasn't sure when that had all happened. He was so painfully shy. She hadn't meant to fall for him. He'd been nothing but trouble in school, then was so strange, barely joining the hymn singings or any social gatherings, seemingly having no interest in girls.

Titus wasn't as big as his father, but his physique implied the life of a logger. She would have to forget about him, stop this foolishness. He would never find her attractive. Besides, she was needed at home and felt guilty even thinking of letting her mother down. Her mother had been diagnosed with MS last year, the crippling disease stealing the healthy cells in her spinal cord, creating loss of movement and speech.

She was the oldest of two, and a willing worker, happy in a secure home, knowing nothing of parental discord or financial hardship. So many blessings, so why this unexplained loss of usual happiness?

And her thoughts went straight back to Titus, sitting there with his eyes lowered. He wouldn't say hi, or even look at her. Likely that loud Isaac had something to do with it, always front and center, always talking, making people laugh. Her mother said if Titus was shy, it was because he'd taken after his mother. Naomi had been quiet and reserved.

Maybe he simply found her unappealing. He came to the singings every Sunday evening, but he hardly spoke to anyone. He had not been this way in school, not at all. So much anger and rebellion, so many problems.

She noticed a deer bounding across a ravine, a golden eagle soaring in the sky, the greening of a south slope, a lump forming in her throat.

Her sinuses burned, tears took away her vision, and suddenly she was crying in great sobs and hiccups as she pedaled along the wet, gravelly road.

She thought she might be losing her mind.

Titus wandered around the house and barn for a week, doing what was required of him, a vacant look in his blue eyes. He wanted a haircut, then complained about the loss of length in the back. Sharon tried to get his attention, joking, bringing the Monopoly game from the drawer, returning it with hurt feelings soon after.

"What is eating Titus?" she grumbled.

Susan looked up from cleaning the floor in her room.

"He's a teenager," she said mildly.

"He's no teenager. He's an adult. Twenty-one. Time he gets a girl-friend, gets married, and moves on out of here."

Susan laughed. "True."

"Are we going to be finished housecleaning before church is here?"

"I think so. We're certainly going to try."

Church services had been announced to be at Isaac Miller's the previous Sunday, meaning there was lots to be done. Susan was proud of her home, and the ability to manage it well was extremely important, so windows would be sparkling, walls, floors, and curtains washed, furniture polished, rearranged, the décor set just right. There were pies to bake, peanut butter spread to mix, dishes to prepare, but most important was the basement, the large open area where services would be held.

Isaac did his share, cleaning the barn, and even the windows were addressed with a bottle of Windex and paper towels. Horses were groomed, fences repaired. Susan lamented about the mud, saying she had never known anything of that texture existed on the face of the earth.

"Like motor oil mixed with superglue and I kid you not," she said, her face red with exertion as she carried yet another bucket of water to rinse the porch steps.

Isaac tried to put an arm around her shoulder, but she shrugged him off efficiently. He pursed his lips, opened his eyes wide, and tiptoed away, winking at Titus.

Having church services at her house was a very big deal for Susan. A meticulous housekeeper, she wanted everything perfect, and often lost some of her good humor accomplishing this and keeping it that way. Isaac was used to it and appreciated her efforts, which he told her many times. This seemed to soften her a bit, but the show had to go on.

Soup and casseroles or eggs and fried scrapple seemed to be what they could expect for meals. They ate it without complaint, knowing the meals took a back seat to everything else.

On the Saturday morning before church at their house, she baked apple crumb pies, the crust filled with a luscious mound of dried apples, brown sugar, and cinnamon. The smell was so delicious that their mouths watered when they came in from the barn.

"Hope we're allowed to have some," Isaac muttered in the mud room, taking his boots to the boot tray, where the worst of the mud would dry and fall into the designated area.

"Allowed," Titus thought. Isaac generally did as he pleased, but with Susan, there seemed to be a certain respect.

This was interesting. But then, Titus thought he'd allow Trisha to boss him around, and gladly, if only he could have her.

"Smells delicious," Isaac said, as he went to fill his coffee cup.

"Don't touch the pies beside the stove," Susan said in clipped tones. "There's a ruined one on the table. You can have that."

They didn't dare ask how or why it had been ruined, but they got down plates and forks, careful to stay out of her way. Red-faced, her neat hair disheveled this morning, yelling at Kayla to get Thayer, the kitchen was prickly with her anxiety.

"Sit down, Susan. Relax for a couple minutes," Isaac said mildly.

She looked at him, caught his eyes and sighed. "Maybe I will."

She filled her coffee mug, sat down, and cut a small slice of pie.

"Is it good?" she questioned, watching Isaac lift half a slice into his mouth.

"The best," he murmured around his mouthful.

"In Lancaster, we just had snitz pie for church. Easy. Dump applesauce and apple butter, brown sugar, minute tapioca, and your filling is done. Twenty-five pies. Done. This is a mess, everybody bringing different pies and you never know what you're going to have. That Abe Louise's cherry pies are so sour you can't eat them and everyone will think I made them."

"You can make snitz pies," Isaac said in a cajoling tone.

"Nobody would appreciate them. Not like Lancaster people do."

She lifted Thayer, who was whining at her knee, and asked when they'd set the benches, her mind already going to the next thing.

"We'll get to it this afternoon, okay?"

"Well, don't wait till late afternoon. When they're set, I'll have mud to clean, you know that."

There was vegetable soup for supper, out of a can.

But by the time the sun sank below the mountain, twilight settled across the land, everything was ready, the basement warm and inviting, benches set, the tables along the side prepared with the small Styrofoam bowls and plates they would need to set out spreads, cheese, pickles, and red beets. There were plates for the sliced homemade bread, a stack for the lunch meat, small ones for butter. Pitchers for water. The coffee filters and large kettle for water to be heated slowly, producing perfect coffee by the time services were over. And the pies.

"You're sure there are no mice?" she asked Isaac, for the third or fourth time.

"No, Susan, there are no mice."

He sighed audibly, fed up, not being too friendly himself.

SUNDAY MORNING THE skies lowered, churned with rain, the downpour immediate and drenching. Women and children scurried into the house, men lowered their faces as they unhitched and put sodden horses into the barn. Titus greeted buggy loads of acquaintances and friends. He watched for Trisha and Millie, but they weren't with their parents, which put his mood about as low as the drenching rain pouring out of leaden skies. But the day was at hand, there was responsibility helping his father with the horses, so he led a small brown mare to a clean stall and tied her with the neck rope.

Men stood in the forebay, little boys by their sides, talking, shaking hands, brushing rain off felt hats. Isaac was holding forth as usual, saying the next time they were well into summer's drought they'd announce services to be at their house, bringing the rain.

The basement was dry, well lit.

The singing rose to the ceiling, great swells of undulating sound, dear and familiar plainsong tying them together in bonds of love and tradition. Remembered songs they all sang back east, before the trek to Wyoming, where *freundshaft* (relatives) and friends still resided. This was home now, this was the life they wanted.

Titus and his father came in late, feeding and watering horses in the barn, seeing which one was unruly and needed to be tied elsewhere, which one needed a bit of space.

There they were. Trisha and Millie.

They must have arrived with friends and he'd missed them. Warmth spread through his body, the comfort of having them here, knowing they wanted to be here at his place. Had they seen him enter?

He hoped so but had no way of knowing if they cared about him. If *she* cared.

By the time the minister stood, cleared his throat, and wished them the Grace of God, the rain had dwindled to an ineffective drizzle, the clouds to the west showing jagged ribbons of color. As the minister spoke, the light increased through the French doors and Titus was filled with a sort of happiness. A small burst of joy, unexplainable.

He dared a look at Trisha, whose face was turned toward the minister. Her profile warmed his heart. He had gone to school with her, attended the same church, had always thought both girls attractive, but had never before experienced this kind of craziness, if that's what it was.

He wasn't sure if it was a good thing, this intensity of emotions, sky high one minute and plunged to the depths the next. But he realized he could not get away from it, and that he didn't want to.

There was a new purpose to his life now, a goal to accomplish. No matter that his heart quaked at the thought of working up the courage to ask her for a date.

He turned his attention to the minister, trained his thoughts to follow the message. All his life he had attended these services, heard the Old Testament stories and about the life and death of Jesus. He knew and understood all of it, but wasn't sure he believed it all. Heaven, hell, the wicked unable to enjoy a blissful life in Heaven. If God was as loving as they made Him out to be, then where was He when it was time to save the wicked ones?

He knew and appreciated his culture, his religion, figured he'd make it to Heaven okay, being Amish and all, but as far as having a one-on-one relationship with Jesus, the way the ministers said it should be, he wasn't very close so far in his life. For one thing, how could you trust Him if He took away your mother when you needed her most?

When he prayed, if he ever did, it often felt as if it went no higher than the ceiling. He guessed he wasn't very religious, but that eventually it might all click. So he listened, halfheartedly. He didn't like the way the minister required so much of a person if he wanted to follow Jesus.

Were they 100 percent sure all the stories about Jesus were true? No one was, really. And if he lowered himself to ask God for Trisha, he could never believe He'd give her to him. It was like a wild shot in the dark, hoping He heard you and felt like answering. "If it was His will," you had to add to prayers, and who knew? It was best to take matters into your own hands and not worry too much about your religion. It was too tangled.

THE TABLES WERE set, the women hurrying to arrange everything, to see to it that the pies were brought and set at equal spaces, water poured, and the signal given for the men to be seated, then the women at their table. Hot coffee was poured and everyone enjoyed the traditional meal and the fellowship afterward.

Susan rushed back and forth, her eyes sparkling with the excitement of ensuring everything was going smoothly. The apple pies were duly complimented, bringing more color to her cheeks. Dishes were washed on a folding table with large totes, hot water brought in buckets, then the casserole put in the oven for the evening meal for friends.

Staying for supper was an old tradition, one that allowed relatives to linger and enjoy one another's company even longer. After that meal was served, the youth would arrive later in the evening for the singing.

It was a long day, filled with sermons, singing, visiting, the preparing of meals, dish washing, and finally, after the last buggy lights disappeared after the singing, to bed at eleven or twelve. Only to wake up early to a mess, a grand mixture of leftovers, mud, and disarray.

Roy Edna patted the couch cushion beside her.

"Come, Susan, sit. We'll help you with supper later. It won't take long to slap that salad together."

Susan sank in gratefully, pushed the button and rested her feet on the footrest, closed her eyes, and said, "Okay, you can go home now."

Everyone laughed.

"Don't you miss your family on days like this?" someone asked.

"I do. In fact, now almost more than ever. But you are my family now."

"That makes me cry," Edna said, sniffing.

"You are. I love it out here. I can honestly say marrying Isaac has enriched my life immensely. And it is so much better, since Titus has changed."

"You mean he's different?"

"He works with Isaac now. And all that bitterness is dissolving. He's just different. Goes to the singings."

Roy Edna nodded. "It's a girl. He's after a girl."

"I wouldn't be too sure. He's never said anything."

"Guys don't."

"Some of them do," Sarah Mast piped up. "Our Harley asked us if we think Eldon Troyer's Barbry Ann would be a good match for him, and that's all he's talked about since."

Roy Edna rolled her eyes and Susan steeled herself for the comeback.

"Well, everyone knows Harley. He talks constantly."

Sarah smiled good naturedly. "That he does."

But Susan knew Sarah had the wind removed from her sails. Should have known better, trying to set Roy Edna straight.

But there was a warmth, an understanding wink from Louise.

The conversation turned to quilts, always a subject of great enthusiasm among the avid quilters. Susan could always hold forth on this subject, her mother a top advisor on the subject, piecing the latest patterns, knowing the popular shades of fabric.

"I'm doing a bargello," Louise said, lifting her hands and sighing.

Murmurs of appreciation.

"When I started, I wasn't sure if I'd be able to finish, but I took my time, told myself I had to stay calm."

Edna lifted a forefinger, meaning serious advice was on its way.

"That's the key. Stay calm till you know you have the hang of it."

"That's right. I was doing okay, but mercy, it is a stretch. Hundreds of narrow strips."

Thayer came crying, his nose running, and Susan got up to care for him.

"Poor boy, having church isn't easy for the little ones. Racing around for a few weeks, then having an upheaval in the house."

Nods of argument, but no one would change a thing. Having church at your house was a blessing, a large part of social life.

In the kitchen, she met Titus, his face tense, eyes large with actual fright.

"What?" she asked.

"Trisha and Millie came with Duane. He decided to stay, which means the girls are staying. What should I do?"

"Show them to Sharon's room. They can change there. We have games."

"But . . ."

"Go on. They'll be fine."

"You don't understand. I don't know how to entertain girls."

"Oh, go on. It's high time you started."

By the looks of it, Titus was in over his head, she thought. She felt a stab of pity. Had his anger actually been a crutch to lean on? Was he so vulnerable, so ill at ease, being terrified of these two girls? The thought struck her. He might well be serious about one of them.

She looked at him, really looked to see if he felt as frightened as he appeared, saw the despair and helplessness. She went closer, put a hand on his arm, said, "You, of all people, should be confident when it comes to girls. I'm sure they would not be staying if they hadn't thought of this beforehand. Perhaps they want to know you better, are curious what your life is like. Did that ever occur to you?"

He blinked, swallowed nervously.

"Where's the Rook game?" he asked, with a lopsided grin.

"I'll get it."

She was filled with a strange little whirl of joy, being the mother of a twenty-one-year-old son who genuinely needed her.

CHAPTER 6

Isaac woke at three-thirty, groaned, and rolled over before
realizing no matter how unbelievable the numbers on the alarm clock
seemed, he had to get up. He found no blessing in hosting services,
and especially having that singing.

His house was in shambles, he had all those benches to carry into
the bench wagon, and he had to put in a full day logging before all that.
He groaned as he shaved, muttered to himself as he brushed his teeth,
wasn't happy with the cold floor on his bare feet, either. Susan had told
him to let that fire go out, the basement was like a sauna, which wasn't
true. It had been comfortable, especially for the old ladies. Could he
help matters if she got so worked up she fairly shot flames out of her
ears?

He stuffed his shirttail into the waist of his denim trousers, bent
forward to inspect the red blood vessels in his eyes. Old. He looked old
and fat and ugly.

He felt two arms steal around his waist, and Susan's face was laid
on his back. He saw the floppy sleeves of her beige robe, like two baby
sheep.

"Good morning, sunshine," she said hoarsely, and laughed.

He held her hands, then bent to kiss them.

"I love you, Susan."

"I love you, too. I'm going to clean floors before the kids wake up,
so I'll make you a breakfast sandwich."

"No need. Apple pie and coffee for me."

She was already on her way to the coffeepot.

Titus came down the stairs without being called, sprang across the cold hardwood floor, and bounced into a kitchen chair, lifting one knee to prop his heel on the seat and slide a white sock over a foot, then the other. Isaac slanted him a cold look, didn't say anything.

Susan blew her nose in a Kleenex, scratched her ribs.

"You're bright-eyed this morning," she observed dryly.

"Yup."

"Your dat wants apple pie with his coffee."

"Fine with me."

They shoveled the apple pie into their mouths between slurps of coffee, while Susan packed both Coleman coolers. More apple pie, ham and cheese sandwiches, pickles, cookies, an apple. It was never enough, so they'd have to buy snacks.

Titus barely touched the floor when he walked, Susan noticed as she set the plastic bucket in the sink and opened the hot water faucet.

Hmm. Did a mother ask questions, or did she stay quiet? He looked pretty happy.

"Do you have a reason for all this bouncing?" she asked.

He said nothing as he got into his coat, but flashed her a wide grin, grabbed his lunch, and was out the door.

As she got down on her hands and knees to scrub the floor, she was lighthearted, energized. That grin would stay with her all day, the work falling away under her capable hands.

TITUS SPENT HIS day in the skidder but was blissfully oblivious to his surroundings until Isaac yelled at him, seeing how he was parked cross-wise on the steep embankment.

He came back to earth with a painful clunk, reality settling in as his father got into the driver's seat and swung the big machine around.

"You better remember next time, buddy."

The words would have stung a year ago, but today they bounced off his head, his mind never absorbing the correction.

She had spoken to him and had met his eyes. He had met her eyes. They were no color at all, and every color of the rainbow mixed with stardust, starlight, moonlight. She had touched his hand. Touched it. To make a point, maybe, but she'd still touched it.

They'd set up the card table in Sharon's room, played game after game of Black Thirteen, a game played with Rook cards. Duane was a great player, Titus learning, but Trisha had gone to great lengths to teach him all the tricks.

Millie was hilarious, which helped draw him out, his shyness like a handicap.

She had looked at Titus, said she didn't know what happened between school and now. He shrugged his shoulders, reddened, but gave no reply. That was when Trisha caught his eye, and there was an understanding there that he couldn't describe but that meant everything.

So he drove the skidder, hopped down to fasten chains, drove the old Cat to shove logs into heaps, but his mind was infused, saturated with the wonder of yesterday. She'd wanted to see his room. Imagine. Said he surely lived in a lovely home. Asked who made his furniture.

He didn't know, and she smiled and said, "Typical guy."

Was it meant as a compliment or had she decided he was no better than anyone else? He wished he knew who had made the furniture, but had no clue. It had appeared in his room one day when he was still in school. Before Susan. The angry years.

She must not have minded too much, the way he thought he might have caught her looking at him when they were singing. And oh, the best part of all. Duane confided in Titus, saying he thought Millie was cute. He might ask her for a date, but would have to speak to his father.

"My mom says you have to pray about these matters."

"Yeah, well, you go right ahead and pray." Titus's voice came out sardonic, bitter.

"Come on, Titus. Lighten up."

What did God have to do with dating, Titus wondered as he sat down on a log to eat his lunch. Human beings had choices to make, and what was He going to do about it? Hit one of them with lightning?

"For God so loved the world that he gave His only begotten son, so that whosoever believeth on him should not perish but have everlasting life."

Out of the blue, the whole long swarm of words filtered into his mind. Now what was this? Where did this come from? He'd heard the words a thousand times in German, knew them like he knew poems from school. He must be going slightly crazy with losing sleep and all these feelings about Trisha.

If God loved the world so much, then why did He allow innocent children to lose their mother? He could have prevented it.

If he believed He sent His Son, he'd have everlasting life. Well, yeah. He figured he did believe, had always believed that, so he wasn't going to hell or anything like that. He just wasn't ready to accept all the love they claimed He had if He allowed bad things to happen. No one would have to know how he felt. It was a private grudge.

He closed the lid of his Coleman lunchbox, wiped his mouth with the napkin Susan always provided, and listened absently to Isaac's talk.

With the price of logs, gas, and diesel fuel costs skyrocketing, they'd have to hustle to get their loads out. That's exactly what he always said, Titus thought. The reason he made all this money. He sawed trees twice, three times as fast as anyone else, and knew it. His chainsaw was like an appendage, another arm.

Titus looked at his father, the pleasant, almost handsome face, the immense bulk of his shoulders, his arms. He looked down at his own arms, felt the muscle with his fingers. He thought he might be getting there, but wasn't positive.

"Hey."

Isaac looked up.

"Why don't you let me cut a while? You can drive the skidder."

"You want to cut? I don't know, Titus. We gotta get these loads out."

So, he said nothing more, but knew he wanted to learn to be as great a cutter as his father was.

"Chainsaws are nothing to mess with," Jason Luhrs offered.

"How will I learn if I never start?"

Isaac tapped his face. "This is where it will get you."

"Not all loggers get smacked in the face."

"All of them experience injury at one time or another."

"So?"

"I guess I have to learn to trust you, Titus. It's hard for me, knowing how dangerous the work is, to allow my own son to make a living doing it."

Titus was amazed to see his father blinking back tears. He really did care about him, if he thought the work might be too dangerous. Titus knew he wanted to do this, knew there was no other occupation quite like it. The open outdoors, nature, the scent of pine and soil, the adrenaline kick starting every morning as his father put on his hard hat, adjusted his belt, and swung his massive chainsaw expertly.

He had made peace with the destruction of trees. There was always reforestation, the company who replanted, sowed grass, cared about the environment. And as long as billions of people on earth would need homes, there would be a demand for lumber. And you had to make a living.

He'd learned so much about nature as a child, wandering the roads with Wolf. And now Wolf was gone. He had died slowly with an untreatable cancer in his stomach, another great and unforgettable sadness. He'd held him in his arms as he faded away, cried bitterly in his bed, refused every gift of a new puppy. They'd never fit.

Someday, he'd get a dog again, but not yet.

His father didn't allow him to cut all week, saying they had to meet the demands of the contract, so Titus drove the skidder, dragged logs, and watched the sky, the nature around him, infused with the same sense of having been blessed by a girl named Trisha.

Trisha and Titus.

Their names matched, which he thought was a good sign, a fair start. How he would accomplish the task of asking her out was a big mystery, but all of that would likely happen in time.

He noticed emerging flowers, found a sense of revival when he saw fescue grasses turning a spring green at the base. He didn't mind the mud sucking at his boots.

Isaac yelled, waved his arms, shouted orders, but Titus went ahead without giving him attention. He guessed he should know what to do by now.

Driving a skidder was not for wimps. Level ground was no different than dangerous slopes, the way you could turn the wheel too sharp and flip the whole machine on a dime. You got the feel of it after a while.

At home, his parents had a relaxed demeanor. Isaac sat around with Susan saying how he couldn't imagine being anything but Amish, what a blessing it was to have church in your house, with Susan smiling and humming all over the place.

Really? Titus thought. Sure didn't seem like a blessing on a Saturday, with a hundred things to do and barely time to do it, Susan with her mouth in a pinched line of disapproval owing to Isaac's perpetual procrastination. It had started on Monday, with a week to get the barn cleaned, the driveway graded, and whatever she fussed about, with Isaac saying "I'll get to it, I'll get to it."

He didn't do anything till Saturday, then saw over his coffee that Susan was sizzling with disapproval. She was meticulous, he knew, and Isaac just didn't share the same sense of urgency when it came to church services.

But it had all gone well, and now was the happy ending to all the tensions and frustration. Susan had helped move the benches from the basement, had mopped and fussed and mopped the floor again, before finally saying it was good enough, she'd go over it later.

The Wyoming mud was like a lurking beast to her, threatening to take away her sanity. She was like a hawk, watching every pair of boots or set of sneakers daring to step into her mudroom. The children were well trained, it was Isaac that was the problem, saying it was hard to unlace his boots every single time he set foot in the house. He used the cast iron shoe brush by the door and wiped his boots on the rug. He couldn't see why she made such a big deal out of it.

Susan was clearly not going to lose this one.

"You can't see what's underneath. All those tracks on the sole of your boots contain mud. When it dries, guess where it will end up. On my floors."

She gave a self-righteous huff and Isaac ground his teeth.

Titus would gladly take off his boots for Trisha. Yes, he would. And evidently Isaac finally admitted defeat, bought a bench and placed it by the door, sat on it to unlace his boots and place them on the tray.

When he padded into the kitchen in his stocking feet, Susan patted his stomach and smiled at him.

As Titus washed his buggy on Saturday afternoon, the sky was an immense dome of the most brilliant blue, the sun's warmth like a gentle touch.

Everywhere, there were signs of spring's arrival. The birds were back in full force, the trill like rushing water, piercing calls, and full-throated songs from spruce trees, telephone wires, and fence posts. A pair of golden eagles soared overhead, tilting their massive wings to ride the current.

The wind never stopped, especially in the afternoon. It blew in from the southwest, bending small trees, ruffling grasses, flapping laundry and loose doors, mercifully drying the ever-present mud.

He slept in on Sunday morning, went down to breakfast without being called. No church today since they had it every other Sunday, the in-between one for visiting and socializing and having devotions at home, a long-standing tradition, though no one seemed to be certain where or how it originated.

Susan was taking bacon from the oven, tilting the pan on an angle to allow the grease to run into a tin can.

She looked up, smiled.

"Good morning, Titus."

"Morning."

He sat down and reached for Thayer, who toddled after him. Thayer held up the two plastic horses he held, saying "*Gaul* (horse). My *gaul.*"

The "gaul" was pronounced in Susan's eastern way of talking, without rolling the "L" at the end of the word. Titus thought it was endearing, the way Susan had never lost her own version of the Pennsylvania Dutch and the two youngest would copy her more than they'd copy Isaac.

Isaac came from the bathroom. "Morning."

Titus nodded. "Real nice outside, huh?"

"Sure is. I was thinking of hitching up and going to the lake."

Breakfast on Sunday morning was like a buffet. Susan cooked every breakfast food she could think of—bacon, sausage, gravy, homemade biscuits, hash browns, pancakes, all of it simply delicious. If there was one thing Titus appreciated about her, it was her cooking. There was always a good supper on the table after a hard day logging.

Sharon came down late, just before breakfast was served, her hair in disarray, rubbing sleep from her eyes. Titus made a face, mimicked her hair, and she thrust out her chin, slanted him a look. Conversation flowed around the table, bits of news from the community, the weather, when Susan could think of planting a garden. Titus heaped his plate, saying little, but thought they were a real family now, everyone blending into a certain harmony they had not experienced before. Sometimes it seemed as if Susan had always been there, his own mother only a dream.

They took turns reading passages from the Bible, in Ephesians, then sang two hymns before lingering around the table drinking coffee, the children playing with the marshmallows in their hot chocolate.

Susan kept humming the hymns as she cleared the table, shooing the men into the living room. Sharon lifted Thayer from the high chair, wiping, teasing him as she took the cloth to his mouth. He turned his face away, grimaced, and yelled.

Titus was filled with a sense of belonging. He imagined roots growing from his chair, growing beneath the hardwood floor, down through the basement walls and into the soil. This was where his parents had raised him. In spite of the upheaval of having lost his mother, this was his home. The clattering of dishes, Thayer's small feet pattering on the floor, Kayla crawling after him, laughing. Isaac already half sleep on his oversized recliner.

He saw Susan pull on a sweatshirt and go out to the phone, something she often did after a busy Saturday, wondering if there was a message from someone.

He knew she missed her family back home in Lancaster. She had been a full-fledged Lancaster girl when she came out to Wyoming to teach school, an older girl who had been on shaky ground, dating someone named Levi who had dumped her, then married her sister Kate after a brief fling with an English nurse he'd met somewhere. Kate had been married to Dan, an unstable man who had spiraled into serious mental disease, leaving the Amish to join a more liberal church, and finally a wild ride on a freeway, where he'd met his death. Titus thought the whole thing was a bit far out. He wondered how that sister of hers could live through all that while raising a family.

He thought maybe that was the reason his father had a chance with Susan, with his size and patched-up face. Susan was good-looking, for him, but then she'd had her heart broken, so there you were.

He looked up when the door opened, having forgotten she'd gone to the phone. He looked again and noticed how swollen her face was, how she'd been crying. A sense of pity overtook him.

She took a deep breath to steady herself, then asked Isaac to come to the kitchen, where they huddled around the kitchen table, talking in low tones. Susan's face kept crumpling, her hand going to the Kleenex in her lap. Isaac looked serious. Titus felt a sense of being pushed away, a juvenile not worthy of serious discussion.

The sun cast a rectangle of light on the gleaming hardwood floor, then faded into a gray area as clouds moved across sit.

Titus looked up when his father called to him, asking him to join them.

The news was not good, leaving Titus in disbelief.

Levi had deserted Kate, seemingly disappearing from work, leaving no clue. Susan was clearly in distress, the love for her sister only intensified because of the distance.

"Why did she marry him? She went through so much with Dan. Oh, I had my misgivings. I did. What causes a person to be so attracted to these men? But the second time around? I guarantee Mam is beside herself."

"You have to go," Isaac said quietly. "We'll manage."

"I'll take Kayla and Thayer."

"Train?"

"Isaac, I'm sorry, but you know how I dislike train travel."

"Alright. We'll find a driver. We'll leave a community message. Someone will want to go back home to Indiana or Ohio. Who is your driver, your favorite one?"

"Just anyone."

Titus was shocked. For a man to leave his wife was a rare occurrence, but if it did happen, a life of loneliness stretched ahead of the poor soul he left behind. There was no hope of having another husband to provide for her, no hope of remarriage, but a life spent raising the family and making a living, somehow. There was always the funds from church, a stipend to fall back on, but it was a hardscrabble existence, supplemented by caring hearts sending well-wrapped cash in white envelopes in the mail, anonymously, always.

Susan was talking, making hand gestures.

"She should have known, Isaac. I tried to tell myself she could win him over with her sweet spirit, that her love for him would be his saving grace. She loved Levi with the same devotion as Dan, total, as if her husband was her god. I'm not like that."

Isaac smiled, shook his head.

"And her men just walk all over her. She's a doormat for them to wipe their feet. How could it possibly happen a second time?"

"She is probably attracted to a weak character, the way you would take pity on a lame puppy or something," Titus offered.

"I think you're right," Susan said, wiping at her blotchy face.

The day's sunshine had somehow evaporated with Isaac sober and Sharon quiet, mulling over the many responsibilities that would be dumped on her at her mother's departure.

She came to sit beside Titus.

"You have to pack your own lunch, buddy. I'll do Dat's, but you're on your own."

"Is that right? Why?"

"Cause you're too picky. I'm not going to all that trouble."

"Whatever," he said, shrugging his shoulders.

In spite of the sadness permeating the house, Titus looked forward to his drive to the hymn singing. He had made plans to go to Duane's house first, but decided to stay home, seeing everyone plunged into trouble like this.

If he was honest about himself, he only went to singings to see Trisha anyway, so what was the use going to Duane's if he wasn't in the mood?

Life sure slammed you sometimes. He felt genuine empathy for Susan and her sister.

He had to hand it to his father, being so generous with the traveling. Almost two thousand miles and back meant the same amount in dollars. A dollar a mile. Or more. Being without your own form of transportation meant being dependent on those who made a living transporting the plain folks.

Titus dressed with care, adjusting his vest and shirt collar just so. He took a last hopeful look in the mirror above his dresser and thought he wasn't anywhere near handsome, but at least he was losing the skinny, boyish look. He looked like his father might have looked at his age, without that ripped-up face held together by whatever it was doctors did. He flexed his muscles, thought he might acquire thick arms after he began cutting.

He had a spring in his step, a light in his eye, remembering Sunday, a week ago. His buggy gleamed, his horse pranced, jingling the rings and snaps. Oh, he felt fine, knew his horse showed proud ownership.

As the steel wheels clattered over loose stones, mud splattered away from the wheels, on them, and on the base of the buggy. He couldn't get away from it, but then, neither could anyone else, so a mud-splattered buggy that was clean underneath was still better than a buggy caked with layers of dried and fresh mud. He smiled to himself, watching a jackrabbit hopping its zig-zagging route through the mud, then disappearing in the brush.

From the rise his horse had taken at a fast clip, he looked down over the sweeping view of pasture, prairie grasses growing in colorful slashes of green, the black cattle dotted like grains of pepper. Everywhere there were round bales of hay, and fences crisscrossed the level land like a giant cake with a knife sliced through icing. James and Frieda Miller raised Angus, same as many others, but he also kept a large number of sheep, which looked like smaller grains of salt in an adjacent plot. They'd bought an old, tumbledown ranch and made many improvements, but the house still resembled the long, low version of all ranch houses. They were built to stand the high winds roaring off the Bighorns, the roof low and sturdy to withstand piles of snow. Squat little houses, as hardy as the weathered inhabitants inside.

His heart leaped as he checked his rearview mirror. Trisha and Milli were coming up behind him, the small horse with his head bent, pulling at the bit. "Hard to hold," the phrase every Amish man used to describe a horse who loved to run, and run fast, especially if there was a buggy ahead of them. Determined to catch up, fighting the bit, they increased their speed even as they felt the pressure of the reins.

He reached down to click the turn signals on, slowed.

He couldn't look in the mirror again. She might see him somehow.

The dreaded shyness again, the handicap. Why couldn't he glance in his mirror, meet her eyes, smile, or wave perhaps, the way most guys would?

He simply could not.

But they were on his heels, or wheels, rather, as he slowed his horses to a walk, pulled up to the barn, and climbed down, watching in which direction the girls would park their buggy.

He'd not forgotten the pickup following him, had still not found enough courage to approach them about the matter. He couldn't follow them tonight, without going too many miles in the opposite direction, so he could only hope they would be alright. He might well be overreaching, with the incident put behind him, and the drive behind their buggy serving no purpose at all.

He turned to greet Duane, who showed up in the deepening twilight, a grin on his face.

CHAPTER 7

Susan had forgotten springtime in Lancaster County, the jarring brilliance of grass and budding trees, the pinks, purples, and lavenders of cultured bushes and shrubs, flowering trees spraying color everywhere. It was a constant delight visually, coupled with the heady scent of blooms and delicate blossoms falling like pink snow on manicured lawns.

"Home sweet home," she thought, as finally, after a long weary drive, one night spent in a motel, and another endless day, they drove up the familiar blacktopped driveway, the blessed back patio, the light lit in the kitchen and her mother's silhouette in the screen door.

A garble of words, her mother soft and warm, exclaiming, welcoming, the drivers on their way to a good night's rest. Her father, aged but sturdy, pumping her hand, his glad cry of welcome a benediction, all she needed to step back into her role as one of David Lapp's girls.

Like finding a comfortable chair and folding gratefully into it after a day of hard labor, Susan became part of her childhood again.

Kayla and Thayer bathed in her parents' blue bathtub smelling of Melaleuca bath soap, the towels worn but serviceable. After fresh pajamas and a bedtime snack they were fussed over, loved, and admired, and then put to bed. Then the hard conversation began.

"Why?"

That was Susan's first question.

Her mother's response was quick, always ahead of her slower father. Ahead and running.

"Because he can. Because he's *goot-gookich* (handsome)."

He had always had a weakness for women. Kate was too easy. "Oh, she let that man do whatever he wanted. To Florida for a month on business. Yes, he did. Said it was for the shop. Soon after, this happened. We know nothing. Mind you, Susan, nothing. It's so hard on Kate. The children. Think about it."

She sniffed, drew in a deep breath.

Her parents had aged, the troubles with Kate causing them pain, her mother's face lined with sorrow. Her voice took on the high quality when anxiety ruled, her sentences short as she tried to express herself. Her father remained quiet, which was his way, nodding in agreement, sadly shaking his head.

"It doesn't seem right, Mam. Kate has always been the sweet, caring one, and her life is always on the verge of disaster."

Her father spoke then, in a quiet, rumbling voice.

"She is sweet and steady, and I believe she stays close to God. Her faith carried her through before, and it will again. Why the Lord chooses to put her through this we may never fully understand, but for now, we're here to help her through. I'm glad you're here."

"Yes, yes," her mother emphasized. "See, Kate doesn't have the common sense you have. She's like a butterfly, all sweetness and light, and like a butterfly, is attracted to the sweet nectar of smooth flattery. Dan and Levi had a lot in common."

She nodded at the wisdom of her own words.

"Like you, Susan. You didn't take Levi back."

"He didn't want me, Mam."

"He knew why. He would never have gotten away with half the lies he did with Kate. Weekends in the Poconos? On business?"

Her mother fairly spat the words.

"Mam, seriously. Did he really?"

"He did."

It was all too awful to contemplate. Kate was so trusting, so dear, and so in love with her man. With Levi, she had a nice home, plenty of money for food and necessities, her husband being a good manager at the shop, the storage sheds rolling out of the lot with precision.

Kate's total devotion blinded her to any red flags she might have noticed. And yet, Susan knew she could easily have fallen into the same trap with Levi. She almost had. A gratefulness for Isaac consumed her, the big steadiness of him, the truth in which he lived and moved through his days.

The next day, Kate met them at the door to her house, her face crumpling as she threw herself into Susan's arms. It was a tender moment, one transporting Susan back to the time when Dan was at his worst, when she had been her rock.

Susan held her away, searched the dear face, still pretty, her figure still slim, her large eyes filled with an indescribable suffering. She was dressed in the latest styles, her dress skimming the tops of her feet, the sleeves tight, no snaps or line down the front, made of a stretchy T-shirt fabric. Her covering was small, her hair combed stylishly.

Levi's influence. A stab of anger shot through her.

Kate led them to the kitchen, a beautifully remodeled one. The house was decorated with the most expensive items, new furniture, battery lamps everywhere, a chandelier placed above the table.

"Sit down, Susan. Mam, do you want your tea? Oh, there's Rose and Liz."

The driver was sent on her way and the two sisters entered, arms outstretched. Enveloped in bear hugs, laughing and crying together, it was a reunion satisfying in the sheer amount of love and longing between them.

"And this is Kayla. And Thayer? Oh, my word, they're so cute!" Rose squealed. "He is going to look like Isaac. But what in the world possessed you to name a poor kid Thayer?"

Typical Rose, throwing out her own observations, letting the words fall where they may.

"I read a book with a boy named Thayer, and he was cute and had a hard life and a I loved the name. In the west, names aren't as traditional as here, where everyone and his brother is named Davey or John."

Liz said things were changed. Newlyweds nowadays named their first baby anything they wanted.

"Not everyone," Mam corrected her. "We still have those who want to hold back, who cling to the old ways."

Rose had certainly not lost any weight, remaining a large woman, still dressed in too-tight clothes, of which she was blissfully unaware.

Liz was more conservative, more obedient to the ordnung of the church, quieter and a lot wiser than Rose.

Susan watched them and admired the little ones who had grown into two-year-olds since she'd seen them. Most of the children were in school, or with the youth, having jobs and learning to navigate the lives of the *rumschpringa*.

"So, Kate, let's stop our fuss and listen to your story," Liz said. There was a breakfast casserole, crisp bacon, overnight French toast with blueberries, a wonderful brunch prepared for her beloved mother and sisters.

"At least I have you," she said softly, attempting a smile, which was unsuccessful, tears springing to her eyes, her sweet mouth quivering.

Rose put up a hand.

"I can't stand it, Kate. I can't take this."

Kate began to weep copiously.

When everyone steadied themselves, the box of tissues passed, and honking, wiping, and sighing ceased, Kate began to talk.

Yes, she had been blind, but not as blind as they thought. Her pride made her keep it all inside, hidden away, the suspicions tamped down, a bright face presented to the world. Isn't that what we were taught?

"Yes, yes," Mam said, nodding.

"Everything is always fine. Even when it isn't. It's our coping mechanism. We hide things away to appear normal, ashamed of being anything less than perfect. And so I let him go. I never once confronted him, afraid of the consequences. He was always nice to me, never cruel, never putting me down or blaming me the way Dan did. But for the last year or so, he . . ."

Her voice trailed off.

"What?" Rose asked, impatient.

"He didn't want me."

"Oh really?" Rose's voice was laced with sarcasm.

Susan bowed her head in the face of Kate's sorrow.

"He left no letter, no indication of where he might have gone, and I know I could probably track him down. He has a phone. But I don't want to. I know he's probably with another woman, and do I really have to know where he is and with whom?"

"No, I agree." Mam nodded.

"Well, I don't," Liz said, her eyes going to Rose, who was turning three shades of red with the effort of subduing her indignation.

"If you don't, I will," she said levelly.

"No, Rose. The Bible teaches us to turn the other cheek. To give the mantle as well as the cloak. I will not chase him, neither will I fight. It is not our way. If I can forgive him, surely you can. I prefer staying nonresistant, the way our ordnung requires."

"But what about finances? You can't live here without a way of making money."

"The house is paid for. We'll get by."

"No, you won't. You have real estate taxes. Heat and groceries and gas. Doctor bills. You have a family."

"The church will help," Mam said quickly.

"I'll get a job."

Rose snorted, turned her head to the side for emphasis.

"And I suppose you'll take him back if ever he comes home," she said.

"Yes. I love him with all my heart. He can't help it if he has this weakness. I believe he tries to work against it. We all have our shortcomings."

Rose slapped the table this time.

"Shortcomings! Oh, for Pete's sake. Running off with another woman, deserting your family, is not a shortcoming, Kate. It's an out and out sin. He'll be living in sin. *Is* living in sin. Sorry, Kate, but I have a hard time with this."

She sniffed indignantly and looked at Liz, who nodded in agreement. Susan spoke then, admitting the spell Levi had once had on her. Besotted, head over heels, she would have done anything to have him, to keep him. She knew his charm, knew his magnetism.

And that wasn't necessarily a bad thing, until he became aware of it and used it as power. His mind wandered, he looked after other women, and became inflated in his own eyes. Arrogant. She had seen only bits and pieces of this, of course, but it was enough.

"And, Kate, I didn't warn you the way I should have. Remember when we dated, and we would spend our Saturday evening with you?"

"Yes, I remember."

"He was attracted to you then."

Kate's eyes lit up. "He was? You think so? So if he liked me then already, there was something there, right? Oh, I just have a feeling he'll be back."

Susan asked if she would please try to see his pattern. When he was with someone, he got bored easily, and wanted someone else. Whoever was the unlucky person to be with him now would likely experience this same loss.

"He's not going to stick with her, either."

"Which means he'll come back to me, right?" Kate said, in her soft, sweet voice, her face alight with hope.

"Okay. I'm done. This is it. Let's change the subject." Rose got up, carried her plate to the sink.

Liz tried to reason with Kate, her mother chiming in, but she would not be persuaded. No, she loved Levi, and with prayer and sacrifice, if she followed the words in the Bible, God would reward her with his homecoming.

The children were all agreed, Emily and Nathan especially, old enough to know the beauty of practicing the life of Jesus, to follow in His footsteps on a daily basis.

"I know I seem simple, but forgiveness and love *are* simple," she finished. "I can't think only of myself and my needs. I have the children, who are at a very tender age. Will it profit their soul to live with anger and resentment? Of course not."

Here was where they all had to agree, where they acknowledged Kate's true goodness. Of course she was right.

But to take him back? Susan wasn't agreed on that one, but obviously would not be able to change anything.

"You see, we are labeled peculiar people, by our dress. Tourists flock to our area to take in this culture. Quaint horses and buggies, neat farms, quilts—it all reminds them of an era when life was better. But in our everyday life, our attitude, our whole way of viewing the world, are we really still nonresistant, carrying the cross of Christ's love? I don't think we are. Prosperity is splintering the true culture. Levi is a driven person, very successful."

She spread her arms. "Look at my home. I have everything."

"We all do," Mam said soberly.

"Which of course is a blessing, but we have a *beruf* (calling) if we want to continue. Remember when I wasn't Amish? We joined that other more liberal group?"

"Yes."

"Well, I learned there, too. We are not here on earth to look out for ourselves, but to give freely, to help those in need, and to spread Christ's love in many ways. We get away from that, through this chasing of prosperity, money, ever bigger and better."

She continued, "I feel as if this was some of the reason Levi was led astray. He got up so high in business, attended these meetings, and it all led to being misled. I will pray for his soul, for his repentance as long as I have breath in my body."

"He wasn't misled," Rose said. "He chose to do what he did."

Kate looked at Rose, then Liz.

"I can see your point, of course. I am always trying to blame everyone else, aren't I? I guess it's because I love him so much."

The remainder of the time with Kate was cloaked in the darkness of disagreement. A sense of unity was simply not there, so the conversation was stilted. Eventually, they turned to lighter subjects that skimmed over the top of the true reason they had come to be with her.

Susan thought of the garden, the barn, mucking stables, mowing all this grass, five children, and finding a job. How would Kate ever manage it all?

Am I my brother's keeper?

This thought flashed into her mind, and she did know the answer. She could not get away from it. Yes, she was her sister's keeper, held the Christian responsibility of seeing she would be taken care of. This she would have to discuss with Isaac.

A great flood of love overtook her. A pure, clean love, one that was grateful to accept the fact she had married a true, kind person, one whose honesty and open-mindedness was worth its weight in gold. A good, decent man who worked hard and enjoyed the fruits of his labor, content with his "frau" till the end of his days. No matter he was gone too much of the time, no matter he procrastinated when church was at their house.

Thank you, she thought to God, the One who directed her steps and knew every hair on her head. As He knew Kate, and loved her the same, even if the plan He had for her life was far beyond their own understanding.

All this crossed her mind as Kate sipped her tea, listening to Rose and Liz, but Susan knew, too, beneath the sweet exterior was a spirit, a heart of steel. She had set her face to what she perceived as truth, and no one would tell her anything different.

Was this, then, why she suffered in life? Why God allowed these trials and sorrows?

The day flew by, as only time does when sisters spend a day together, especially when they live a great distance apart.

Back home with her mother, she spent another hour discussing Kate's plight with her parents, who assured her they would do anything to lighten her load. It was only their parental duty, and others would do the same without complaint.

They visited grandparents, uncles, aunts, and old friends, went to dry goods stores, and stopped by the market where Susan used to work. It was all a dear homecoming, in every sense of the word.

Susan's family promised to visit her in the summer. They would bring Kate this time, and the children. So Susan hugged her dear parents and wished them a loving farewell, her eyes blinded with tears as she climbed into the fifteen-passenger van. She could barely see to strap Thayer in his car seat.

But as they moved through traffic and passed horses and buggies on the wide shoulder of Route 340, she set her face to the west. She longed for Isaac and the homestead, and knew it was her home.

Mark and Elmer had been especially dear, and warm circles flowed around her heart. She loved them both, as well as their dear wives and little toddlers. They were men now, with beards and straw hats, owning homes and starting a construction business of their own. Elmer had mentioned a longing to move somewhere else, a place life would flow at a slower pace, but thought Wyoming was much too far. And besides, her covering was weird. They all had a good laugh. Elmer's wife, tall, skinny, and as sweet as her name, Rosanne, put Susan's covering on her head and modeled it for him, turning this way, then that.

It was hilarious. Brothers were easy. They didn't nitpick or carry around prickly little grudges and talk about you behind your back.

They were guys, and guys weren't like their female counterparts, being hurt about every little remark, taking offense easily like her sisters.

Especially Rose. Now she was a piece of work, that one.

But love flowed for her, too. She'd be taken down a few notches by life, likely by those fancy girls of hers. Poor Amos, the long-suffering husband. He seemed to be doing alright, still watched his overweight, effusive wife with a twinkle in his eye. Now there was another good, solid man.

And so her thoughts tumbled between conversations with the driver and his wife on their way to Holmes County, Ohio to pick up the remainder of the passengers.

SHE WAS WEARY to the bone, her back muscles aching from the van seats. She strained to see the brown buildings melding with the landscape, the pine and spruce trees growing in clumps on the greening pastures dotted with black cattle and grazing horses. There was so much emptiness, dust, and wide-open space containing nothing but an endless blue sky and a constant wind blowing as free and as ancient as the mighty Bighorn Mountains.

Isaac and Titus had stayed home from their logging to welcome her. Sharon had everything in perfect order, her friend Elizabeth staying with her to ease the loneliness. Susan hugged Sharon, then Isaac, but only welcomed Titus with a smile. He was not, and hadn't been for years, available for a hug, and this was an understanding between them. But his eyes searched her face, and that was something.

It fit like a glove—the house, the home, the familiar scent of Wyoming. She sat with Isaac after the children were in bed, and between tears and the grabbing of Kleenex, Kate's story tumbled out. Isaac listened quietly, shaking his head.

"For some men, I guess, it's like an addiction, something they can never quite conquer."

"Yes. And Kate. Seriously, Isaac. How is she going to manage? I think she's still in denial. She talks like it will be easy to get a job and manage everything else herself. Plus, she thinks Levi is coming back and she plans to let him."

"We'll help her."

Susan put her face in her hands and cried. Isaac drew her into his arms, thinking he'd done something wrong, but between hiccups and the blowing of her nose, she managed to tell him how much she loved and appreciated him, the truthful goodness of him. She hadn't known how he would feel about helping Kate, had dreaded asking.

And then she told him about being her sister's keeper, the words she had remembered.

"Yes, Susan. We are our brother's keeper. Sister, in this case. If God blesses us with plenty, it's our duty to share, and when something like this comes up, of course we will do it."

"But like, every month?"

"That's what I was thinking. We'll just put it in the mail, with a letter, explaining our belief. She'll accept it, won't she?"

"I think so."

"I feel so sorry for her. Does she have any idea where Levi went?"

"Absolutely none. It's all a big mystery, but I'm sure someday he'll try to contact her, out of guilt."

She inhaled the scent of his flannel shirt, laid her head on his massive chest, closed her eyes, and allowed waves of gratitude to wash over her.

"I love you so much, Isaac."

"And I love you. The day you came into my life was a blessed one, and my journey has been far easier ever since. There is not one single thing I have ever done to deserve you."

AFTER THE HOMECOMING, it seemed as if their love reached a new level, a deeper connection of love and understanding. Titus and Sharon both realized this and felt a new sense of security.

The days turned warmer, the garden was plowed and tilled, seeds dropped into the almost too-wet soil. Calves were born at the neighboring farms and frolicked in the pastures with their loving mothers, anxiously calling when they became too reckless. Every day the sunrise was so beautiful. Susan had her devotions on the back patio, her heart filled with God's love to all mankind, the sheer amazement of that sun rising fresh and new each day, with all the turmoil humans had created on His fresh, clean earth.

A part of her stayed in Lancaster with Kate, however. She found she could no more separate herself from her sister's sorrows than she could from her own arms or legs. It was as if God kept reminding her of the need to pray, to flail at the throne, begging Him to help, to ease the burden of losing Levi to his wanton ways. And she prayed for him, too.

No matter how disgusted she felt, he was one of God's children, too, and afflicted with his own thorns of the flesh, his own desires to quench.

She could still remember how he had won her through his easy charm, his smooth character. She had resisted at first, had tried her best to untangle herself from his web, truly believed he loved her.

How many women had he conquered in this manner?

She shuddered, thinking of his charms, even waitresses and store clerks responding, and she too taken by him to realize his greatest weakness.

Her mother left a number of messages during that first week back. She had kept a serene face to her girls, but deep down, she was enduring a marathon, running a race by keeping her faith in God's love. She felt to blame. "What have we done to deserve this, Susan? Why us? We should have seen it in Dan, first of all." And so on.

Susan did what she could to calm her mother's fears, but in the end, her mother would need to find solid ground again.

TITUS WAS AT the singing on Sunday evening and was determined to talk to Trisha about driving home with Millie. It wasn't safe, especially after another encounter with what he knew was the same pickup truck. He'd gone to Duane's house on Tuesday evening for a few horseshoe nails, and coming back, his heart leaped in his throat, realizing he was being followed again, the engine repeatedly revved, gravel spinning beneath tires. He was driving his father's Standardbred gelding, Artie, the one so hard to hold, and for that, he was glad. He loosened the reins and let him run, the wheels flying over potholes, spitting gravel, swaying around curves, as if he were traveling on two wheels.

Artie flattened his ears as the driver lay on the horn, but kept up his speed without showing fear. When the truck finally skidded around him, so close he could see the driver's profile, he pulled on the right rein, instinctively trying to get away.

He was scared. He could feel the gun barrel poking out of a window, although he had no reason to believe these men meant actual harm. He turned into the long winding driveway, thankful to be home, appreciating Artie's speed and common sense.

He walked to Isaac, who didn't seem concerned, said probably some boys out having a good time. He wouldn't worry too much, as long as they didn't actually stop and get out of the truck.

CHAPTER 8

SHE SAID HELLO, AND SO DID MILLIE, BUT HE COULD NOT GET UP the courage to bring up the subject until after the singing, when the women served coffee and snacks. She was close, close enough he could call out her name quietly, without creating attention.

"Trisha."

She hadn't heard, so he tried again. This time, she turned to face him, her eyebrows raised in question. In the lamplight, she was so perfect, he lost the use of his voice, but the overriding fear for their safety quickly made him regain it.

"You'll likely think I'm foolish, but I worry about you and Millie getting home."

"Oh? Why is that?"

He told her about the two incidents, and how he was afraid for what could happen, especially in the open buggy. His words were low, and he felt them come out garbled, but he had to say it.

She searched his face. "Oh wow," she breathed.

"Yeah. Dat says he wouldn't worry, probably someone out having fun with the Amish teams, but still, you never know."

She said nothing, and he knew a deep misery, berating himself for the offered protection she didn't want or need.

"Yes."

She took a deep breath.

"I wish we had someone who could pick us up. My dad is not completely okay with Millie and me taking our own buggy. If he heard this, he most certainly won't be. We'll just have to see, I guess."

"I could."

"No, oh no. It's way too far out around. I could never require that."

"Our barn is full of horses. Some of them are pretty good." Emboldened by her polite refusal, he told her he planned on following them home that very evening. She nodded, then told him they would be fine though. Really, what were the chances?

Afraid to voice his own opinion, afraid of what she would think of him to insist on following, he gave in. He gave a short laugh said yeah, really, and edged away, got up and left the room. He thought of his father, the booming opinions, the courage to say what he thought and let the opinion be taken where or how it may.

THE NEWS CIRCULATED among the community fast. Abe Mast's daughters, the ones who drove their own horse to the singing, had experienced a terrible thing. Two men in a pickup followed them for miles in the open buggy, clearly trying to scare the horse. Parents tightened their grip on children, watched every vehicle on seldom-traveled roads. School teachers were warned.

Darlene was preparing to leave and didn't take it seriously, thinking it was only some bored ranch kids out for a lark. Every opinion voiced added to the fray until the incident was considered, taken apart, added on, and speculation ran wild. Titus heard most of them from Susan, who had gone to Roy Edna's house for coffee and came home with the dire prediction of someone being kidnapped or worse.

Titus called Abe Mast's number and left a message saying he'd pick both girls up at six-thirty on Sunday evening. He could hardly believe he'd actually done it, but since no one called back to deny him that privilege, he thought they must be alright with it. He found himself looking forward to Sunday evening with a certain giddiness, an almost childlike anticipation.

Oh, it was nothing. He told himself this repeatedly, and held out the hope that perhaps later, in years to come, she might actually detect a few good qualities and consider him.

He washed and waxed his buggy, cleaned the windows with Windex and paper towels, washed and groomed his Friesian horse, brushed the mane and tail until they rippled and gleamed like a dark waterfall. He polished the black harness, then dressed with the same amount of care, giving plenty of detail to his blond hair, using cologne. He smiled to himself and thought there was nothing wrong with making an honest attempt.

He had, after all, spoken to her, and she had spoken to him. Not just light bantering, the way you did in games, but a real normal conversation in which he could remember every single word.

The evening was one of those times in spring where he ached with a nameless emotion, the beauty of the west singing to his spirit, or his soul, whatever was the part of you that felt things deeply.

He loved nature, loved wide open spaces with endless sky and deep forests with the acrid scent of pine needles, ravines, and tree roots like gnarly snakes. He loved the quiet time before a snowstorm. He relished the high hot winds in the middle of summer's drought, the choppy, cold winds of autumn before the hunt began, the elk and mule deer like needles in a haystack, the mountains, ridges, and cliffs hoarding their wildlife like rare prizes.

He knew the area well, knew where the bald eagles nested by the fast-flowing Crazy Woman River, and the golden eagles who lived farther away from the water. It was all a part of him, and he a part of this vast land, the extensive forests and gigantic mountains, filled with the innumerable secrets of nature.

This new restlessness was a part of nature, he assumed. It was natural and right for a man to want someone to share his life, to live with and love, to enjoy the time here on earth as long as your days lasted. And he felt a sense of happiness, a new lease on his future, to know and appreciate this fact. As he approached the home of Abe and Louise

Mast, he was calmed and comforted by his own thoughts, the realization that wanting a companion was good.

It was nature. Or maybe God, depending how you wanted to word it. Weren't God and nature the same thing? They were to him.

He wasn't sure what the proper procedure would be. Should he pull up to the barn, tie his horse, and walk to the house, or should he pull up to the house and stay sitting? He decided on the latter. Easier on the nerves.

Everything was quiet, the farmhouse small, friendly with a wide front porch along two sides, wooden rocking chairs, a swing. An old dog with a graying muzzle came up behind him, gave a short unenthused bark, wagged his tail enough to let him know he was okay with his arrival, and wandered off. Titus said "Hey, buddy," but let it go at that, seeing the front door open and Abe Mast himself making his way down the porch steps.

"Hey there, Titus. How are you?"

"I'm doing okay. And you?"

"A lot better now that I know you're taking the girls. I guess you heard what happened, right?"

"I did."

"You warned them."

"Yes. But was afraid of being a sissy, too."

"You mean, insisting you accompany them?"

"Yeah."

"Well, you should have. But then, maybe it scared Trisha enough that she takes it seriously. Thank you so much, though, for being willing to take them. I hope you know, you're going to put some miles on."

"Kernel can do it."

"Kernel? As in C-O-L-O-N-E-L?"

"No. A nugget. A kernel. When he was born, he wasn't bigger than one, hardly. We raised him. He's mine."

"You like horses?"

But Titus gave him no reply, his eyes losing focus at the sight of Trisha and her sister coming down the steps. Like two spring flowers wearing small black sweaters.

"Uh, yeah. Yes. I do like them."

Abe Mast had to stifle a grin. He didn't want to embarrass this earnest young man, but no one drove an extra eleven or twelve miles out of the goodness of their heart. Usually, there was a bit more involved.

"Okay, Titus. Be careful. Bring them back safe and not too late."

The three of them on the seat was a tight fit, but Millie seemed quite comfortable in the middle, chattering on, offering him a piece of chewing gum, with Trisha being quiet, riding along without comment.

"So, what do you think, Titus? You think the guys following us were the same ones?"

"Could be. Tell me about it."

The ride through the dark countryside was much the same as his own, the two times he'd been followed. There was no way of knowing if there was any real danger involved, or if they were merely pranksters. At any rate, the whole thing was unsettling.

Trisha said she didn't know what would be best if a truck pulled in front of you and tried to block your path. Should you turn your horse around or pick up speed to run past them?

The enormity of the situation made Titus lose his shyness and he spoke freely, telling them it was far better to keep going at a high rate of speed, hoping to elude them. To turn around would be to stop your horse, allowing them time to grab the bridle, and it was all over after that. If they meant bodily harm.

He had to admit, he was proud of his horse. He knew Trisha loved horses, appreciated a good one, and now was aware of the powerful gait, the springy, rocking sway of the Friesian, coupled with the speed of the Standardbred. His black mane and tail rippled in the evening wind, the buggy drawn as an afterthought.

"At any rate, I'd hate the thought of trying to stop this horse. He's pretty awesome," Millie said, popping her gum and waving a hand for emphasis.

A car approached from behind. Titus glanced in the mirror, released a breath. A blue car, not a pickup. Harmless. They soon drove around, waving.

Titus lifted his hat. Trisha looked sideways, then looked ahead. Titus pointed across the level plain.

"Mule deer. Two of them."

"Two doe," Millie corrected him.

"I never said it was a buck and a doe."

Trisha caught his eye, smiled, then looked straight ahead again, hardly knowing how to be comfortable in any other position. Titus lifted his hat again and shook his hair away from his face before settling it lower, lifting the reins to urge his horse on.

"So tonight on our return, who will be the watchdog?" he asked suddenly. "I thought maybe one of you would offer to keep an eye out, and if there's a possibility of our being followed, we'll turn the lights off and make a quick detour. A side road, or a bit of woods, whatever, I don't know, we'll have to see how this all goes."

"You're expecting to be followed?" Trisha asked, suddenly.

"We don't know. Just in case."

"Maybe we should just stop going to the singings for a while. At least until we know what's going on."

"We won't know if we stay home," Titus offered.

"But aren't you really scared?" Millie wanted to know.

"I don't think so. Not with Kernel. He's pretty intimidating."

The singing was held at Dan Weaver's, an older couple who raised a few cattle, a scattering of sheep, and kept a few dogs and sleek, fat barn cats. They'd made their living back in Illinois, and now spent their retirement enjoying the west, away from the crowds, like Dan had always dreamed. They cared deeply about the community, gave everything to the strengthening of bonds, like hosting the singing for the youth, befriending them all. Their house was small, but there was an attached garage, the windows welcoming with squares of yellow light, a few buggies parked in the yard, a wagon in the barnyard to tie horses.

The girls helped him unhitch, remarking at the lack of hard breathing, as if he hadn't run so many miles. Titus smiled and glanced at Trisha, who caught his eye and smiled back.

"You're proud of your horse. I can tell."

He didn't answer. The moment was too much—the scent of a spring evening, the color of her dress, and the understanding in her eyes.

He felt more at ease with her, felt as if he were headed in the right direction, but there was always the insurmountable hurdle of actually coming right out and asking. The thought always made the self-doubt and insecurities pile up like debris, trapping him with their weight.

How did one go about it? He tried to imagine the words: "Do you want to have a date?" "Would you agree to a date?" "May I ask if we can start a friendship?" She already was his friend, so that was lame. He could not imagine those words coming out of his mouth, could not visualize the scene at all.

He sat beside Duane and Lester, helped sing the many hymns, talked to some of the parents when they talked to him, and knew where Trisha was seated, when she got up to leave the table, and when she came back. There was a sense of longing, but it was harnessed to his own failure, his own lack of courage. For a fleeting moment, he realized Abram was watching Trisha, his dark good looks in contrast to his own. His heart leaped in his throat and despair gripped him.

Now he had to add this new dimension to every other roadblock.

Of course someone else might want her, too. And she might well want him back. He couldn't deal with this. He wanted to get Kernel, hitch up, and flee, head back to the homestead and bury himself beneath the quilts on his bed, forget about any romantic inclination. If Abram was in the running, there was no competition. There could only be one winner and it certainly was not him.

He drank coffee, but his mouth was too dry to think of eating a snack. He smiled at Duane's jokes, said very little, saw Abram make his way over to the girls, and allowed misery to have its way.

Yes. There he was, bold as ever, approaching Trisha.

He spoke to her. Smiled. She spoke, smiled back. Millie and Linda joined the conversation, which seemed to go on and on.

Finally, Titus had enough, so he got up and walked out. Duane followed, asking what was up.

"Getting some fresh air," Titus answered.

The night was velvety with the softness of spring, the air heavy with moist soil, newborn calves, and emerging growth. He felt a renewal of his spirit, a calm, being away from the spectacle inside. Surrounded by nature, the one thing he knew and understood, he regained his breath, found the firm ground under his feet, and knew the seasons would always come and go, as sure as anything he knew. If things didn't work out the way he wanted, the way things often didn't, he would have the world around him, the natural world he loved, to fall back on.

This was his way of accepting the inevitable, admitting defeat, and giving in to whatever came his way. It did not necessarily include God, or the word God, but it was an obedience, a giving in, to a force much bigger than himself. All this occurred while Duane chattered away, and he nodded in monosyllables, his mind a thousand miles away.

"Hey, are you going to haul the girls around now?"

"For a while. See if that truck follows anyone."

"You're lucky."

"I'm surprised you say that."

"Why? You know I like Millie. Always have. I'm waiting till she's allowed to date. I think she likes me, too."

"Wow."

"What do you mean, wow? Aren't you happy for me?"

"You don't have her yet."

"Well, that isn't a problem. It's just a matter of asking."

"Hm."

"What?"

"It's a pretty big matter, Duane."

And so Titus found a huge difference in the way two people thought about themselves. Duane never imagined her saying no, thought she liked him too, and it was only a matter of time, while Titus struggled with the mere thought of asking, was convinced she would not accept. And now the giant obstacle in the road. Abram.

He took a deep breath. He had the whole way home to look forward to.

He was disappointed when Millie plopped herself in the middle again. Buggies were perfect to be seated close to someone, but it would have been nice to have Trisha beside him. Perhaps that would be asking too much, and perhaps she did not want to be close to him at all. He might be repulsive.

As usual, Millie chattered away, her stream of rhetoric punctuated only by an occasional acknowledgement from Titus or Trisha.

"You guys are awful quiet," she said finally. "Trisha, that Abram was being friendly tonight. He'll probably ask you before too long."

Titus held his breath.

"Mm-hmm."

"That's lame, Trisha. Don't you think it's exciting?"

"Not really."

Titus breathed again.

"I don't know what you're waiting on. You're not getting any younger. Mam married Dat at your age."

"I know."

Kernel wanted to run, knew the horse's instinct of heading home. Titus concentrated on driving, his eyes constantly going to his rearview mirror, hoping no headlights would shine through the dark. The air was becoming chilly, so he told the girls there was a lap robe underneath the seat if they needed it.

Every moment was a pleasure, and he remembered to appreciate the fact they were with him, had agreed to be in his company. If he was repulsive, they would not have agreed to go with him.

Millie was saying they should go riding. Next Sunday. Maybe Duane would go. Ride out to Bear Lake. Have a picnic.

Did Titus want to go?

The unexpected invitation took him by surprise, so he took his time answering. Bear Lake was a good distance, and Duane would have to come to his house.

"I probably could."

"Good. We'll plan it then. You ride to our house and we'll go from there. If it rains, or the weather isn't good, we'll go another time."

No headlights shone though the dark and the ride home was uneventful, except for the unexpected milestone Millie had accomplished. He was elated, frightened, a whole kaleidoscope of emotion tumbling over him at once. He knew these girls were expert riders, had no way of knowing if he'd pass their standards. He remembered the ill-fated rodeo as if it were yesterday.

ALL WEEK, HE struggled with internal emotions, causing raised eyebrows between his parents. Sharon told him he was a grouch, and if he couldn't take coming home that late, he might as well give up hauling those girls to the singing.

Then Isaac suggested he learn to cut trees, saying it was a good time, the ground being solid, no snow or ice. Titus shook his head, unsure.

"I don't know, Dat."

"Titus, you're old enough. Strong enough. You've watched me time after time. I thought you wanted to?"

Titus shrugged, didn't answer. Suddenly he felt bound to be a miserable failure, bound to make a mess of things. Cause an accident.

"You won't find better terrain. We're basically working on level ground, okay? Most of these trees are straight, growing the way trees do in thick forest. Come on."

Titus bowed his head, looked at his saw. Fairly new, gleaming. He had only used it to de-limb. It took him twice as long to cut branches from a fallen log as it did his dad. Titus was afraid of the saw blade. Twenty-five inches of deadly chains moving at an unbelievable speed, spurting smoke and too many decibels of raw sound. His father made it seem effortless, but he knew it was an acquired skill, one he would likely never conquer.

Slowly, he bent to pick up the saw and nodded to his father, who immediately turned, striding to a sturdy pine, a perfectly straight beauty.

Titus looked to the top, evaluated distance.

He felt the usual stab of accusation, the murdering of healthy trees.

He swallowed, felt his mouth go dry.

"Okay, buddy. It's all yours."

"Dat. I can't do it. I won't be able to calculate the distance for the face cut. I know I've watched you a million times, but . . . "

"But what?"

"I don't know."

"Look, we all have to learn. I don't expect perfection. First, you make your face cut. Hold your saw at an angle."

He waited. Slowly, Titus started his saw, winced at the dangerous power.

"One cut, not quite to the center," Isaac yelled.

Titus estimated. Sawdust flew like sparks. The saw whined. He withdrew, held the chainsaw by the handle.

"Turn it off."

Titus obeyed.

"Okay. Here's the deal. Your next cut will be level. Below the face cut. As near as you can tell, make a perfect wedge. After you have that done, turn off your saw and we'll continue."

Titus bit his lower lip, then clenched his teeth. He nodded curtly.

A logger now, he couldn't waste energy talking.

The saw whined.

How far? Estimation was the hard part.

He drew the saw away from the cut, was gratified to see his father reach down and knock the wedge loose.

"See this?"

He pointed to the injured tree. "That center of the tree, a few inches of the core, is your holding wood. That is all that will hold the tree until it falls, plays a big part in the proper direction. Think of a toothpick,

Titus. Snapped in two or twisted? If this tree twists, it will slam in any direction."

Titus said nothing.

"Now, your next step is to cut the whole way around. Level with the bottom of the face cut."

Titus jerked the chainsaw to life, felt the acrid smoke in his nostrils. He planted his feet the way he'd seen his father, bent his back. He felt the muscles play in his upper arms, felt them tighten in his lower back.

The chainsaw roared.

"Whoa! Hold it!" his father screamed.

Titus pulled the saw free, searched his face.

"Not sure. You went a little deep." Isaac reached into his belt, extracted an iron wedge, then handed him the mallet.

"Okay, three of these. Space them. You've seen me do it. Alright. I want you to understand this, Titus. Right now, the only thing holding this tree is a few inches of that core. The holding wood. If you place your wedges properly, make the final at the face cut, the tree will fall right there."

He pointed a thick finger.

"Place the wedges."

Even more confident now, Titus hammered the first one, then stood to search his father's face.

"Looks good."

He brought the mallet down on the second one. Isaac was watching the top. Titus saw his gaze, saw the top of the tree shiver, as if it was in its death throes. He felt a sense of pity, a sadness for the life of the tree, and wished he could undo the damage he'd done.

"Whoa!" Isaac yelled.

Then, "Run!"

Titus dropped his mallet, scattered the wedge, turned, and ran through the soft bed of leaves, twigs, and soil. Behind him, he heard the earsplitting crack of the tree tearing, twisting the holding wood, teetering precariously before cracking. He kept his eyes on his father, who veered to the left, then threw himself full length as the tree crashed behind them.

Titus felt a blow from behind, as if tackled by a large man, and was thrown and pinned securely to the ground.

CHAPTER 9

H E COULDN'T BREATHE AT FIRST. THEN HE GASPED, TOOK SIPS OF air. His face was smashed into a mess of leaves and soil. He tried to turn his head, tried to call out for his father. He felt flattened, all the cells in his body smashed into millions of particles. In the distance, he heard his father's stentorian yells.

Another sip of air. His face felt bloated, his body elongated. He heard the whine of the chainsaw. His father gave a resounding kick and the heavy branch was off his back.

In a terrible voice, his father called his name.

Titus turned his head. He was answering, or thought he was. He felt a large hand on his shoulder, a tender touch, then another.

"Are you okay, Titus?"

"Yes."

He wanted to say that, thought he had, but found himself spitting dirt and moss and bits of leaf. He twisted his body, but felt no major pain, only a stiffness. He sat up. He wiped at his eyes, spat, reached for his handkerchief. Isaac was on his knees, swiping at his face as if he were a child, noticing the gash on Titus's cheek, the swelling of his nose.

"You were slammed pretty hard," he said, tears welling.

And Titus saw the tears like diamonds on his father's face, trembling on his eyelashes. He saw the loosening mouth, the handkerchief brought to his nose, and realized that was for him, for what might have been.

"You're okay then?"

His voice was hoarse, tremulous.

Titus got to his feet, shook leaves and dirt off his body, and grinned. He felt his nose, but quickly took his hand away. That hurt.

"You're bleeding," Isaac said.

"Yeah. Is it deep?"

"Not bad."

"What happened?"

"The cut was a mite deep. When the wedges went in, the tree twisted. Not your fault, Titus. I should have let you practice on a smaller tree."

"Maybe I'm not a logger."

"Sure you are. Everyone has to learn. Tell you what. We'll wrap up for the day, make sure your face isn't too messed up, see a doctor."

"No. They won't do anything for a nose. It isn't broken, I don't think.

They walked out of the woods together, each carrying his saw, sober, the bond between them strengthened by the mishap.

Suddenly Isaac spoke.

"Now don't go thinking you're a failure, Titus. I twisted quite a few trees. Why do you think my face is held together by plates and screws? I had my nose broken more than once."

"Yeah, but you think I'm cut out to be a logger? You think I have the skill?"

"Of course not. Not now you don't. But you will. You'll get the hang of it. I'll tell you what, Titus. It takes courage to be a logger. You can't go around being afraid of your own shadow. Very few men actually make the cut, being a good cutter. Excuse my pun. But I think you have it in you. I can tell you're already building the physique, and you have the right idea, the way you planted your feet."

"Seriously?"

"Yep. Absolutely."

Titus felt a surge of adrenaline then. His nose was throbbing, the cut on his cheek stinging, but no matter, his father had faith in him. Mentally, his shoulders squared, his height gained a few inches, his chest expanded. Could it be he was not a failure after all? That one broken, twisted tree did not mark you forever?

Jason Luhrs, on the loader, saw them coming. He knew instinctively something had gone wrong. He cut the engine, climbed down, saw the swelling and the blood, and shook his head.

Like father like son, he thought.

TITUS WOKE THE following morning with his eyes swollen shut and his nose twice as large as it had been. He groaned, rolling over. Excruciating.

His father had escaped injury entirely, grazed by a few branches, but here he was battered and swollen, and Sunday was looming. He could not let Trisha see him like this, could he? He leaned into the bathroom mirror and peered through a line of hazy vision. There was no way he could go on Sunday.

He took only a day off, then it was back to driving the skidder, careening around on level ground, but careful now, knowing one turn made too sharply and he could easily flip the machine. Inclines were easier, in a way; these machines were made for treacherous terrain.

By Friday his eyes were fully open, but his nose was still large and discolored. The cut was healing, leaving an angry purple scab. He reconsidered, deciding not to cancel Sunday plans. He cut more trees, smaller ones, getting a better grasp on the complexities, the need for a face cut and properly placed wedges. That first time he'd cut too deep, then not deep enough. He understood now more than ever the importance of the holding wood.

He laughed. He talked. He watched the sky, asked Jason to check the weather for Sunday on his phone. Clear and beautiful, windy.

He cleaned and oiled his saddle, then went to the harness shop and bought a bridle, complete with rosettes and intricate detailing.

He felt like a bower bird, preparing its home for a possible mate, and was deeply ashamed. Then elated, humming under his breath.

Sunday morning he was awake at first light, but stayed in bed, determined to hide his anticipation from his parents. He hadn't told Susan, or his father, so he would not give away his feelings now.

Breakfast was the usual array of delicious food Susan always made on in-between Sundays, one mouthwatering dish after another. An egg and cheese casserole, bacon, sausage gravy with homemade biscuits, French toast with maple syrup, shoofly pie.

Shoofly pie was an item originating in Lancaster County, and Susan's were the best. His own mother never made them, so he had one taste of the brown goo on the bottom, topped with a brown sugar cake and a dusting of crumbs, and was hooked.

"What are you doing today?" Sharon asked, after devotions.

"Going riding with Duane."

"Where to?"

"Bear Lake."

"Uh-huh. And you wouldn't happen to be going with Trisha and Millie, would you? Just accidentally dropping by?"

Sharon was shrewd, way too perceptive. He tried to deny it, but was cut off completely.

"I talked to Millie," Susan confessed. "Remember, we clean Dan Katie's house every other Thursday?"

"Oh. Well, whatever," Titus said, admitting defeat.

He looked up to see his parents watching him, their eyes shining with the good news. Here was proof Titus was being a normal young man, going to the youth gatherings, the Amish gateway to meeting a young woman of your choice, learning what was a true attraction, waiting to have prayers answered.

Yes, this was good news on a beautiful spring morning in May.

Sharon, however, pouted. She had hoped there was a chance of going with Titus, but she could tell that would never happen. A few more months, and she would be allowed to join the group of teenagers, but not yet. At least she had that to look forward to.

Titus wore denim, a blue denim shirt. He would not go riding in his Sunday trousers, he didn't care what Susan said. She actually became quite persistent about his appearance and even asked if he didn't want a bandage on that cut on his cheek. She looked way too long and too hard at his broken nose before going back downstairs.

She thinks I'm not good enough for Trisha, he thought. *Probably I'm not, but I may as well not overdo it.* He thought of the bower bird again, but this time just chuckled to himself.

Charger was a brother to Sharon's mare named Dusty, fathered by Isaac's snorting stallion, the one he'd been riding when he met Susan down at Roy and Edna's. He was huge at four years old, as brown as the cliffsides at West Bend, with a reddish black mane and tail, completely unsafe until he had a few miles under his pounding hooves. Titus had trained him mostly by himself, but lately, he had not been getting the exercise he needed, so it took all his effort to saddle him.

With every turn of his head, he felt the stiffness in his neck, the ache in his shoulders, the fullness in his nose, but the anticipation remedied any physical aches and pains. He had to make repeated attempts to get himself in the saddle, Charger sidestepping or lunging forward. His father stood on the porch, watching, which only made a bad situation worse.

Why was he always intimidated by him? Why was every single thing he did measured by the approval or disapproval of his father?

For a moment, he recognized this, before making one desperate attempt to get it right, which was what he did, then flew past the house in a cloud of dust, a hand waved in the air, a fleeting grin for his father's benefit.

He watched for one in return, and all was right with his world when he saw the flash of his smile.

Approval. His day would be blessed.

TRISHA AND MILLIE rode horses he had never seen before, but then, quite a few years had gone by since he had last ridden with them. Duane rode the big gray he bought last year. Trisha's horse was a fiery sorrel, Millie's a small palomino with a cream-colored mane and tail.

Charger was the largest horse, and also the one misbehaving. The other horses watched him, ears flickering for commands from their riders.

The color in Trisha's face was heightened and her eyes sparkled. Millie was talking as fast as possible, saying anything and everything all at once, the way she always did, only even more.

"What happened to you?" was the start, followed by an outpouring on the dangers of logging, which led into describing her best friend's cousin's broken nose, and then the amount of blood thinner medication they gave her grandmother at the hospital, and then how the scratch on Titus's cheek could become infected.

Trisha caught his eye and smiled, a slow, meaningful smile setting the tone for the perfection of the entire day. His whole being was filled with hope.

They started off, the creaking of saddles, the scent of leather and horses all familiar. Charger's ears were flickering, alert to the commands of his rider. He wanted to run, wanted to race the horses surrounding him, but was constantly drawn back by a steady pressure on the bit. Titus felt the hopping, bouncing gait, knew the horse would wear himself out fighting the bit, so he allowed him to forge ahead a bit to wear off the excess energy. He bent low over the saddle, felt the surge of power beneath him, the rhythmic beat of hooves on gravel, the wind in his face.

The empowering sense of flying hooves, the effortless gait of a smooth ride, was as exhilarating as always, and Titus found the same happiness he'd first experienced on a fast-moving pony. He reined in after a few miles, then turned back to join the remaining riders.

Duane laughed and shook his head.

Trisha said he'd calm down after that run, which was the case, Charger obedient now, his neck stretched out, loose reins in Titus's hands.

All around them there were signs of spring, the sun warm on their shoulders. Ahead of them, the Bighorns rose in the distance, imposing, their stark beauty dwarfing the vastness of rolling terrain dotted with cattle, an occasional outbuilding or low ranch house.

The slopes were covered in trees, mostly spruce and fir, as if the grassy sections decided to grow sideburns or a moustache. Birds called from leaning, weathered fence posts, barbed wire slung loosely between them. Ravines sprouted wildflowers, small tufts of forget-me-not and windflower, and bunches of tufted fescue grasses watered by spring runoff.

Soon enough, the lack of adequate rainfall would dry up even the hardiest flowers, but for now, they remained healthy and colorful, blown in the stiff gale.

Titus turned in his saddle.

"We turn here?"

"Yup."

He nodded and pulled lightly on the right rein, the horses all turning as one. The road turned to the left soon after, bearing down into a steep spruce-covered incline, the sunlight dappled with the shade of cottonwoods and pine trees.

He noticed the way Trisha rode, the way she became part of her mount, moving easily with the gait, leaning slightly forward, her back straight, her covering strings blowing behind her. She, too, had been raised with ponies and horses as a way of recreation, but she had acquired a skill beyond most other girls. Admiration rose in him, a flowering emotion still not fully understood, the thorn of his own inadequacies suppressing the joy of experiencing first love.

Oh, she was amazing. When her horse was spooked by a flapping canvas on a passing truck, she merely moved with him, fully prepared for the sideways movement beneath her. When she rode downhill, she sat back, relaxed, let the horse pick his own way. And sometimes she rode beside him, close enough that he could have reached out and touched her, which, of course, was unthinkable.

She asked him quietly if he'd experienced much pain. He said some, but it could have been much worse. The ground was soft with leaves and moist soil, so he was spared the worst.

"I'm glad you weren't hurt worse."

"Yeah, it could have killed me. I guess. Although it wasn't the main tree, only a branch."

"Bad enough." Then, "Do you work with your dad?"

"Yeah."

"You like it?"

"I do now. It took me a while. At first I felt bad, butchering the forest, as if I was personally murdering trees. The wild creatures, wrecking their habitat, being responsible for misplaced animals is not good."

She was silent, the creaking of leather and iron horseshoes on gravel the only sound.

"That means you have a soft heart."

"I don't know if I ever had it checked."

She laughed softly. She rode only slightly lower than him, the sorrel a good-sized horse, so when he glanced at her, they were surprisingly close. He caught her eye.

"You think pitying wild creatures has anything to do with having a soft heart?" he asked. "Or do I feel bad for them just because?"

"Let's just say I know guys who wouldn't think twice about killing small creatures for fun," she said.

There wasn't much to say about that, so he didn't.

"You're a hunter, though, right?"

"Yes, I am. Darlene was a great teacher. You probably think this is weird, but she and I spent hours together. She was raised with a father and brothers who were big game hunters. Traveled, you know. She taught me more about hunting than my dad. But he's too busy logging to go much. He's obsessed."

She glanced at him. "Do I detect a note of bitterness?"

Titus shrugged.

"You do get along with your dad, right?"

"Yeah, better than I used to."

"And Susan?"

"She's okay. For a stepmother."

"You'll think me nosy. I'm not. I just remember you in school. You were a lot different back then. So angry. Mam always said you were hurting about your mother. 'Hurt people hurt people,' she said."

Titus looked puzzled and forgot himself for a minute, before he nodded.

"Guess she was right. It hurts to lose your mom."

"I'm sure it does."

Behind them, Duane said it was five more miles, so why not take a break? They agreed, reined in their horses, and dismounted. Charger pulled on his bit and lowered his head to munch on tuftgrass growing by the side of the road. Titus stretched, then asked if anyone had been smart enough to pack cold drinks.

Millie reached into oversized packs, one on either side of her horse, and produced ice-cold cans of Coke, which brought a whoop from Duane. She smiled into his eyes as she handed him one, and he blushed to the roots of his hair.

The lake shimmered in the sunlight and the grass had a lush thickness not found anywhere else, especially where cattle grazed year-round and rainfall was never quite adequate. Small white flowers grew in charming clumps, their scent intoxicating. The earth seemed resplendent, promise shimmering on the moving ripples of the lake surface, the glow like an abundance of diamonds.

They tied the horses and spread the saddle blankets and a cloth for the food. Ravenous, they devoured the meat and cheese, the crackers and potato chips, the homemade chocolate whoopie pies, somewhat crushed but retaining every bit of flavor. They stretched out on the lake bank, the sun's gentle warmth relaxing them as they made light conversation, Millie being the main speaker as always. She was a delight, the way she described events and the folks around her.

Titus was so glad to be a part of this excursion, to be close to Trisha. The smile never quite left his face, even when he put his head on his saddle and closed his eyes.

Trisha observed him from her vantage point, the still swollen nose and eyes, the bruised cheek, the shape of his mouth, the cleft in his chin. His hands were large, and she bet the palms were calloused.

His body showed the rigors of his job in the thickness of his shoulders, in the muscles constantly playing on his forearms. Today, she loved his shirt. The denim was a good brand, the western cut attractive, the blue bringing out his tanned skin, the blue of his eyes. He had no idea of his own attraction, unaware of his powerful magnetism.

Humble. He was a humble person. Not cripplingly self-conscious, but merely thought little of himself, was not blown way out of proportion by his own outsized ego the way many handsome young men were.

He was seasoned beyond his years by life's hard knocks, and the anger sustaining him had evaporated, leaving the good, solid foundation of who he really was. She watched his chest rise and fall, wondered if he knew much about spiritual matters, if he knew Jesus in an intimate way.

Did he pray? Did he believe in Christ?

He had made no commitment to the church, past the age when most boys accepted Jesus into their hearts and were baptized, a joy to their parents, another soul won, another obedient child to help build the church.

Would he join the Amish if he hadn't yet? Sometimes, they simply never did, but chose an alternative lifestyle, breaking hearts, moving on into a different existence, casting off the Amish culture like a heavy backpack.

Why did these thoughts enter her mind now?

Questions without answers circled restlessly, a hungry pack of wolves threatening to attack and devour her peace. Was this love, then, this tremendous longing for another person, coupled to the anxiety of being in a free fall, a headlong pitch into the unknown?

She heard Duane ask Millie to go for a walk, heard her sister's soft reply, and watched them move off together. She swallowed her insecurity.

Would Titus notice they were alone? Was he actually asleep?

The water on the lake rippled and shone, the sun slanted through treetops, the breeze swaying them, creating patterns of light and shadow. A meadowlark whistled.

He sat up, looked around, then rubbed his eyes, winced.

She busied herself, lifted the flap of a saddlebag, rummaged around and came up with peppermint LifeSavers.

"Where are Duane and Millie?"

"He asked her to go for a walk."

There was no answer. He pulled up his knees, rested his elbows on top, his back muscles straining against his shirt. He squinted, watched the lake.

Should she move down the grassy incline to sit beside him? Would that be too bold?

She decided it would.

He wanted to ask if she wanted to go for a walk as well, but knew he could never push the right phrase from his terrified mouth.

So they sat, awkwardly. The lake rippled on. The pine trees surrounding it bent and swayed. A duck called, then another. Both felt the need to say something, but were held back.

She realized both of them were older, had tested the waters of trials and disappointments. Especially him. She gathered courage, got slowly to her feet, then moved down to sit beside him, careful to keep just enough distance.

"Water kind of holds you in its spell," she said softly.

He nodded.

"Dat took me to the ocean when I was a small boy," he said. "We went to Lancaster to deliver a horse and it died. So we went to Virginia and we sat on the beach, watched the endless waves crashing in. That's an amazing thing. This is more peaceful."

"I never saw the ocean."

He said nothing. In his mind, he said, *maybe someday I can take you.*

"It's really something."

"Was Susan a part of your life then?"

"Sort of, but she didn't live with us at that point."

"I forget how that all went."

"I broke my leg, wandering around with Wolf. Remember?"

"Yes, now I do. And she came back out to Wyoming, wanting to help."

"I don't know how my dad managed to get her to marry him."

Trisha laughed. "They make the perfect couple."

When he gave no answer, she wondered what went through his mind.

She glanced at him, saw his profile, and pitched headlong again.

Even with a swollen nose and slightly swollen eyes, he had the most arresting profile. It was the Titus she had gone to school with, but a certain maturity had leveled out the puckered anger, the features bunched with unhappiness and loneliness. She longed to know him better, to know so many things about him, but knew it was not proper to make the first move. She was also afraid she might push him away if he found her too bold.

"Do we want to see where Duane and Millie went?"

Her heart leaped. "We can."

Side by side, they walked around the lake, the path littered with pinecones and rock. She imagined holding his hand. He imagined touching a hand to her waist. Imagination did nothing to step up the stilted conversation, so they both felt the first shadow of dismal failure.

When they spotted Duane ahead of them, a rush of relief was almost palpable. Millie's chattering took away the rigid self-awareness, and they joined in the easy banter, the normal conversations of youth and bright expectation.

The sun lowered, the need to start the return trip apparent, but no one wanted the day to end. They skipped rocks, watched a pair of bald eagles, saw fish leaping in a grand display on the surface.

There was the scent of warm, moist grass and pine sap, the stamping of horses' hooves and swishing of tails, the taste of more smooshed whoopie pies.

All of it was like a bit of paradise on earth for Titus.

He copied every image of Trisha in his memory. Her white bowl-shaped covering with a top of burnished curls, her tanned, lightly freckled skin, eyes like a clear spring. The way her nose rounded at the end.

She had eaten her lunch meat and cheese in a roll and wiped her face with a napkin, dabbing gently at her mouth. He must remember to eat slower, better. Couldn't spray food around the way his father did.

She had beautiful hands, perfect nails. He wanted to feel her hand in his, wondered if they were as soft as he thought they must be.

Her dress was moss green, the leggings she wore underneath were black. Her boots were of a good quality.

Millie giggled a lot, smiled at Duane and looked at him. Trisha did none of this and he desperately wished she would at least try to steal his attention.

She was so tall and quiet, so hard to figure out.

She was perfection, and this thought alone was frightening.

CHAPTER 10

Titus was put to work on smaller trees, cutting one after another with varying degrees of success. Sometimes, his estimations were good, other times, the tree shivered, twisted, and exploded in the wrong direction. Titus was left holding the saw, scratching his head in bewilderment. Mostly, his father laughed, told him to keep going.

He wore the leather belt with loops and pockets, carried his own cast iron wedges and mallet. He took to putting red hot fireballs in his mouth, sucking on them the way Isaac did. He drank Coke and Mountain Dew, began greeting the occupants of the general store the way his father did. He even slapped a few forearms.

One Wednesday morning, Susan informed him there was a work bee at Dan Weaver's. He wanted his back lot cleared, the logs cut into firewood. He'd come down with pneumonia in February and hadn't been able to regain his strength. He was worried about his depleted woodpile.

Titus figured they'd probably not be home from work in time to go, so it was no big deal.

That day, his father threw his chainsaw in the back well before Titus expected him to. When Titus questioned him, he said they were going to the work bee. Who else would fell trees?

He hadn't thought this one out.

Would he be able to show his skill to his group of friends? To Trisha? Perhaps the girls weren't invited. Either way, the prospect was as thrilling as walking through a field of thistles in your bare feet, so he sat back, crossed his arms, and pouted. Staying up late mid-week was not his cup of tea, not at all.

Back at the house, he loaded his chainsaw and belt, grudgingly accepted the round Tupperware container of cupcakes from Susan, and drove off.

Halfway there, he opened the container and ate three cupcakes. He let his horse walk up small hills and pitied himself.

He disliked work bees. Working, sweating, dressed in ugly everyday clothes, with the girls looking as pretty as always . . . it wasn't fair.

He wasn't confident enough of his cutting skills to do it in front of his peers. He imagined himself in his patched denims and his steel-toed logger's shoes, his hind end in the air most of the evening with his face to the ground, red and swollen. Walrus-like.

He was late. A few trees had been cut, split, and stacked, but they were waiting until he arrived to cut the larger ones. Prepared to be the laughingstock, he smiled, said polite hellos, stalked off, and set to work, hoping Trisha had declined and was at home with her family.

He evaluated the first tree, a thick lodgepole on the verge of death. Fairly straight, but there was only one direction for it to fall safely. He focused, yanked the rope, and made his first cut, so focused he became unaware of his surroundings. He made another lower cut, then a cut around, and pounded in the iron wedges. He took a deep breath.

The tree shivered. He started his saw, made the final cut, and stood back, willing the tree to go where he directed it. Not bad, but not as good as his dad could have done.

He cut three thick pines, then two aging cottonwoods, before de-limbing. His confidence had risen a rung or two, so he felt the dance in his legs as he walked along the top of the log, de-limbing, focused. The whining of more saws meant the firewood was on its way, so he took a break, removed his hard hat, and wiped the perspiration from his face.

He removed his belt, placed it beside his saw, then saw what he was most afraid of. A gaggle of girls arriving with Thermoses of cold drinks.

And yes, Trisha among them.

Nothing to do but face her, nowhere to hide now.

"Hey, Titus!" Millie beamed at him.

"You were amazing. You're a real logger. I mean, I didn't know you could do that. Wow!"

Linda chimed in with more nonsense, but Trisha said nothing. He had no idea how to take a compliment well, especially covered in sweat and sawdust, his hair matted to his forehead by the tight-fitting hard hat.

So he shook his head no, looked at the toe of his boots.

And Trisha's heart swelled.

Millie poured him a lemonade. He looked up, straight into Trisha's eyes that held a perplexing message he did not understand. For days afterward, he would try to figure it out, berating himself for allowing his imagination to run crazy. If she had approved, he was still only himself, and she'd only meant it to be kind, pitying him standing there red-faced and perspiring.

DUANE ASKED MILLIE for a date, and she said yes. He asked Titus if he was attracted to Trisha, and he shrugged his shoulders and wouldn't answer. Duane suggested they could go for a double date.

Titus mumbled some gibberish about not being ready.

"How old do you expect to be before you finally ask someone?" Duane teased. "Forty?"

It was no laughing matter to Titus. How could he tell Duane of the crippling sense of hopelessness, the impossible task of asking Trisha? It was like jumping off a forty-foot tower into a sea of icebergs. He knew it was cowardly, knew he was not quite like other young men, simply thinking it was no big deal if a girl said no, that there were other fish in the sea.

Fish. Really?

Young people simply did not take this thing seriously enough, he thought. To choose a young lady to be your companion for the rest of your life was no walk in the park, no easy stroll down a rose-scented pathway where you could reach out and pluck the one you liked best.

There was a whole tangle of feelings involved, insecure thoughts telling you there wasn't a chance. The way you looked, acted, spoke. If you went too fast you were bound to spook the poor girl, who very likely wanted nothing to do with you in the first place. Maybe out of the kindness of her heart she would say yes, then get the blues later on and break your heart.

Trisha was kind, very kind, which meant she would probably say yes but only because she didn't want to hurt his feelings.

No, the whole thing was an impossibility.

It was only later in the week that the thought struck him. Millie would ride with Duane now, leaving him to provide a ride for Trisha. Alone.

He was sitting on the ground, his back against a pile of logs, lost in thought as he ate his second sandwich. The thought was so unexpected he choked on lunchmeat, hacking and coughing and carrying on, until his father asked if he was okay. Wiping tears, he nodded, put the rest of his sandwich in his lunch, and stalked off.

They were working in the foothills of the Bighorn Mountain range, an elevation with a sweeping view of the vast Wyoming territory. The astounding view never failed to ignite a sense of wonder, imagining the brave settlers traveling from the east with plodding oxen, tattered wagons with flapping canvas, weathered men and tough wives, children used to cold and heat and unthinkable hardship. And here he was, living in a beautiful home with all the comforts he needed, a lucrative job, parents, a community in which he thrived, and he still had his own personal journey, his own hardship to endure, self-imposed or not.

It was getting to the point where he realized he needed help. Should he talk to Susan? To his father? He dismissed both.

What about God? Should he get Him involved if he wasn't even sure? How did one begin to pray? Did God even care about him? It seemed unlikely that God would hear his relatively insignificant thoughts when he had over eight billion people to oversee.

Besides, he was a sinner. A hypocrite. He dressed in plain clothes, turned a righteous face to the church, and wasn't sure he believed in God at all.

Ministers blathered on every two weeks, got all worked up with revelations of their own, imposed their meaning on the whole congregation, and not one member of the congregation could stand up and disagree. He often wanted to. All this talk of how much God loved them simply couldn't be true, or He would not have taken his precious mother. God did whatever He wanted and gave you no reason to trust Him.

Should he get down on his knees? Lift holy hands? Should he merely direct his thoughts to the clouds? Where was God? He supposed He was in Heaven, and Heaven was somewhere beyond the galaxy, the dark void of outer space alive with moons and stars and planets whizzing and whirling precariously, narrowly missing each other.

He figured God had created that. No one else could have done it.

But when He was done with all that, and humans were created and all, did He still care about what went on in the world below? People kept having babies, in poor countries, where they starved as children. What sense was in that? Some babies were born into abusive situations, and God just let the sun come up every morning and go down every night as if there wasn't a thing wrong.

He sat down, absentmindedly sifting pine needles through his fingers, and wondered about these things. He found no sense of peace. When he got to his feet, he knew he must keep these thoughts locked away. There was not one person who would understand.

HE PICKED TRISHA up on Sunday evening, as usual, telling himself he would not need to carry a conversation. Nothing mattered. She didn't want him anyway. He'd decided to give up, get rid of this battering volley of feelings. She was just another girl.

It was a warm, early summer evening, when the light was golden, the earth was still green from spring rains, the trees at the height of producing healthy leaves. The tips of fir trees produced new growth, creeks and ponds were filled, the air was alive with chirps and warbles of birds.

She was a vision in a pale blue dress, her scent like a flower garden, or a hillside covered in lupines. She greeted him warmly, sat beside him and smiled, setting him alive with every ounce of love and longing he had ever felt since the day he noticed her.

"How are you, Titus?"

"Okay."

"Did you have a good week?"

"Ordinary."

"What's ordinary?"

"Cutting trees. Driving the loader or the skidder."

"Sounds dangerous."

"It is. But you learn."

"I suppose so."

There was a space of silence, the only sound the jingling of snaps and rings on the leather harness, the clapping of hooves and the rattling of steel-rimmed wheels. The thought of another nine or ten miles with her loomed before him, dread seizing him as if a slavering dragon would come trotting toward them.

He cared about her. He loved her. She set every fiber in his body alive. Now what was he supposed to do?

"It is simply a gorgeous evening," she said softly.

"Sure is."

"Titus, I hope you know you don't have to drive so far to pick me up, now that Millie and Duane are dating. I'm sure Abram would offer if you decided it was too far. He only lives a few miles in the opposite direction."

"I know where he lives."

"Oh. Okay."

"It doesn't matter. If you'd rather go with him, it's okay. But I don't have anything else to do on Sunday afternoon, and my horse needs the exercise. Horses, I should say."

"You have a pile of them, don't you?"

"Dad keeps the stable full."

"Millie and I have our riding horses, but Dat doesn't want to feed too many. He's a cow person. His herd of cows is his life."

"That's a good thing out here in the west."

"It is. And he's good at what he does. Has some of the nicest calves around. This year he had a hundred percent success rate."

"Wow."

"Yes. I thought so too."

The miles sped away, with easy talk between them. She was the one who led the subject, and before he realized what was occurring, he was talking more than she'd ever heard him. His face came alive as he spoke of his job, his eyes glowing with the thrill of keeping up with his father, which of course was not possible.

"He's crazy," Titus said, shaking his head.

Trisha laughed.

"My dad talks about it. Said he's the best logger he's ever heard of. Like a legend in his time. So, you'll follow in his footsteps?"

"No. I can never fill his shoes. He's like a giant."

"Looks as if you're well on the way, watching you take down those pines at the work bee. I was watching from the house. I'd say you're pretty good."

"You never saw my dad."

She placed a hand on his arm. He felt the touch of her fingers, the softness like the feather of a bird.

"Titus, don't compare yourself with your father. Sometimes we need to find out who we really are by stretching the ties that bind. Your father is a powerful man, but so are you for someone who is starting out."

She took her hand away.

When he said nothing, she glanced over, saw the working of his mouth, and knew she had hit a painful depth.

"I didn't mean to hurt your feelings."

The words were spoken so softly he could barely hear them. She was so kind, so easily concerned about the feelings of others, he realized anew. It was a lovely trait, one making her sweet, and the true description of it, not a light observation, but a truth in every sense of the word.

"You didn't. I don't know how to take a compliment. I'm not good with words, as you probably know by now."

"Don't say that. We can talk."

"Yes, we can."

He glanced at her, saw she was looking at him. He turned his head slightly and smiled into her eyes, allowing the smile to spread to his eyes.

He saw her eyes weren't really green, but brownish green with yellow lights dancing in them, little points of light that seemed magnetic, and he could not take his eyes away from hers.

There was a honk of a car horn from behind.

A quick pull on the right rein. Nothing was said.

THE WORDS OF the German hymn rose from the singing table, a blend of youthful voices in harmony with their Creator. Hymn singing was an old tradition for the youth raised by concerned parents in the Amish community, a teaching that would stay with them as they grew into maturity, many of them unaware of the impact these words would have on their character. Many of them were more interested in the foibles of youth, their thoughts taken up by their own appearance, or who was watching whom, wondering about the events following the songs of praise, but it was and always would be a Christian setting where the angels hovered, directing young souls to Christ Himself.

Titus sang, but his thoughts were on Trisha, wondering at the look they exchanged on the way. Her hand on his arm, conveying her faith in him.

Could he ever explain that away?

He looked forward to the ride home with childlike anticipation.

But while hitching up his horse, he watched with a sinking heart as Trisha was approached from behind, a voice stopping her as she stepped into the circle of headlights, and was drawn back into the shadows. His horse stamped one foot with impatience, tossed his head, jingling the snaps on his bit. His heart pounded.

He counted every second, and the seconds turned into minutes.

He felt nauseated.

So, this was where it all ended then.

Duane walked past, Millie beside him, talking, laughing.

"Hey, Titus. See you later. Have a good week."

"Yeah."

Millie stopped. "Where's Trisha?"

"She'll be here."

"Okay. See you."

"Yup."

He swallowed hard. He reached into his vest pocket for a piece of his favorite chewing gum. He unwrapped it and popped it into his mouth, his tongue gone dry.

He had never felt so alone.

Buggies were drawn to horses, traces fastened, snaps connected. Girls hurried to hit the steps, get settled on the seat, before the driver fastened the neck rein and hit the steps as the impatient horse moved off, anxious to catch up with the buggy ahead of them.

And still he waited.

When she finally appeared, she climbed slowly into the buggy and drew the light lap robe over her lap as he hooked the neck rein and drew back on the driving reins.

"Whoa," he called, before leaping onto the step as the eager horse moved off.

He had his hands full, keeping the horse under control until they turned on the macadam road and he allowed a fast trot. When no words were spoken, he experienced an impending sense of doom, as if led to his own execution.

There was nothing to say, he supposed, after someone had taken her aside and asked her for a date. The road home loomed as if fraught with untold danger.

When she drew the lap robe away and reached for her dress pocket, extracted a tissue, and lightly blew her nose, he realized she was weeping softly.

Every word he needed to say was scattered by overriding doubt in his own ability to make this situation bearable, so he said nothing. As the miles wore away beneath the lunging horse, he accepted this as their last ride together, sure of the reason for her tears.

Then, "I'm sorry you had to wait," she said in a barely audible voice.

"It's okay."

She drew a long breath.

"You must wonder what that was about."

He said nothing.

"It was Abram. He . . . asked me for a date on Saturday evening."

At least five different responses crowded out the words he wanted to say, so it only served as an effective stop to anything.

From behind, there was the revving of a diesel engine, the headlights brilliant on the fast-moving horse. He glanced in the mirror, recognized the hood of the dreaded vehicle. Again, the engine was given an acceleration, slowed, sped up again. Titus shook the reins, asked for more speed, his mind instantly recognizing the long, lonely stretch of road ahead of them.

He calculated the speed required to get through it.

"Who is it?" she asked, her voice trembling.

"The truck."

"You mean . . . ?"

"Yes."

He bit his lower lip, grimly. If they went around, he had to come up with a plan. They had talked about this before, but the reality of the situation now made that plan laughable. The only hope was the best Standardbred horse his father owned, the one between the shafts now. Kernel was powerful, but not as obedient as this one.

"Just hold on," he said, between short puffs of breath.

The engine was powerful, roaring as the vehicle pulled out, leveled with them, and stayed by their side. He reached over and pushed Trisha back, without turning his head.

"Stay back as far as possible," he hissed.

Insults were hurled, curse words tinged with malice. An arm appeared, waving an object. Adrenaline surged as Titus recognized the gleaming silver of a deadly weapon, the western pistol, held by one finger close to the trigger.

He saw a masked face.

Trisha whimpered.

"Stay back," he hissed.

The truck moved forward with a roar. The horse lunged, ears flickering as he waited for the command for more speed. Titus saw the truck move to the shoulder of the road, brake lights like an evil omen. The passenger door opened, the figure of a man appeared, followed by another. They stepped into the middle of the road, spread their arms.

The road was level and Titus calculated his chances. He knew this horse would obey the command of his driver over any obstacle in his way, so he loosened the reins, shook them, urged him forward with a loud call.

He responded by the lowering of powerful haunches, lunging into the collar as his muscled legs dug into the macadam, his iron-shod hooves digging in.

The wheels sang, the buggy swayed. Would he be held responsible if he ran them over? But he knew no other way.

On they came. He saw the masked faces, the terror, before they were upon them, leaping away at the last instant.

He heard their yells and obscenities, but they were past. When the truck pulled up behind them again, he was resigned to his fate. If this was how he was meant to die, at least he'd be with Trisha.

Spare us, spare us. Let us live.

He didn't know how to pray, only knew his thoughts, every ounce of his being was directed to a higher authority, to a God who had created the world with a spoken word.

Another screaming of the engine, and the truck roared past, leaving an acrid black cloud of diesel smoke and fumes. Titus stayed focused, kept his eyes on the receding taillights, wondered at the ability of the horse to keep up this pace. If they pulled off again, he didn't know to do any different, seeing as the first time might have done the job.

"Titus?"

"Sh. Not now."

But the truck moved on, the red taillights like malevolent red eyes taunting them, the diesel smoke taking up residence in their nostrils.

Titus did not take his sight off the long stretch of road until the lights disappeared from view, the turn in the road obscuring any sign of them. The horse had slowed of his own accord, flecks of white foam flying like insects past the brilliance of the headlights. He was completely soaked in sweat, breathing hard, so Titus drew back on the reins even more.

"Are they gone?"

"I think so. But I have to keep an eye out. You can sit up." He had to concentrate to keep his voice from shaking.

"Who would do such a thing? Do you think they meant serious harm?"

"I don't know."

He was glad she hadn't seen the pistol. Best not to mention it now. He felt something should be done, but what? The Amish were taught to be nonresistant, to turn the other cheek. Though, Titus was sure no one would give him a hard time for acting to protect himself and Trisha. But what if the masked man had fired the gun? Even if he hadn't intended to, he might have been scared with the horse charging at him and fired without thinking.

"I'm . . . thankful," Trisha said.

"I just did what we'd talked about before, remember?"

"Yes. But I honestly never thought it would happen in real life."

"Well, it did."

She smiled in the dim light, but he didn't see.

When they arrived at her place, she said he'd have to let his horse rest, and perhaps it was best to stay the night in the guest room.

"I don't want you going home alone. What if they return?"

They sat in the buggy, the reins loosened. The horse dropped his head, leaned on the shafts, sweat and foam running. They unhitched, led him to water, gave him a light feed.

Then they stood in the dim light, unsure, awkward. This was like an actual date. Boy takes girl home, they go to the house, sit in the living room and get to know each other. Titus couldn't go there, couldn't allow her to think he had it on his mind.

"Would you like to come in? Duane and Millie will soon be home. They were staying to play games later."

"No."

"Okay. So maybe we can find something to sit on while your horse is resting."

"I should go."

"Not yet. Let your horse rest first."

There was the sound of munching, the rustling of hay, a dripping faucet, as they stood awkwardly. Titus had to know what had occurred between her and Abram, the week ahead an eternity if he had to go on without the knowledge of a yes or no. He had come through a fearful incident, but this, this was worse.

"Titus, I know you must wonder what Abram asked."

His heart plummeted. Here it was, then. The end of everything.

"I had started to tell you, but the truck interrupted. Yes, Titus, he asked me for a date. He's a really nice guy."

Titus literally stopped breathing.

"But I don't know if he's right for me, so I told him not for this time, I needed to sort some things out. Just some insecurities about someone else."

He resumed breathing, but only on account of actually being lightheaded. He felt like he might as well fall over dead.

CHAPTER 11

H E WOKE ON MONDAY MORNING, THE EVENING BEFORE ENVELOP-
ing him in a dark cloud of dread. He knew things had gone badly,
the way he left in a rush, with no words of reassurance. He only knew
there was another young man involved, and she had used the word
"insecurities," which meant she wanted him, but wasn't 100 percent
sure he wanted her.

Well, so be it.

He was out. She could find someone else to look out for her safety.
This thing of asking for a date was a complicated maze, in which you
wandered around completely lost. He should never have given himself
the foolish thought of standing a remote chance. The worst of it was
there was no one to help, no one to confide in.

As he brushed his teeth and peered at his reflection, he wondered
at the fact she'd agreed to ride in the same buggy. The old anger and
self-loathing returned. He was short with Susan, he slouched in the
back seat of the truck on his way to work, and he ignored his father and
refused to go into the store for his usual cup of hot coffee.

He was getting better at cutting trees, the only bright spot in his
day. He knew instinctively now how to cut to keep the holding wood
intact, the tree falling closer to the intended spot. His father's praise
buoyed his spirit as he struggled to loosen the ties to Trisha.

Life simply wasn't fair. He felt a reincarnation of the sickening loss
he'd experienced as a child, bereft of a mother, only this time, it was

hard in a different way. He knew if he stayed in the Amish community, he'd have to see her, see her going home with someone else, even attend her wedding, which was unthinkable. He tried to come up with a plan, a way of escape, but could not imagine leaving Wyoming.

The land got into your blood, the strength of nature, the open air and vast spaces, which he knew were a part of who he was.

He couldn't imagine running to another community, starting over. Then he was accosted with the thought of his own cowardice, and the self-loathing that followed. Again, he wished for half the confidence his father displayed, the exuberance for life, the world and the people in it.

As it was, on Wednesday evening, the family was all tired, relaxed, lingering at the supper table after the garden had been tilled and watered. Susan, who often missed the efficiency of soil that held moisture accompanied by frequent rains, managed a few remarks about gardening in Wyoming, which Isaac allowed to bounce off with ease.

That was another thing.

How could you allow disparaging remarks like that to slide off like water? How could he go ahead with the tiller and smile at her a few minutes later? That was a piece of the confidence puzzle right there. His dad was okay with Susan's put-downs, his confidence clicking in immediately, thinking she didn't mean it the way it sounded.

"So," his father began, shifting the toothpick from one side of his mouth to the other. "When are you going to think about a girl?"

He felt the heat in his face, felt the failure to find a proper comeback, so he looked at the food residue on his plate and shrugged.

When no answer was forthcoming, Isaac tried again.

"I guess I should ask about your commitment to God first. You haven't made a move about giving your life to Jesus."

Susan swallowed nervously. Sharon got up to clear the table. The perfect answer came into his mind, but stayed there.

How did one commit to someone they didn't know?

Who was Jesus?

He was a picture in the Bible Story book. A man with long brown hair and a beard who wore a white robe and sandals. A man who died a shameful death on the cross, died a barbaric death and supposedly rose again, and had enough power by going through all that to save people from their sins. He'd heard it from his mother, heard the whole story over and over in German, from various preachers whose beards wagged and whose eyes watered with the depth of their emotion. People who honestly felt this unseen Jesus lived in hearts and provided strength and guidance.

He'd never felt a thing. Not once. He wasn't sure if he wanted to. He could handle things pretty well on his own. Why give away the little bit of power he had to someone you couldn't find?

His thoughts were cut off by his father's voice.

"You can't have a good relationship with a girl without faith."

Before he could stop, the words came, short, clipped, and angry.

"Faith in who?"

"What's that supposed to mean?" Isaac's face was stern.

"Just what I said."

Sensing the beginning of an argument, Susan shifted her feet and cleared her throat. She put a hand close to Titus's arm, and he met her gaze.

"Titus, it's okay. I know how you feel."

"No, you don't."

"Titus." A stern warning from his father.

"She doesn't."

Susan sat back, brought to silence. Kayla began singing her lullaby to her doll, rocking in the corner. Thayer pounded his rubber ball on the kitchen floor, welcome sounds of distraction.

"She never lost her mother," he said in the general direction of his father.

"Titus, isn't it about time you buried that hatchet?" Isaac sighed.

"What's that supposed to mean?"

"You know. You've been carrying around this personal grudge against God, never accepting the fact He giveth and He taketh away. It was her time to go. Her time on earth was finished."

"How do you know that? Maybe you didn't do everything you could have done."

"She had the best care available."

Isaac remembered the doctors, the looming five-story hospitals, the chemotherapy and radiation boosted by alternative protocols. In spite of it all, she slipped away, surrendered to the hovering angels by her bed. The pain of those days lessened, but never went away completely; the only thing now was the comforting presence of Susan, the best thing that could have happened to him.

"Titus, our life is not our own. Can you understand this?" Susan asked.

"Whose is it then?"

He knew he was being obstinate. Knew he was hurting his parents, but the hurt inside him was entrenched too deeply to care. Why must he be the one carrying all the hurt alone?

"God's."

"Yeah, well. He skips a few of us down the line."

"Let me put it this way, Titus," said Isaac. "Jesus stands before the door of your heart and He knocks, never giving up hope that you'll listen. He loves you more than we are capable of. Hopefully, soon you'll open the door and let Him in."

Susan nodded. "God created you. He knew before you were born that your mother would be taken to Him and I would become your stepmom. It's all an act of love and caring on His part. We have to accept Him as the Master of our lives.

"So, He does stuff like kill your mother? That makes sense."

"Let it go, Titus. Let go of the tragedy of your mother's death," his father said, with no small amount of sternness.

Titus sighed, shook his head.

The truth was, he didn't want to let go. He wanted to keep her close. To feel the nurturing from his soft, warm, breathing mother. The way her housecoat gave off sweet powdery scents as he sat on her lap and read all the Berenstain Bears books. The one where they got in trouble at school. The one where they learned how to do a good job. He thought of the hot chocolate and warm coconut oatmeal cookies she had ready when he came home from school. He still loved her with a fierce, possessive kind of love, the memory of her burning as brightly as possible.

If he let go of that, he would have to surrender to something else, and nothing could take its place.

HE DID NOT go to the hymn singing on Sunday evening, but stayed in his room, read old westerns he'd read ten times, ate pretzels, and drank Coke warm out of the can. He was thoroughly miserable.

The day was so beautiful, it ached. Every rise in the level land was dotted with wildflowers on the southern slopes, birdsong and the cries of hawks resonating through the air like liquid gold.

Toward evening, he was restless, so he let himself out the front door and called Duane, forgetting the fact he was dating. One ring turned into six or seven and he remembered, then felt foolish and hoped Duane wouldn't notice his number on the caller ID. He shoved his hands in his pockets and walked down across the horse pasture, climbed the fence, and made his way to the high ridge surrounding it. He'd hike for a while, get rid of the restless feeling in his legs.

He breathed deeply, the scent of pine and decaying leaves a boon to his spirits. Birds twittered at his approach. He thought of Trisha, wondered if she was getting dressed to go to the singing, and which one would pick her up. She could go with Duane and Millie, or perhaps she'd take her own buggy again, although he doubted she'd be brave enough.

Or crazy enough. His mind searched the list of young men who would be interested in her. Other than Abram, he could not imagine one other person, most of the guys being much younger than she was.

One thing was sure, he wouldn't think of dating anyone else until she was married. Gone. From his mind and his heart.

Linda wasn't too bad. Could he love someone besides Trisha? Surely it would be without fireworks and heart palpitations and knee weakness, which might be nice.

Then there was this matter of faith, his dad sounding like a real minister of the gospel, with Susan as his helper.

Whatever.

He had no reason to believe any of that stuff mattered as much as they let on. Still, if he thought about it, there was plenty good in their lives. Plain good. Susan, for sure. She cared so deeply about neighbors. There wasn't one neighbor on Sky Road she didn't know and who didn't know her. She was always baking someone cookies, bringing them a meal, or inviting them in for coffee to listen to their woes. It didn't matter whether they were Amish or English, she seemed to love them all the same.

He stood on the side of a high ridge and watched the black cattle milling across the green pasture, a sight to behold. Before long, the green pasture would be brown and yellow, the sun and the wind drying out most of the green. Haying would begin. He could feel the ache in his muscles, hauling those bales around.

Trisha said she and Millie did most of it. They drove the horses hitched to the baler and everything. He shook his head, feeling an arrow of pain and loss. Which seemed to be his lot in life.

Trisha was unlike any girl he'd ever met. She was assured and humble at the same time, besides being beautiful. Perhaps this was his punishment for thinking too highly of himself, thinking he wasn't a homely looking loser after all and stood a slight chance.

Her horse riding was beauty in motion. She rode so easily, as if she and her mount were one. He couldn't take his eyes off her. He never could. She completed him, that's all there was to it.

Trisha lay on her bed, her hands propped behind her head, listening to Millie who bounced from closet to the bed, laying out first one dress, then another, viewing them from different angles, clucking and fussing like a mother hen with a brood of freshly hatched peeps.

"Oh, just put one on. Guys don't know or care what you're wearing," she observed dryly.

"Well Trish, obviously I'm doing something right. I'm the one who got what I wanted. I'm dating."

"And I'm not."

"Yeah well, you guys have issues."

"Issues with what?"

"Who knows? You should think about why he's bringing you home. Maybe he wants to."

"He was right about the danger."

Trisha and Millie's dad had called the sheriff, saying there was a time and place for getting the authorities involved and this was it. But the sheriff had said there wasn't much they could do without a license plate number to track them down. The singing had been canceled, the decision made to keep the youth off the roads for a while. So Duane was coming over with a driver to pick Millie up.

Millie held a dress up to her chest, considering it. She paused and glanced over at Trisha. "Call Isaac's. Leave a message. Ask Titus to come over."

"Are you kidding me, Millie? I would never."

"Of course you wouldn't. That's why I'm dating and you're not. You are way too proud to even think of flirting one tiny bit."

She shrugged into a dusty green dress, turned sideways in the mirror, and smoothed the pleats over her hips.

"What do you think?"

Trisha nodded.

"Millie. I do too know how to flirt. I told you about our night. I even invited him in, which was awkward. I also told him about Abram. And . . ." Here she paused and slanted Millie a sheepish look. "I should have worded it differently. I told Titus about telling Abram I'm insecure about someone else. Do you think he might think I meant another guy, when I really meant him?"

"Think, think, think, meant, meant. Why don't you say how you really feel?"

"I can't."

Millie turned away from the mirror and reached out to slap Trisha's raised knees.

"Sometimes I can hardly believe you're older than I am. I guarantee you Titus thinks it's all over. He doesn't think very much of himself and you know it. Why would you have told him that?"

Millie was fairly shrieking now.

"Sh. Mom will hear. I don't know why I said that."

"I do. It's your foolish pride."

Trisha rolled over, sat up, and slid to the floor. She stretched one leg out to the side, bent to touch both hands to one foot, then the other.

She kept on for ten repetitions on either side as Millie secured her apron, then opened a drawer to search for the best white covering.

"Aren't you wearing shoes?" Trisha asked.

"No. I hate them."

Trisha looked at her feet. "I don't like being barefoot. My toes are ugly."

"What? Boy, you two would make a wonderful couple. He doesn't have enough gumption to swat a fly, and you sit in your room cringing about your toes."

Trisha laughed, a full-throated sound that reassured Millie.

"I'm going to leave a message at Isaac's."

"No. Don't. Please don't. If God wants us to be together, it will happen."

"Huh. He's going to need some help from me, I bet you anything."

But Trisha's heart contained the peace of a believer, fledgling though it was. In her own simple way, it affected her life, this faith in God which amounted to bursts of song, bouts of Bible reading, and kneeling by her bed to pray every evening without fail. She had never experienced a soul-shattering trauma like losing a mother to cancer, had always been secure and loved by both parents. Her idea of God was an outreach of the love she experienced with her parents, the sweet security of protection and safety.

So now, when she went for her own walk in the fields surrounding their property, the niggling doubts of her misspoken words were handed over to God, who knew all things, and would take care of it.

If He had a plan for Titus and her, it would work out in His own time. She believed this amazing sense of attraction for the very one she had never noticed before was from God, a hand ushering her down the path of finding a life companion.

LATE SPRING TURNED into the dry heat of a Wyoming summer. Singings resumed after there were no more sightings of the mystery truck, but Titus did not go that whole summer. He perfected the art of felling trees, or at least became much better. His father no longer praised him, seeing him gain confidence on his own. He slung bales of hay as lightly as a football, developed muscle, and thought of Trisha constantly. He trained two-year-old foals to ride and drive and kept himself separate from the social whirl of the youth.

His father's right shoulder acted up, causing severe pain at night. He swallowed Advil, increased his fluid intake, and still went to work every day.

From him, Titus learned what sheer determination could accomplish, gradually stepping into his father's footsteps. His workload increased, his muscles burned with overuse, his legs became as sturdy as the young trees surrounding the large ones. And deep inside, he carried the sadness of what might have been. His blue eyes took on a look of impenetrable sorrow and his mouth curved downward in perpetual seriousness. He found no joy in everyday life.

A certain lifting of his spirits occurred only when he took long hikes into the foothills of the Bighorn Mountains and searched for wildlife through the lenses of his favorite binoculars, his heart beating rapidly at the sight of a magnificent elk or mule deer, a black bear rolling along in his distinctive gait.

Susan spent much time in prayer for her stepson. She knew what was missing in his life, knew too that only God alone could provide the necessary ingredient, the Spirit that dwelled in hearts opened to Him.

Sharon turned sixteen years old. The party was postponed until Susan felt stronger; she had been taken by a severe bout of morning sickness after she discovered another little one was on its way. For weeks she lay on the couch every morning and evening, the nausea keeping her in its grip. She consumed chlorophyll and ginger tea, plus other remedies from well-meaning sisters and concerned parents, but they all failed. Finally, she told them all to leave her alone with her misery, that nothing helped anyway.

Kate wrote long letters of gratitude and undying hope for Levi's return, while a vile bitterness roiled in Susan's stomach. It literally made her sick, reading those letters. Some of them went unanswered, the disgust was so overwhelming.

Isaac was ecstatic about another baby. He yelped and bounced and brought her raspberry ice cream, the only food she could think of. That and white American cheese sandwiches with mustard.

Titus thought this aspect of married life absolutely bewildering. Why keep on having more babies when Kayla and Thayer were plenty? He could not see the elation of having your wife go through all this physical misfortune and thought his father a moron at best.

When they finally sent out the invitations for Sharon's birthday party, cleaned the basement, made a cake, and hung paper decorations, Titus had accepted the fact that Trisha would be dating Abram or the mysterious person she talked about.

He believed he had surrendered to his fate and promised himself he would not look forward to seeing her, if she even decided to come. If not, then it would seal the direction he was taking.

Sharon was a winsome, petite girl, opening to the possibilities of being included in a group of young people. Blond and blue-eyed, with a quiet charm and a manner that spoke of her dutiful life at home with her stepmother, Titus realized a true sense of pride in his sister. For her sake, he dressed in a light blue shirt. He thought derisively of the miserable attention to detail he had followed to win Trisha. Look where it got him. He had struck out completely.

He brushed his wet hair with no thought of his appearance and went down to the basement to open windows before the party's arrival. He teased Sharon about being nervous and was met with Susan's protective arm around her daughter.

"She's barely sixteen, Titus."

And Titus felt old, seasoned, though he had no desire to go through all that youth stuff again. He was thinking of getting another dog. Now there was unconditional love, the kind you could depend on to take you through your days stress free. He had heard that old Ben Schmidt, over on 636, had raised a litter of Siberian huskies mixed with German shepherds. He was thinking of going over one evening soon.

When buggies began to arrive, he tried to capture the old feeling of anticipation he felt a few months before, but an overriding dread replaced it.

Who was the mystery man who made Trisha feel insecure?

He would find out soon enough, he supposed, and was not going to be caught lurking in corners for a glimpse of them.

Parents arrived, some of them bringing Sharon's young friends. There were the usual youth driving their own teams, clattering up the drive with an array of horses. Titus envied them, the youthful optimism found only in the very young, before life's disappointments and realities hit you in the face. Before wanting someone you could not have.

Susan did her best to be a good hostess, but her face was about the same shade as the icing on the birthday cake, her eyes large and dark. Thayer didn't like the commotion and threw a fit, hanging on to her skirts and crying. Isaac, as usual, was holding forth, a group of men around him laughing, drinking coffee, all of them unaware of Susan's plight.

Titus left Duane's side, scooped up his younger brother, and placed him squarely on his father's lap. Isaac looked up, found Titus with disapproval written all over his face, and took Thayer and quieted down.

Titus thought his dad might never change, but in the meantime, he could give him a hand in seeing himself.

Sharon was radiant. She cut the cake, opened presents, talked and giggled with her group of friends. Susan beamed by her side, despite the nausea that continued to plague her. There was talk, later, of how Susan simply took that girl under her wing as if she were her own, and to watch them you'd never know she wasn't. But then, she'd been younger when her mother died, had never been strange like Titus.

And Titus told himself it was okay if Trisha didn't show up. It was easier than having her appear with a new boyfriend. He had started to relax, laughing and joking with Duane and Lester, when he looked up to find her standing inside the basement door, a young man he had never seen beside her.

His heart sank.

So this was the one. Strangely, they resembled each other. The young man had the wavy hair, the tanned skin, and from what he could tell from a distance, the almond-shaped greenish eyes.

His hair was not cut according to the "ordnung," and he appeared to be unaware of his surroundings.

CHAPTER 12

He asked Duane.

"The guy with Trish?" Titus did his best to conceal the anxiety creeping across his face.

"Why do you ask, Titus?"

"Just wondered. He isn't from around here, is he?"

"No. It's their first cousin from Iowa. He was at a boy's camp, like a rehabilitation place for anger issues, and other stuff. Millie said he didn't want to come along tonight, but Trisha thought he should."

Duane asked where he'd been hiding, why he didn't come around, and Titus shrugged. Sometimes there was too much to say, so you said nothing.

"I don't know what's keeping you from asking Trisha."

"It's complicated."

"There's nothing complicated about it. Just ask her."

"Abram did."

"She obviously said no."

"There's someone else. She told me."

"She didn't say who it was?"

"No."

Duane looked at Titus, hard. "You know, for someone as intelligent and hardworking as you, you don't have a clue when it comes right down to it."

Titus gave him a glare, "What's that supposed to mean?"

"She told you there was someone else?"

"She said she told Abram she wasn't ready, that she was insecure about someone else."

"Which is probably you."

"Me? Why would it be me?"

"Oh, she talks to Millie, makes her promise not to breathe a word, but she tells me everything. It irks me, Titus, how you always stay on the outskirts, looking in. Like a wolf. Sneaky. Scared to be yourself. You should see a good counselor."

"What for?"

"Just stuff. You need to get over your mom, try a little harder to accept yourself and the people around you. As soon as stuff doesn't go your way, poof! You're gone."

"That's a mouthful."

"Really. But it's true."

Lester joined them at that moment, and talk turned to light-hearted banter, Duane talking excitedly about fly fishing on the river.

They ate cake and ice cream, played a few games, watched the younger ones play a game of volleyball. Trisha did not come over to talk to them, or try to make herself available to Duane or Titus.

Should he talk to her?

He thought of watching for when it was time for her to leave. He could offer his help at hitching up.

There was talk of another episode with the roaring diesel truck, a young married couple on their way home from a friend's house very nearly upsetting when the horse was frightened and ran through a ditch alongside the road. The police were called as usual, and they came out to talk and get a description of the vehicle, which was sketchy at best, so there was never a buggy ride after dark without a certain amount of apprehension.

If only he were like Duane, just walking up to Trisha to ask her how she was doing. Maybe he could ask to be introduced to the cousin from Iowa. It was a big relief that he wasn't an actual boyfriend.

He watched them drive away, hating himself and his lack of courage, angry at Duane for daring to mention a counselor. He didn't need anyone to tell him how to live his life, or to dig up old stuff. It was weird the way people thought because certain things happened in the past it created a monster as an adult.

Duane had no idea the amount of self-loathing, the agony of approaching Trisha. He couldn't do it, and that was the bottom line.

But there was reason to hope. She was not dating, which meant he should go to the next singing. He thought staying away would give her a chance to date the one she wanted, and Duane thought it might be him.

Why would it be?

HE DID GO to the singing, a distance of about fifteen miles, but only at his parents' urging, saying it was his duty to take his sister now.

He knew that, but had hoped they wouldn't require it.

His father had given him quite a lecture, with Susan nodding in approval.

He felt the old rebellion well up, could taste the bitterness of his anger, but controlled it successfully and was pleasant enough by Sunday.

Church at the neighboring ranch had been an ordeal, which he could not explain away. There had been a visiting minister from Ohio, and one endowed with a special talent. All day since the service he'd felt like crying. During the sermon he felt goose bumps, the hair on his neck rising. He coughed, swallowed, cleared his throat, did his level best to control his emotion, but this guy dug deeper than most.

Life wasn't always easy, the minister had said. Stuff happens that we don't understand, so we run from God. We say we can handle it ourselves, but we can't. If God is not our Master, we're only kidding ourselves.

Titus wondered if God was a feeling. If He was alive. If Christian people everywhere could feel Him, or if they just thought He was there. Why did he feel as if he should start weeping, genuinely crying, with an unexplainable ache somewhere in the region of his chest?

He had never come so close to realizing he might not be able to handle everything.

Trisha. It was Trisha, completely bringing him to his knees.

But he fought. This wasn't the way it was supposed to be. Nothing he had ever read made this sound normal. Perhaps he was not like other people, but went around with a mental disorder, thinking he was okay when he actually was not.

THERE WAS A message on voice mail saying Susan's father had been diagnosed with pancreatic cancer, stage two, which sounded treatable, but often with that type of cancer the prognosis was grim.

Susan wept quietly into the dishwater, wept as she hung out laundry, then turned a brave face to Isaac and said she'd be fine. But the atmosphere in the house was quiet, a sadness permeating the air, and Isaac told Susan to start preparing, that they were going for a visit.

"You can't get away from your work," she protested, but it was not in earnest.

Isaac insisted, said it was high time she went home to her family. He'd call, make arrangements, and no, not the train, Susan was not in shape physically to put herself through that grueling trip. They'd hire a driver, take the family, see some sights, sleep in a nice hotel.

Susan's eyes sparkled. The color rose in her cheeks. She put a forefinger to the calendar and muttered to herself, Isaac at her back, a hand on her waist.

She opened the sewing machine and sewed all week. They went to town and bought new footwear for the children. Isaac shut down the logging operation for two weeks, give or take a few days, paid Jason Luhrs and told him to enjoy his leisure a couple of weeks. Titus saw Jason's gratitude and devotion and knew his father had a special talent with the employees. He wished he were his father, with all that gumption, the decisions coming easily.

Luggage was brought from the attic, wiped clean of dust, and filled. Titus had misgivings, wondering how he'd get through this, wandering around stuffy Lancaster County. He'd be terribly out of place there, a bumbling country hick from Wyoming. But he would go for Susan.

She seemed so happy about his decision to go, which was a bit bewildering. Did she care so much about him? He decided perhaps she did. He found her upstairs going through the shirts and Sunday trousers in his closet, turning guiltily to ask if he was sure he had plenty of clothes.

"Don't worry about me," he said, and almost added "Mom."

Dave and Amanda Baugh were the drivers, a retired couple who had sold their ranch and now lived in a cozy bungalow an Amish builder had built for them. They made some extra cash on the side by driving the Amish to places they wanted to go for a dollar a mile—plus waiting time, if they sat in parking lots too long.

Everyone knew Isaac Miller, so the chance to drive over four thousand miles with him was readily accepted. Susan would have gone by train, by any rattling old conveyance, as long as she got to her parents' house sometime soon. But she was grateful for the comfort and convenience of being driven.

Titus could see how much Isaac's sacrifice meant to her. She hummed beneath her breath, she touched her husband continuously, put an arm around his shoulders, reached up to touch his face, smiled and sewed and looked forward to seeing her family. Titus knew he would do the same for Trisha, and gladly.

He knew this last singing would be important to him, before they left on their trip, but for what reason, he didn't know. Sharon was eager to go, with the youthful optimism of a sixteen-year-old, so he tried to relax, go with the flow of her conversation, and stop worrying about Trisha.

The singing was uneventful, the songs, the faces, the benches behind them lined with parents. As usual, he knew where Trisha was all the time. He knew when she got up to leave the room and when she came back. He watched her fluid grace, the way she smiled, her profile etched in his mind.

He had to talk to her. He had to. He couldn't go to Lancaster without having spoken a word again. He felt the pounding in his chest, felt the fear of disappointment crowd out his breathing, and knew he simply couldn't do it. The embarrassment, the sheer thought of approaching her, was too monumental.

He hitched up his horse, feeling lower than he ever had. He waited on Sharon, who he knew was not ready to leave. Singings had turned into a misery for him, like running a marathon without training. Exhausting, hours of sheer endurance.

He loathed himself afresh, the cowardly hiding, peeping at Trisha like a wounded dog. Twenty-one years old, considered an adult, and worse than a sniveling child.

She came out of the circle of lights in the mellow summer night like a vision. She walked up to him, put a hand on the black shaft of the buggy, and said in her soft voice, low, a bit hoarse, "How are you, Titus?"

He swallowed. He cleared his throat. Her face was tense, her eyes large and darkened in the dim light. She did not smile, other than the quick lift of the corners of her mouth.

"Okay."

"Just okay."

"Well, yeah. Sort of."

No. I'm not good, he wanted to say. *I am held in the grip of some ongoing spiritual struggle and completely miserable about you. I'm afraid of my own shadow, and there's no end in sight.*

"I hear you're going to Lancaster County. I'm sorry to hear about your grandfather."

"He's not my grandfather."

"Oh, I guess not biologically. Right."

He wished he could retrieve the harsh words, but the damage had been done. Trisha sensed the bitterness.

There was an awkward silence.

"So, now you have Sharon to accompany you. Do you enjoy bringing her to the singing?"

"It's okay."

"You don't enjoy Sunday evening, do you?"

"Not really."

"I miss our rides together."

"Yeah."

"That last ride, though. My word. I don't think I was ever so afraid in my whole life."

He nodded. He went cold, then hot, became dizzy.

She'd missed their rides. She had missed being with him. How could a person hear these words and stay on his own two feet?

"But it was ridiculous, you driving all that way out around. But I have thought since, if I would have been with anyone else, a less powerful horse and a more timid driver, things could have been very different."

"Oh, I don't know."

He looked down at the toe of his shoe, scuffed the dust, ran a hand through his hair, the words he wanted to say disappearing beneath the disbelief of what she had said.

"You showed a lot of courage that night, Titus."

"Courage?" he asked, dumbly.

"Yes. You were very brave, really. Goading your horse toward those men. Like a movie or something. And I bet you anything you never told your parents. If it wouldn't be for me telling everyone, the incident would have been forgotten by now."

"What do you mean?"

"Everyone is talking about it. Saying how you're developing into your father. I hear you're getting good at cutting trees."

"Oh, I don't know."

"Come on, Titus."

She laughed softly. Did he imagine this, or did she step closer?

"I'm not as good as my dad. When he cuts a tree, it goes within inches of the intended spot. I can't do that."

"You're still young."

"I guess."

There was another space of silence.

Then, "So you won't be here for a while?" she asked.

"No."

"Will you go to the singings in Lancaster?"

"I didn't even think that far. I have cousins, I guess. I don't know."

"I'd love to see Lancaster County."

"Come along."

The words were out of his mouth without a thought behind them, but his heart was exploding with a thousand words. *Oh, come along with me. Sit beside me in the van and share the sights and sounds and new experiences.*

She laughed again, very softly. And now she did come closer. He could detect a scent of flowering trees and new spring grass and the subtle scent of the sun on fresh water rippling over glistening rock.

"Would you actually want me to accompany your family?" she asked.

If you were my special friend. My girlfriend. If I had the courage to ask you for a date. She'd told him he had courage, had been brave.

But this . . . this was harder.

"Of course."

She drew in a breath, held it. Then she laughed, a trembling sound he wasn't sure was actually a genuine laugh, or something else.

"Are you sure? Wouldn't that be a bit strange?"

"Not for me it wouldn't."

She stood quietly.

Ask her.

He heard the words as clearly as if someone had spoken them in his ear. It took his breath away, but he couldn't do it, told himself it was all his imagination, his heightened senses because of her nearness.

Ask her now.

"How are you coming to the singings now?"

"With Abram."

"You're with him?"

"You mean, am I dating him?"

He nodded.

"He asked me again."

Sharon erupted into the circle of lights, a vision in pale lavender, breathless, apologizing, ready to go. Quickly, Trisha stepped up, whispered, "I said no."

Then she left, slid away from him, and vanished into the dark.

SITTING IN A van barreling down one interstate highway after another for hours on end was a lesson in patience. His body was used to working hard, not sitting still in a cramped van.

Half of him wanted to be at home, his thoughts constantly going to Trisha, but he knew this trip meant a lot to Susan.

The scenery was much the same, sagebrush and cactus, wide open spaces with distant mountains, towns, farms, cattle, horses. Road signs advertising anything from cars to dental work. Lonely ranch houses crumbling in the wind and the sun, tumbleweed piled beside the porches like dead landscaping, rusted trucks yawing to the sides.

Titus often wondered what the stories were behind these weather-beaten houses, vacant now, the broken windows like grief-stricken eyes, the sturdy walls bravely keeping the house intact. At some point in time a family might have filled the house with color and light, footsteps and voices, so that the house itself was like a living thing.

Maybe the family had been lonely and decided to move to a more urban area. It might have felt too isolating to stay in the old house handed down for generations. Or maybe they lost their jobs and had to move where there was more work available.

He felt a certain sense of loss for old houses along the way. It made him wonder if he was too sensitive.

Trisha had said no to Abram again. He returned to that thought again and again, wondering why she had rushed to tell him that before Sharon joined them.

He still felt the same desperation, the same feeling for her he'd always had, but he needed to get his priorities in order first. He had only a vague idea of what that meant, but the fact of it was there, like a distant roadblock shrouded in fog.

At the motel he stayed up too late watching shows on television, thrilled to see one featuring the last frontier in Alaska and how people lived there. Alaska was something to see. He would love to go, but Amish people didn't fly on airplanes, even those little bush planes droning through the sky like giant dragonflies. It was a rule, an *ordnung*, though sometimes exceptions were made for emergencies.

Did he want to be Amish, for sure? It meant living within a circle of people forming a boundary around you, the restrictions voiced by the bishop in spring and again the fall, a set of rules to live by, to obey and to honor.

He thought about what it would be like to say goodbye to parents and siblings, set his face to that wonderful land, and experience all the character-building hardship he had seen the folks on television living with. He truly loved nature, found peace in the amazing views of the west, marveled at the intricacies of a beaver dam, the flight of the golden eagle.

He also loved Trisha.

He loved her with his heart and soul. He could never leave her for Alaska. So, if he loved her, it meant his future was set before him, to become a part of the Amish community, live within those boundaries for the remainder of his life.

The thought was not depressing at all, but rather very peaceful. There was comfort in knowing who he was, knowing the path stretching before him had been walked by his father, and his father before him. He thought about the timeless safety of tradition. *Die "fore-eldra"* (forefathers). . . how often had he heard it said that it was a blessing to walk in the path of one's forefathers? The righteous path of tradition was God's way. So, could you walk this road without fully trusting God, or even knowing whether He cared about you? Was tradition enough?

These were the things standing in his way.

His parents had no idea, and he was ashamed to bring up his questions. He could already feel his father's impatience.

"You think too much," he'd say. "Why can't you be like other young men? Just follow the path. Go, and the rest will follow."

The message he seemed to get from the people around him was that as long as you honored your parents' wishes, you had already embraced all that was necessary.

But was that truly all that was necessary?

He did not know.

IN THE MORNING, Titus knocked on the door of his parents' room and found Susan with her book of devotions on her lap. She closed it, a question in her eyes.

"Did you sleep well, Titus?"

"After I quit watching television."

She grinned. "What were you watching?"

"Alaska."

"Good for you. At least it was something decent."

"Where's Dat?"

"He went to get us some coffee."

Titus nodded and lifted Thayer, who was still in his pajamas. Kayla smiled up at him, asked to go with him when he went for his coffee. So he dressed Thayer while Susan dressed Kayla and held their hands as he walked across the parking lot to the convenience store, gas pumps like beehives, men and women in dueling cars and pickup trucks, casting curious stares.

Titus did not welcome the ill-concealed curiosity. He hated being dressed in the Amish garb in places like this. In North Dakota, folks weren't used to seeing Amish people around.

Titus was very conscious of his broadfall trousers and hair cut in the customary bowl cut. His father, on the other hand, was always oblivious to how odd they looked. He would just smile at gawking individuals and strike up a conversation about the weather.

Sure enough, there he was, holding two cups of coffee, standing beside a bearded man with a long gray ponytail, his motorcycle helmet in his hand, a gleaming Harley Davidson beside him. They were having an animated conversation, and Titus felt the slow release of full-on embarrassment. He tried to sneak past them with the kids.

No luck. "Titus! Come over here."

"I'm getting coffee."

"No, come here. I want you to meet this guy."

It was rude to keep going, so he made a detour past a few vehicles, stepped across a curb, and looked at the two of them, wishing the macadam would open up and swallow him.

"This is my son, Titus. And these younger ones are Thayer and Kayla."

A broad grin, a smile of accomplishment.

"This guy is a logger. Drives a skidder." He gave Titus a sturdy slap on the back.

Titus nodded, tight-lipped.

"I hear you're pretty good," the man said, his eyes showing genuine interest.

"Oh, I don't know. I haven't been doing it very long."

"Not everyone can do it, you know."

Titus nodded. Isaac beamed and went on about the logging industry, then told the man his coffee was getting cold and he better get back to his wife.

Titus wondered what the point was. Why strike up a conversation with someone you had never seen before and who you'd probably never see again?

He bought coffee, granola bars, and lollipops for the children, then made his way back to the motel room without making eye contact with anyone.

Breakfast was a jolly affair, his parents both in high spirits, eager to be back on the road. Titus was unusually quiet and he found Susan's eyes searching his face more than once. She tried to include him in conversation, but failed.

Once back on the road, she tried to involve him in conversation about the surrounding scenery, but when there wasn't much response she gave up. He was sleepy, having stayed up late, so he soon stretched out with a pillow under his head, the humming of tires on macadam lulling him to sleep.

CHAPTER 13

LANCASTER COUNTY WAS A WONDER, TITUS THOUGHT. ALL THIS rain, all these growing things, farms wedged against farms surrounded by roads and places of business, main roads packed with vehicles, horses and buggies traveling alongside on the wide shoulder.

Titus observed the red lights at intersections, horses standing amid vehicles, obedient, accustomed to all forms of moving objects. He watched in mild disbelief as a horse pranced, swayed from front to back, the driver a middle-aged woman who looked unperturbed, talking to her passenger as she waited at a red light.

As they approached Susan's parents' home, he remembered only parts of it, having been much younger when he had last visited. He found himself wishing he hadn't come. He felt awkward and out of place. He hung back while all the handshaking and hugging was going on, desperately hoping no one would try and hug him.

Mercifully, no one did.

After the initial flurry of greetings, they were shown to their rooms upstairs, windows open, curtains fluttering in the summer breeze, the drone of traffic permeating every room. The rooms were spotlessly clean, the beds made to perfection, the scent of mothballs in closets offset by air freshener and traffic fumes.

He sat around the kitchen table with his parents as they opened the discussion about Susan's father being diagnosed with cancer. He looked thin and pale but spoke honestly about the past, when he'd felt exhausted to the point of collapse, then developed pain in his side, and went to the family doctor who sent him for tests. He was still in the early stages of pancreatic cancer, so there was a ray of hope. He was one of the lucky ones, catching it that early, he said. But didn't look forward to the treatment at all.

Susan was relieved, finding the news much better than she'd hoped, so there was a sparkle of joy in her eyes as she listened to her father.

The sisters and husbands, cousins and kin descended on the house like a swarm of African locusts. Titus was unimpressed and stayed in the living room pretending to read a hunting magazine as voices rose and fell. Children shrieked and banged doors and ran back and forth without being noticed, their parents engrossed in loud conversations.

He had no idea how he would ever get through the week.

He saw Susan turn back into a Lancaster girl again, her speech returning to the more clipped pronunciation, not the Susan he knew. Sharon rolled her eyes and smirked.

It suddenly felt obvious that they were not her children, not really. They were Isaac's, and they were from the west, where customs were different, where clothes were made in the western style, bowl-shaped coverings and dresses made in a more modest fashion, where language was softer, the r's rolled into a soft burr.

They felt isolated, unsure how to act among the colorful dresses and different pronunciations of familiar Dutch words.

Rose arrived, husband in tow, a pile of children like brilliant birds. The oldest daughter, who looked to be around Sharon's age, introduced herself as Caitlyn. "But call me Kay, everyone else does."

She smiled at Titus and gave Sharon a hug that was not really a hug, more of a sliding of her arm around a shoulder, then a frank stare of evaluation before saying they were both "cute."

She was dark-haired, dark-eyed, with hair rolled up over her head in a style that was unusual. Her small covering barely clung to her head with the few straight pins holding it, a heart-shaped white covering as unusual as the hair. Her dress was lime green, the hem brushing the soles of her shoes. A black apron with a bib up the front was tied around her waist.

She had just started "running around," the term used to acknowledge the age of sixteen, when she was accepted into the circle of youth, and was having a blast, she said, talking around the large wad of gum in her mouth, popping it as if to accentuate her words.

Every five minutes she pulled a small phone out of her sweater pocket and viewed a display of something or other before slipping it back.

Occasionally, a tweet alerted her to some message or other, which she would read before smiling, or drawing her eyebrow down, holding the small device in both hands as her thumbs flew across the screen.

She sat back, crossed her legs, and swung a sandaled foot.

"So, tell me, what do you do out in the boonies?" she asked.

Sharon looked puzzled, but Titus wasn't about to be the bumpkin she made them out to be, and answered, "We build campfires to cook rats and eat them."

She howled with delight, fully and unabashedly. "You're funny."

He grinned at her, and she grinned back.

"I guess you don't drive a car, huh?"

"No."

"No Saturday night parties, huh?"

"No."

"What do you do?"

"I just told you."

She laughed again. "You're funny. You're cute, too."

Titus decided he genuinely liked her. There was no guile in this girl, she was merely being honest and open about her observations, shrugging her shoulders if she didn't understand some of their descriptions of home.

Titus forgot about himself when he was with Kay and found himself saying and laughing more than he thought possible. Kay and Sharon went upstairs and returned wearing each other's clothes. Sharon giggled, her face pink with embarrassment, but she made a perfectly lovely Lancaster girl. Kay was doubled over with the hilarity of the situation.

She took pictures with her phone and wanted to send them to Titus's phone. She was incredulous when told he had none. No one in the youth group did.

"Mercy days. Really? How do you stay in touch?"

Titus caught the frown from his grandparents.

Rose told Kay to put that phone away and stop being impolite.

Kay fired back a retort to save her pride, marched off into the living room, and flopped on the couch, petulant now.

"I can't stand my mom. This dress is hot, and I don't mean it's awesome. I'm warm. Let's go trade again."

So Titus wandered out to the back porch, sat in the shade of the house, and listened to the children playing cornhole in the back yard.

It wasn't long before Kay and Sharon joined him, Kay plunking herself down beside him on the swing, moving even closer to make room for Sharon. Titus was a bit uncomfortable. He could not remember a time when any girl had ever sat this close, even in a buggy. But she was at ease, her hands expressive as she described her job to Sharon.

She offered to take them to the Saturday night party, saying Sharon could wear her clothes, but Sharon shook her head, saying they weren't used to any of the things she had described.

"Oh, come on. What do you do for excitement? You're stuck with these horribly dull lives. Titus, don't you even have a girlfriend?"

"No."

"Seriously?"

"No. I don't."

"So what do you do? I mean, like, during the week?"

"I cut trees and drive a skidder. I'm a logger."

"Wow, how cool is that?"

She popped her gum, checked her phone, rocked the swing.

"Yeah. You guys are so laid back, which is awesome, really."

There wasn't much to say to that, so Titus said nothing.

"Sharon, what about you?"

"I help my mom. A friend and I clean house for an older lady in our church."

"Oh man, I'd like, literally die."

Titus felt sorry for Sharon then, but was glad to see her take it in stride. He was proud of her, could see the good manners, the quick evaluation of the divide in cultures. She knew there was no contest, so she sat back and accepted it.

"Tell you what. Let's do a tour of the markets. I'll show you where I work. Would that be cool?"

"Sure."

"Cool. I'll get a driver. The guys who haul me all over the place are all at work. The Amish guys. I don't even know anyone that doesn't have a vehicle. We get around in cars on the weekend."

She went on to describe her "crush" of the week, a guy named Jason King. He was the one she really wanted to hang out with, but he was drunk half the time and not ready to settle down yet. And besides, he wasn't sure if he was going to be Amish or not, and her dad would have a royal hissy if she never joined up.

Titus listened, grinning inside. This was truly a different world, but told through the refreshing views of this Kay, it was enormously entertaining. He'd heard from Susan about these markets around Lancaster and surrounding areas, and couldn't imagine fifty or more vendors under one roof. Many of the stands were owned by the Amish.

He looked down at Kay, and she looked up at him. He smiled and she smiled back. She slapped his thigh.

"I think you're really cute." She giggled. "Probably I shouldn't tell you that, huh? I'm not even your real cousin. We could get married someday, even."

Titus smiled, then he laughed.

"You wouldn't marry a country logger from Wyoming."

"No. But I'd love to give you a haircut, get you a really nice car, teach you how to be a Lancaster guy."

"Is that what's important?"

"Well, yeah."

"Is everyone like this?"

"No, of course not. I'm in one of the top groups. The aces. There are thousands of kids and they all belong to different groups. Some of them have cars, others get around in teams, some are real decent, it goes from one extreme to the other."

"Hm. Interesting. Who decides this?" Titus asked.

"Well, a lot depends on the parents. If your parents aren't worried about ordnung and are cool with stuff, you're going to be like them. My mom doesn't worry about anything. She's cool."

"I thought you couldn't stand her."

"Not when she wants to act all *chide* (decent) and strict when plain people are around. As if she cared one iota about anything. Dad does, she doesn't. But she wants people—you know, strict people—to think she does. I hate when she does that."

"I see," Titus said, nodding. He looked down at her, liked the contours of her pert little nose, the flash of dark eyes. She was just adorable. He thought how easily he could ask her for a date. Just ask, and she'd be kind and open and honest. Why couldn't he be relaxed around Trisha?

The back door opened and Dave came out, his protruding stomach half-covered in black trousers, giving him the appearance of a partially submerged Easter egg, his yellow shirt a perfect shade. His round face was framed by a thick brown beard, an abundance of hair like a well-thatched English cottage. He was carrying a gray tub filled with something edible. He headed for the grill, lifted the lid, and pressed a few buttons, turned a few knobs. He turned to Titus, curiosity on his round face.

"You look like an interesting chap. You sure have grown."

He lifted his shoulders, flexed his arms.

"I can see your strength. Logger, huh?"

Titus grinned. "It's what I do."

"You look it."

So now he was cute, according to Kay, and strong, built like a logger, according to Dave. Was this what Lancaster folks did, handed out compliments? But he'd take it. He found himself drawn to this Dave, an amiable person exuding friendliness, curiosity. He asked so many questions, Titus felt as if he were being interviewed by a professional, but liked him immensely. He got off the swing and helped with the burgers and hot dogs, kept up a running conversation.

The meal was delicious, the burgers crisp on the outside, juicy on the inside, cheese melting down their sides, lots of mayonnaise, homemade zucchini relish, tomato, onion, and whatnot piled on top. Mothers cut up hot dogs, squirted ketchup onto paper plates, poured drinks and shooed children off the porch so that if they spilled lemonade, it didn't have to be cleaned up. Talk flowed easily, laughs erupting like small breezes here and there. Kay was teased and flung back her own sharp retorts.

Through it all, Titus caught Susan watching her father with an anxious expression, and it stabbed his heart. Here was a picture of love. She had left everything she knew, moved thousands of miles away to be a mother to someone else's children, flinging doubt and caution to the wind, just going out and doing it. Successfully.

Nothing was perfect, ever, but here, seeing the look of pure love for her ailing father, Titus realized the sacrifice she had made for them.

Regret for the years of anger struck him, but he did not know how to go about remedying that now.

TRUE TO HER word, Kay rode to her grandparents' house with a hired driver, drank a cup of coffee, and picked at an apple fritter while Sharon and Titus got ready to join her for a tour of the markets.

Susan watched her warily. As they went out the back door, she told Sharon to be careful and gave Titus a meaningful look.

Of course, Susan would be concerned about Sharon, knowing well how easily a sixteen-year-old could be impressed. But Titus liked Kay, figured he'd have a good time.

The traffic on Route 30, then on 283, was unlike anything Titus had ever experienced. He found himself gripping the edge of the seat, leaning forward as if to help the driver with a second set of eyes. There had been plenty of traffic around the major city bypasses on the way in, but this was ridiculous. Lancaster wasn't a huge city, so why all the traffic?

He asked Kay, and she waved a hand, said it was the never-ending swarm of tourists descending on Lancaster County every year. Any time of the year, except summer was worse.

"Tourists love to look at the way we live," she snorted. "They have no idea."

Titus agreed. Seen from the outside, the charm of a horse and buggy traveling slowly down the road, a farmer in a field driving six Belgian horses, or a team of plodding mules, the driver wearing a wide-brimmed straw hat—it all took them back in time. It reminded them of a slower, better time, when life was not filled with too much information, religious and political strife, anxiety. And so the charm remained.

But from the inside, there were plenty of imperfections.

Plus, the Amish were not immune to worldly influences. So many new things cropped up—an invasion of gadgets to entice the curious, a new way of making phone calls, the internet available at the touch of a screen, the whole world at your fingertips. The ministers strove to keep the flock free of worldly invasion, with limited success. Among the Amish, as with the rest of the world, one conscience was not the same as another, folks allowing themselves the freedom of a newer and more modern way of life, rejecting the old, simple way.

Kerosene lamps were all but obsolete, replaced with battery lamps powered by the rechargeable batteries, now widely available. Solar panels appeared on roofs, the sun providing energy to power freezers and refrigerators, automatic washers. And so there were disagreements, conservatives yearning to go back to a simpler time while the more liberal embraced the changes.

The foundation of the ordnung were the contented souls who cherished and appreciated the old customs but strove to keep the love of Christ in their hearts toward the younger and more adventurous.

Church members were lost, excommunicated, as they joined a church where cars, electricity, and cell phones were accepted as a way of life, serving Christ with a disregard of senseless man-made rules. When folks wanted church members that were more like-minded, the world was their palette, and they could start a new church, one producing the colorful fruits of their way of thinking. All of this was allowed, usually remaining in harmony with the church they had forsaken, as long as the basic rules of ordnung were kept intact.

Harrisburg was a large city bordered by a wide river named the Susquehanna. Spanned by bridges, buildings towering close by, mansions lining the streets by the river, they made a few turns and approached an old brick building.

"This is where your mother worked for a long time," Kay informed them. She was a great tour guide, pointing out various places of interest as Titus had been occupied by his thoughts. Now he was drawn in by the immense building, the number of cars in the parking lot, and the crowd going in and out of the market.

He'd never seen so many diverse people. Black people jostled along with whites, Hispanics, Asian people—there were so many different people all coming to buy whatever this market had to offer. He was eager to see what it was all about.

Kay smiled at Sharon. "You okay? It can be a bit intimidating at first."

"I'm fine." Sharon smiled.

Titus looked at his sister. It would take more than this to frighten her. She was a wonderful rider, sticking to her horse like a burr, unafraid of even the wildest animal. She was a true western girl, and Titus was proud of her.

The market was a wonder. Titus was uncomfortable at first, the crush of people working on his nerves, but Kay pointed out so many interesting things, especially the deli where Susan had made sandwiches, a long sub they called a hoagie, for many years.

To go from this life to Wyoming was indeed a huge change, one she must not have taken lightly. He felt the familiar regret.

Kay was animated now, touching his arm, showing off. She smiled and waved, said, "How's it going?" or "Hey!" to many of the vendors, and what a variety of folks there were. Plain, solemn men, dressed in old-fashioned clothing, selling cheese and cuts of meat, saying "good morning" in humble tones, in the reserved manner typical of the Amish. They worked side by side with girls dressed like Kay, in brilliant colors and rolled hair, their small coverings pinned precariously on the backs of their heads. And there were older women in every size and description at cash registers, taking orders, bagging items as they talked to customers.

Kay pointed out the immense bakery, filled with a variety of Amish people working methodically, and the glass cases filled with all manner of pastries. There were whoopie pies of every description, cookies and loaves of bread, pies and cakes, muffins and doughnuts.

Titus bought a box of six chocolate whoopie pies, the white filling between the two chocolate cookies as thick as the cookies themselves.

"Find a table, if you can," Kay ordered. "Sharon and I will get coffee."

Titus spotted a family leaving a table and slid gratefully into a chair as soon as it was vacant. He wished he was his father, who would not feel one stab of embarrassment, but would strike up a conversation immediately with the most available person.

Titus wasn't sure if the proper thing was to open the clear plastic box and help himself to a whoopie pie or to wait, so he sat. He was careful not to make eye contact with anyone.

"Hello."

He looked up to find a smiling young man in a bill cap, a beard trimmed close to his face, wearing a button-down shirt and broadfall trousers. Amish, evidently.

"Someone said you're Susan Lapp's stepson from Wyoming."

Titus wasn't thrilled to be singled out, but he nodded.

"Good to meet you. I'm Ben Stoltzfus, her cousin on her dad's side. Sorry to hear about her dad."

"Yes. It's why we're here."

"I imagine. Must be tough for her. So, how're things in the west?"

"Oh, pretty good."

Ben slid into the chair opposite him.

"Well, you're a nice-looking fellow. Often wondered what her husband looked like. She could have had a bunch of guys around here, but had a tough time of it, it seemed like. So she took off for Wyoming."

Titus didn't know what to say to that blunt observation, so he said nothing.

"Must have been a huge change for her."

"I think so."

"They had children together then, I hear."

"Yes."

"So you're a mixed family, huh? And how's that going for you?"

"Good."

"Good, good. Well, I gotta get going. I own the barbeque place. Come get yourself some dinner. On the house."

He stuck out a hand, soft and pale. Titus gripped it and gave him a small grin. Ben shook his hand, commented on his hard palm.

"What do you do?"

"I'm a logger, with my dad."

"Really? Wow. You look it. Guess you think I'm a real weirdo, working in here, huh?"

Titus shook his head.

Ben patted his shoulder, said, "Good to meet you," and hurried off.

Kay and Sharon returned, bearing three cups of coffee.

"I didn't know what you liked, so I got you a black coffee."

"I drink it black."

"I got a caramel latte. Sharon, too."

He didn't mention the fact he had no idea what a caramel latte was, afraid she'd think him a hopeless backwoods hillbilly, so he nodded. Kay eyed the whoopie pie package.

"Go ahead. I'm not touching those high-calorie things."

"Me either," Sharon said.

"Some Ben Stoltzfus came to meet me. Said he was a cousin. Said we should get some of his barbeque for lunch."

Kay snorted delicately. "His stuff is gross."

Titus lifted his eyebrows.

"He makes a killing with that stuff. Owns three places. I can't stand him."

So that was the second person she couldn't stand. Her mother and this cousin. He supposed honesty was a virtue, although in this case, a dubious one.

He thought of a woven rug, loosening along the edges, becoming frayed. He wasn't sure why the thought entered his mind, but he felt the change of the fabric of Amish life. Perhaps Kay was an exception.

"Okay, if the barbeque isn't good, I'll start on the whoopie pies," he commented, opening the plastic and helping himself.

"You're so cool," Kay giggled. "I can't believe you're single."

Sharon caught his eye, winked.

Titus ate three whoopie pies and grinned at the effusive comments from Kay, who stated unabashedly she'd weigh three hundred pounds if she ate like that.

He went and got some barbeque chicken, despite Kay's warnings, and found it delicious.

Kay sat opposite, picking at a turkey and spinach wrap, eating mostly spinach.

Sharon ate some of his barbeque and told Kay it was actually really good.

Kay waved a hand, dismissing the whole episode.

Kay was the product of a modern Amish home, one where new ideas were adopted and attitudes often paralleled those of the world. She was unabashedly herself, comfortable with her own values, unafraid to speak her mind, which was refreshing.

After the market, they visited a woodworking shop, a huge building filled with the smell of lumber, paint, and varnish, and a showroom with sturdy oak furniture for exorbitant prices.

Another place manufactured sheds, anything customers wanted. Garden sheds with copper birds on top of cupolas, any type of windows or doors, the whine of saws and tapping of screw guns a thrilling sound.

He imagined working indoors, pumping out sheds as fast as possible, and knew he was blessed beyond what he deserved.

He could not do without the wide-open spaces, the scent of rain and drought and wind from the snow-capped mountains. To wander the foothills on any given day, to feel a sense of awe and wonder as he walked among pungent spruce and Douglas fir, was a privilege he would never again take for granted.

He felt sure God had something to do with it all.

CHAPTER 14

THEY ATTENDED A NEIGHBORING CHURCH SERVICE, WHICH TITUS found similar to their own, except for the number of people who came on foot. Everyone lived so close, there was no need to hitch up the team. He observed a quiet way, an inhibition, no emotion displayed among anyone in the morning, but after services the atmosphere seemed to loosen up. A few of the boys spoke to him, but many of them didn't bother.

He noticed the difference in the girls' dress and could see Kay was pretty liberal, the girls in church showing a more circumspect demeanor. He supposed it was all normal among the thousands of Amish families, with varying levels of adherence to the ordnung, and who was he to judge?

He was curious about the Sunday evening singings, and later that afternoon, he asked Susan's sister Kate, a petite, quiet, lovely woman with the saddest eyes he had ever seen. She often sat by herself, observing quietly, saying nothing, so he sat beside her and brought up the question.

"Oh," Kate said, "very likely only a few, if any of the youth at church, attend the same singing."

"What?"

Titus looked at her, incredulous.

She nodded. "Yes. There are so many different groups with different levels of dress and behavior. You can pretty much choose which group suits your idea of 'rumschpringa.' Parents take their children to visit different singings, see which one they want."

"Are you serious?"

"Yes. It's actually very nice. There are conservative groups, parent supervised groups, very liberal groups, and just about anything in between."

"What about Kay?"

Kate smiled. "Well, you've seen Rose. Kay is just a product of her family. Not to judge them, but they're always stretching the rules."

"I like Kay. She's very honest. There's no guessing what she's thinking."

"Same as her mother," Kate said with another smile.

Titus wanted to ask her many questions, about her life, about Levi, but felt it would be an intrusion of her privacy. And he simply didn't have the gift of talking candidly with anyone. He was always afraid of being obnoxious, or stupid, or simply not knowing what to say, so he didn't say much of anything.

"So, I hear you don't have a girlfriend yet," Kate said, smiling at him in the sweet guileless way of hers.

"No."

There was a space of silence as they watched Susan's mother move past the swing with a large bowl of snack mix, children racing around in the back yard, Rose and Liz sitting around the patio table all talking at once, the men huddled around the grill, flicking knobs, arguing about heat, evidently. Susan's father was lying down in the bedroom, a fan blowing the warm air around him, feeling tired out from going to church.

It was wonderful, the way the family stuck to one another when they came East to visit, losing very little time while being together.

Titus felt a certain kinship, pride in the fact Susan was from this place.

"I'm sure you could have a girlfriend," Kate said softly.

"I'm in no hurry."

"As you shouldn't be. I have many regrets."

Titus had heard about Kate's life, an almost unbelievable chain of sad events. Her first husband had untreated bipolar disorder and died tragically, and the second, Susan's former boyfriend, left her and moved to Florida for another woman.

Titus did not know what to say.

"I didn't choose wisely. I thought I prayed and asked for guidance, but I didn't really. I just fell hard for an attractive man and took the consequences, I guess."

She looked up at Titus, her soft eyes liquid with unshed tears.

"But Levi will be back. I truly believe he will. I pray constantly."

Almost, Titus snorted. Almost, he told her not to hold her breath, that God didn't always answer prayer, and sometimes He left you floating without Him. Instead, he nodded.

"You could go to a singing tonight. You and Sharon. Kay would be glad to take you. She'd find a girl for you." Kate giggled.

Titus was aware of the fact that she was a hopeless romantic, always imagining the unreality of a fantasy world. Levi would come riding in on a white horse, swoop her off her feet with chivalrous apologies, and all would be well.

Well, she'd suffered plenty, and he allowed her these unrealistic moments. He smiled and said, "I don't know about that."

"Yes, I know. They're pretty wild. A lot of her friends don't stay with the Amish, but choose other churches."

"Well, it stands to reason."

"You're so wise for your age, Titus."

So now he was good-looking, built like a logger, and wise. He'd go home with enough confidence to ask Trisha . . . at least until he saw her and tried to say anything.

SUSAN WAS UNUSUALLY quiet on the return trip. Isaac tried his best to keep her spirits up, but gave up somewhere in Ohio and allowed her the sadness she needed. This time, saying goodbye had been especially hard, with her father's failing health, her mother's stoic acceptance.

Titus watched all this from the back seat and thought it was good for his father to feel as if he wasn't capable of fixing everything with his loud voice and effusive manner.

Glad to be back home, Titus fell out of the van, carried luggage and bags, breathed deeply of the pure, sweet air, and felt a spring in his step and an unusual gratefulness welling up in him.

This was home. He reveled in the feeling of belonging to the land, the mountains, the wide-open spaces.

Lancaster was pretty, the way a groomed, expensively dressed lady is attractive, but Wyoming was like a slender young pioneer girl, skirts and hair blowing in the wind, pure and clean and free.

That evening he rode his horse to the ravines by the river and watched the parched grass sway in the wind, like a whisper from Mother Nature, telling him all the secrets he needed to know. He felt fulfilled, at one with his world, the flowing wind, the dust raised in small whirlwinds, like a hello, welcome back. The river was reduced to a trickle in the dry season, footprints of deer and coyotes, wolf and badger along the sides where the soil was dark from the small trickle of water.

He breathed in the scent of the horse's mane, heard the creaking leather of his saddle, felt one with the generations of hardy folks who had been here before him. He thought of all the men and women from the East, leaving lives of ease and relative comfort to settle the West. Didn't all men have the drive for adventure, the seeking of new horizons, or was that merely a thing of the past?

He sat on his horse, watched the blazing sun go down over the land, found colors he could not name, the open sky and beauty of the land filling his chest, his lungs, and finally his heart. He bowed his head, knowing there had been a Creator whose mind was far above any imagination of the human brain to design anything as beautiful as this.

And this was only a fraction of the universe, the universe only a fraction of the galaxy exploding with planets and hurling stars, bypassing each other with infinite precision.

He turned his horse, leaned forward, and loosened the reins, feeling the power beneath him, the wind in his face.

THIS TIME, IT was especially hard for Susan as she went about her duties, doing laundry and straightening the house. Everything was off kilter somehow.

She felt afresh how much of her heart stayed in Lancaster and fought the tears that threatened to run down her cheeks. She tried keeping her spirits up and failed miserably.

She told Isaac she hadn't slept well, had a pounding headache, and could they buy their breakfast sandwich and get lunch somewhere? Then she went back to bed and allowed the self-pity to wash the tears out of her eyes and into her pillow.

Isaac said it was okay, but he wasn't his usual self either, quiet on the front seat, the miles falling away as they sped toward the logging site two hours away. He was not quite as obnoxious with his effusive manner, only responding with the curt "Morning" when an acquaintance spoke to him.

By lunchtime, he had his old enthusiasm back and said he was starving, they'd take a few hours to find a good diner, as a special treat.

There, he was surprisingly well known by other loggers, ranchers, and farmers, all waving and calling out greetings, to which his father responded in his usual loud manner. And as usual, Titus was the afterthought, was nodded to, acknowledged minimally.

The food was good, the service pleasant, and Titus felt himself growing sleepy, a lethargy stealing over him on the return trip. He guessed he was lazy after the week in Lancaster, all that good food and rest.

The skidder broke down about an hour after their return, so Isaac and the driver went for parts. Isaac was red-faced and walking with a stiff-legged gait, the irritation radiating like a rash. Going to the diner was enough time off, and now this.

Titus shrugged, picked up the chainsaw, and went back to cutting trees. It was hot, the sun beating down on his back as he bent to his work. It was a gnarly old pine, the tree on an incline, so it was harder to judge, a bit difficult to make a good cut.

But he was confident, had done it many times.

The saw roared, Titus giving it all the power possible. He straightened, stood back, felt the pride as the tree fell close enough to the projected distance.

He drew his eyebrows down when he saw the bent sapling it had taken down with it, a lethal trap ready to spring. It had happened before, knocking him to the ground with its velocity. He considered the situation, thought he'd wait until his father retuned, then thought of his ill temper.

His pride won out. No use letting his father see this.

Titus stepped up to the bent sapling and evaluated the proper way to release it, his heart pounding. Fully aware of the danger, he hesitated, then lifted the saw, eyed the pine.

If it rolled before he could step back and away, he was history. He pressed down on the saw.

He felt a moment's confusion, almost a surprise, then a blinding smack full on to his face. He knew he was hurled backward, knew his saw went flying, felt his hard hat ripped from his head. He lay on his back, his world rocked by pain unlike anything he'd thought possible.

He reached up. His hand came away sticky, red with his own blood. But he was fully conscious. He knew it was bad and he was alone. He put a hand up again. Blood dripped between his fingers, and he knew he had to get help, and soon.

He got to his feet, held on to a tree for support, struggled to stay conscious as the earth tilted.

Got to go. Got to get to the road.

He had nothing to stanch the flow of blood. Not even a paper towel from his lunchbox. He lurched down the logging trail, no idea if he'd make it to the road, but he had to try. Stumbling, he knew there was no way. He would lose too much blood before his father returned. But the thought of dying alone was terrifying, goading him on. He wasn't sure God cared enough about him to take him to Heaven.

A mind-numbing regret paralleled the agony of his broken face. He was keenly aware of the steely rebellion against the loss of his mother. As he stumbled along, the pain of his remorse was worse than the severe injury to his face. So much time in his young life had been wasted on bitterness, so much time wallowing in anger.

He walked, fueled by determination and the fear of dying, his shirt front soaked in blood. He noticed nothing of his surroundings, his brain exploding with raw pain from his left cheekbone. His thoughts churned.

He could not die. Would not. The human body contained gallons of blood, didn't it? He wasn't really sure.

He tried to keep up a train of positive thoughts, which became shattered by the onslaught of a debilitating fear of dying.

Through the haze of pain, he heard the grinding of gears, a truck making its way down the canyon road. There was hope, if only a small thread.

He hurried on, stumbling over tree roots, felt the weakness in his arms, the muscles in his legs turning soft. He became aware of things being distant, as if he were looking from the outside in, or through a dark glass. The sound of another moving vehicle helped him to propel himself forward, helped him hang on to one more positive thought.

He stumbled again, righted himself, and drew to the bend of the macadam road. Would his father return? Would he be the one to find him? His thoughts jumbled, jammed like floating logs on a dam.

A car stopped. A blue car.

He dropped his hand, peered through impaired vision to see a white horrified face. A woman. The driver's door opened, a man, of average height, overweight, his face blanched with fright.

"Hey. Oh my. Were you shot?"

The woman yanked the car door open, strode over, screamed, and backed away. "I told you I didn't want to see the West up close on these creepy back roads, Ron," she yelled.

Titus opened his mouth, but the effort to speak was too much.

He made another effort.

"Logging. Logging accident."

That changed everything. The man turned on his heel to retrieve a black duffel bag from the trunk and a roll of paper towels. The woman returned and helped mop the blood from his face and get him out of the blood-soaked shirt.

They arranged a pillow on the back seat and covered him with a blanket, the shivering suddenly uncontrollable. A cell phone was produced and he heard urgent voices, felt the movement of the vehicle.

WHEN HE AWOKE, the white light hurt his eyes. He knew immediately he was in a hospital somewhere. He reached up to find his face swathed in bandages, a doctor and two nurses in the room.

"Is the patient awake?"

"Yes, he is."

The doctor was there, smiling. "Hey buddy."

There was nothing to say, so he nodded. It hurt.

"How are you feeling?"

He nodded again.

"You're all patched up. That tree packed a pretty good wallop. You're a fortunate young man. A few inches higher and you'd be in the morgue. Walked out by yourself?"

He nodded.

"You'll be fine. Tough, that's what you are."

He turned to the blond nurse.

"Heard anything?"

"They're on their way."

"Your family will be here soon."

Titus rolled his eyes from side to side. That hurt. It hurt a lot. He turned his head, which was no different. It would take a while for things to return to normal. A needle poked into a vein on the top of his hand and was attached to a thick plastic hose leading to an IV bag hanging from a pole.

He was wearing a gown, covered in a white blanket. His tongue felt dry, his lips cracked, broken open. His whole face was a mass of throbbing pain. He drifted off, dreamed of clipped bushes and lines of traffic. He didn't know how long he slept, but was awakened by a hand on his shoulder, his name spoken in a terrible voice, his father's face by his bedside.

"Titus. Oh my word, Titus. What you put us through!"

Susan was beside him, her face working, tears seeping from her worried eyes. She grabbed a few Kleenex from the small box on the bedside table, hand to his arm, a gentle squeeze.

"So glad you'll be okay, Titus."

The doctor spoke, explaining the procedure. It had been a five-hour surgery. There were plates holding the cheekbone intact. Broken nose, but the jaw was mercifully intact. A grave injury, but Titus was young, he would heal with minimal scarring.

Isaac showed the doctor his own face, which was astonishing.

"Talk about following in the old man's footsteps," he said.

He would require a night's stay, but Isaac and Susan stayed till visiting hours were over. Isaac gave them both a colorful account of his return to the logging site to find no sign of Titus, a sighting of blood, then another. The chainsaw and hard hat, the felled pine and the twisted sapling.

"It was plain as day. As if the trees could talk. As if I was trailing a deer, except it was my own son's blood. Got to the road, found your shirt. Soaked. It was soaked. In blood. You just cannot imagine the thoughts, Titus."

Isaac had flagged down a passing car and used their cell phone to call the closest hospital. It took what felt like a lifetime to confirm that Titus had been there but had been transferred to another hospital for emergency surgery. So he was alive. Isaac almost hugged the man whose cell phone he was using. The man was gracious, insisting he stay until Isaac could get through to the other hospital. When Isaac learned Titus would be in surgery for at least a few hours, he made the decision to go home and collect Susan before heading to the hospital.

Isaac's face showed the pain of the past hours, the time of imagining the worst. He was reminded of Titus's days of being in the wilderness with a broken leg, as a child, but then, that had brought Susan into his life, which was the greatest blessing.

He reached for Susan's hand, smiled deeply, searched her gaze. They asked Titus what had actually occurred, but it hurt to talk, so they agreed to wait.

There was a slight knock. Isaac called for the nurse to come in but was surprised to see a middle-aged Amish couple step through the door, shy smiles on their faces. Isaac and Susan got to their feet, met the extended hands for the traditional Amish handshake.

"We are Simon and Betty Bontrager from Oak Bluff community."

"Oh, yeah. Heard of it, just have never been there. How do you do?" Isaac boomed, till Susan asked him to quiet down, they were in a hospital.

"We heard there was an Amish boy here. Logging accident?" Simon asked, glancing at Titus, but looking away politely.

"Yes, indeed. Logging is one of the most dangerous jobs on earth. My face is patched together, and now it happened to my son. Same thing."

"Huh," Betty said, her small, bright face as curious as a bird.

"Isn't that something?" Simon exclaimed.

He walked to Titus, held out a hand. Titus took it.

He smiled, a warmth radiating from his eyes.

"I wish you better days, young man. Looks like you really got clobbered, didn't you?"

Susan asked Betty what brought them here to this hospital.

Betty said their nineteen-year-old daughter was a recovering leukemia patient, being sent home in the morning after her last hospital stay.

Susan expressed the empathy she felt, asked how she was doing.

"Oh, she's come a long way. She started feeling bad at seventeen and has endured more than many others endure in a lifetime."

"I'm sure."

"She'd be glad if you'd visit."

"Not tonight. Our driver is actually waiting."

There was more small talk, a few words of comfort, and they were on their way. They turned back to Titus, who had already fallen asleep, the mixture of medication in his IV putting him in a state of much needed rest.

Isaac patted his shoulder, said, "Sleep well, buddy," and put a hand on Susan's elbow to guide her out.

THE FOLLOWING MORNING, Titus's face felt as if a ton of bricks had fallen on it. He pressed the button on his bedrail and asked in a rasping voice he barely recognized for more pain meds. The IV was taken out of his hand and he was given pain pills and a small paper cup of water.

He was handed a tray of Cream of Wheat without sugar and canned pears. He was so hungry he sucked the tasteless mush off his spoon, smashed the stringy pears and ate them, too.

He was so glad to see his parents that he gave them a bit of a smile and a thumbs-up. He saw the love and caring, and for the first time in his life, he allowed it to stream into his soul, his heart swelling with a returned love.

Susan brought a hand mirror. He could not believe the disfigurement. His eyes were a deep black, purple, blue, and green, swelled into mere slits, his nose easily twice the normal size. A jagged line of stitches zigzagged across an unnatural cheek, the protrusion unaligned with the uninjured side. He was hideous.

Immediately, his thoughts went to Trisha. The small amount of hope he'd felt was dashed to the ground.

He handed the mirror back, said nothing.

When the doctor came in, he seemed pleased with the surgery.

No bandage, just Vaseline on the stitches. Don't allow a scab to form. A prescription was sent to the nearest drugstore, keys tapped on a computer wheeled into the room, a form signed, and he was told to get dressed, he was free to go.

Isaac became his true ebullient self then, praising the doctor's skill, his voice too loud, his speech laced with the genuine appreciation he felt in his heart.

"Thank you. In a year or so, he'll be as good as new."

They shook hands and the doctor left quickly. Too many things to attend to, doing his best to make every second count.

They were escorted to the waiting area, but had been released sooner than expected, meaning the driver would not be available for another hour.

"One of the quirks of being Amish," Susan sighed. "You okay?"

She looked up at Titus, concern in her soft eyes. He nodded assurance, said he was ready for a burger and fries.

They were surprised to see the Bontragers seated in an alcove behind a potted plant. They had their daughter with them, seated a bit off to the side, a magazine open on her lap, her head bent.

They expressed the surprise, the coincidence of both being released earlier and drivers being asked to return at eleven.

"Oh, yes, of course, we need to introduce Rachel. Rachel, this is Isaac and Susan, their son Titus. He was in a logging accident."

She looked up, a smile lighting the tanned face. She stood up, extending a hand to Titus. Her hair was growing back, dark blond with lighter strands, as if the Creator had changed his mind at the last minute. Her eyes were unusual, almost the same color as her hair.

Titus took the small brown hand. She looked into his face and said, "You look as if you ran into a brick wall."

"Worse than that," he grated out.

"Well, I'll trade your face for my leukemia. Want to?"

She tilted her head to the side, smiled her wide smile, and Titus knew she reminded him of someone, but who was it?

She moved away from the parents, asked if he wanted to join her, which he surely did. Completely unselfconscious, she asked about logging, never mentioning her own difficult battle, waving away the fact she'd suffered.

"Hurts to talk, right?"

He said it did.

"Then we'll just sit here and enjoy our time together till the drivers show up. I can talk."

And she did, in a low musical voice, bordering on hoarse. She said her voice sounded like an old smoker, she knew, but it was the chemo treatments.

Now he knew who she reminded him of. It was Kay. Like her, she was completely comfortable in her own skin, the talk flowing from her like a bright river of sparkling water.

Titus watched her from swollen eyes, pondering.

CHAPTER 15

Back home, Titus fell into a state of deep depression. He felt buried in a mountain of dark matter suppressing every normal urge to do anything.

He lay around the house, read old westerns and Archie comic books, snapped at Sharon and refused to take her to the Sunday evening hymn singing.

Susan applied plenty of patience, but with Isaac gone for the greater part of the day, she was at her wit's end after a week of this.

Titus quit looking in the mirror, knowing it would only make him feel worse. He forgot to apply Vaseline as often as he should have, then yelled at Susan for not reminding him, then stomped out of the house and went for a walk.

The pastures were brown, the grass brittle and coated with dust. Little puffs of dust rose up with every step. The garden was trying its best with regular hours of watering, but it was nothing compared to the Lancaster gardens. He again thought of all Susan had given up and felt badly for his behavior.

He recognized the fact that he missed Trisha. He needed to speak to her, be near her, to feel the craziness of his heartbeats when she approached, the sweetness of the blood singing in his veins.

But with this face?

He cursed his own bad luck, reveling in the familiar bitterness.

Why did nothing ever turn out right? He kicked blindly at the dust and watched a hawk circling over the ridge. He wanted to go back to work again, but he also felt a wave of anxiety whenever he thought of it.

After a month, the swelling in his eyes was almost completely gone, his nose returning to a better place except for a bump along the top. But the scars on the cheekbone were many, raised bumps appearing like earthworms forever embedded into his skin.

It was gross.

By this time, Sharon had a neighbor boy take her to the singings, and talk flowed again about the diesel truck terrorizing young people in buggies. Sam Detweiler's Ivan had a run-in with the same truck, but was closer to his home, turning in the drive as they roared away, leaving the poor sixteen-year-old scared out of his wits.

Titus was consumed with raw anger over the incidents. He told Sharon he was going to the singing the following Sunday night. He slapped a Band-Aid on the scars and dressed in his best shirt, thinking of Trisha as he combed his hair.

Susan sighed with relief and Isaac shook his head. After that miraculous deliverance from death or a far more serious injury than he received, you would surely think he would appreciate God's mercy and show a bit of love around the house.

Susan said it must have been his obsession with Trisha, feeling the loss of his good looks, but Isaac was adamant, saying there was no sense in his childish behavior. Everything was always about Titus. They both knew what he needed, which was the saving grace of Jesus in his heart, something he'd heard from the ministers all his life but never seemed to grasp.

"If this injury hasn't touched him, surely nothing else will," Isaac sighed, weary of trying to help his son.

"We never know. God's ways are far above our own. What we think should do the trick doesn't make a dent in his armor."

"Huh. Dent is right. He's as hard as nails."

"I just wish he'd ask Trisha. Girls can do so much to help young men like Titus. Millie says she'd take him in a heartbeat."

"Millie says a lot of things," Isaac said with a grin.

IT WAS AT the singing, the familiar long table prepared for the many youth, that Titus noticed the difference. Abram was ecstatic, his eyes sparkling, his voice strong as he sang. Trisha kept her face averted, but he noticed a glow of happiness, her striking beauty even more pronounced. Millie spoke to him, checked out his face, but kept her distance, and Duane, he noticed, was plain acting weird.

Sharon told him on the way home, but only when he asked.

Yes, Abram and Trisha were a couple. This was their third date. He breathed out. He felt his chest cave in, did not want to draw another breath. He wished he could just fade out like fog and disappear.

He wished the tree would have finished him off.

But here was Sharon beside him, the strong horse charging down the road, the night soft and dark, with no explanation whatsoever. The earth revolved on its axis, the quarter moon sailed on, and why did any human being on the face of God's earth think He cared about them when you were nothing but a slimy piece of bacteria somewhere in the mud beneath the stagnant waters of a farm pond?

All the old bitterness welled up, the anger coming in thick waves like nausea, leaving an accelerated heartbeat and a vile taste on his tongue. He listened to Sharon's voice trying to comfort him, but understood nothing, only the pattering of her words like gravel spitting away from the wheels. When he heard the mocking backfiring of a diesel engine and felt the surge of the horse as he spooked, adrenaline fed his veins, his pulse throbbing in his neck.

"Bring it on, guys. Just try it tonight." He felt no fear, only a wild surge of anger toward one more incident to take him down, to take him beyond himself. He no longer cared about his own safety, his own good reputation, or his looks, whatever was left of them.

The truck stayed back, a true hunter stalking his prey.

Titus told Sharon they were being followed, but she had nothing to worry about, certainly not this time, driving Sambo, the Friesian

Standardbred mix standing two hands higher than any other horse in the stable and as black as midnight.

Sharon raised large eyes to his face, clearly frightened.

"Let's turn in at Adam's place. Aren't we close?"

"Not really. Three, four miles."

"What should we do?" Her voice sounded panicked.

"I'm here, Sharon. I'll do everything I can to protect us."

"If we had a cell phone, we'd call the sheriff."

"We don't have one."

"Could we turn into an English place? They could help us."

Titus watched the truck draw closer, saw the headlights illuminate the night, could see the uneasy flicking of the horse's ears.

"I'm not afraid, Sharon. We'll be okay."

It all happened in less than a few minutes—the truck pulling out, roaring past, coming to a stop and two men leaping out, projecting a human fence across the road. Titus bit down on his lower lip and reached under the seat for a whip, the one thing putting his horse in a frenzy. Titus stood up, leaned out the window, and cracked the short whip just above his back, sending him into an immediate lunge, followed by a wild panic-induced full-on gallop.

Sharon screamed, a high-pitched sound rending the air like a fire siren. The buggy swayed and rolled, tossing them like eggs in a basket.

Titus wanted to spare them no pain, wanted to see the massive hooves pound them into the dirt. He stood up, cracked the whip, and yelled.

The horse never wavered and this time the young men couldn't get out of the way fast enough. There was a bump when the front wheel went over an object. Titus didn't glance back, but he had a feeling both guys had felt hooves and one or both were run over by a wheel.

They rounded a turn and the buggy skidded and swayed. Almost, they overturned, but Titus hauled back on the reins, spoke to the horse, looked in the mirror and knew they would not be followed.

Sharon was crying, but he told her to brace up, the worst was over. He drove slowly on home with the heaving, foam-flecked horse and relived the satisfaction of that nasty bump.

He really had done it this time. He doubted anyone would be harassing horses and buggies for a long time to come.

He slept very little that night, his chest heaving as if the weight of a stone was crushing him into the mattress. He didn't care how badly he had hurt those men in the road. He was consumed with this loss of Trisha.

Why had she accepted Abram and how could she look so pleased?

Everything and everyone was against him. His fate was constant disappointment. Even the trees hated him, smacking him in the face like a boxer. He couldn't live without Trisha to look forward to, without the thrill of asking her out sometime in the future. She was all he ever wanted. She was perfect.

Why hadn't he asked her when he had the chance?

Because he was a sniveling coward, that was why.

Well, he'd proved his worth tonight. His face held together by a surgeon's skill, he had driven his horse right over his tormentors. He might get in trouble, but he didn't care. He'd sit in jail for the satisfaction of that bump.

WHEN ISAAC AND Susan heard what happened from Sharon, they were not pleased. They became deeply concerned about Trisha dating Abram, knowing what a hurdle this would prove to be for Titus.

Isaac and Susan questioned him about the incident, dismayed to find him surly, defensive.

Titus shrugged his shoulders. "Ain't my fault."

"What isn't your fault?"

"That the guy was run over. They can't go around doing this and you know it. They probably believe all this nonresistant crap, so they think they can go around harassing whoever they want. Well, they messed with the wrong guy."

"You don't sound very respectful, Titus, calling our beliefs crap."

"Well, they are."

"You realize those men may have been seriously injured. You have a responsibility to let the authorities know what happened."

"You want me to turn myself in? Those guys could have gotten *us* killed. Aren't you even happy that I got Sharon out of there safely?"

There was a long sigh from Isaac, then an uncomfortable silence except the creaking of the porch rocker.

"Titus, we thought you would change this summer, and it seemed as if you were well on the way. And now Trisha is dating."

"So what? I have nothing to do with Trisha. Never did. I don't know where you unearthed that fairy tale."

Susan's heart sank, clearly understanding the hurt and the fury efficiently covering it.

"Titus, surely the logging accident helped you see you were not ready to meet God. What if the tree had done what the doctor said might have happened?" she asked.

He looked at her. She held his gaze but shuddered at the cold refusal in his eyes, the challenge to try to change him.

"You don't know if I'm saved or not."

"True. That's God's job. But surely . . ."

Her voice drifted off.

"I know what you mean. Surely I'd be a better person by now. Fruits of the spirit and all that. Well, you can just leave me alone, because I can figure it out. I'm an adult."

And with that, he left the porch.

Isaac called the sheriff's office and gave them a brief description of the situation and told them someone needed to go down there and see if the men were badly injured. By this point, probably another motorist would have found them and gotten help if they needed it, but you never knew. These guys were likely young men, possibly Titus's age, and Isaac flashed back to following the trail of Titus's blood out of the woods. The troublemakers were someone's sons, too.

The next morning, Isaac and Susan were still reeling from the events and conversation of the night before. They stood together and stared unseeing across the back yard where Thayer and Kayla were rolling a volleyball back and forth, running, tumbling in the dry brown grass, the picture of sweet innocence. For a moment, Isaac felt the responsibility of shaping these little souls, felt a failure with Titus.

He reached over, took Susan's hand.

"I feel every mistake I ever made with that boy. Remember how often he was alone with practical strangers at the house before you came? I should have been there."

"Don't look back. Don't, Isaac. Sharon was there, too."

She squeezed his hand, laced her fingers with his.

"Evidently, with all God is sending him, he's pruning the wild shoots of the grapevine, as the Bible says. He feels as if nothing is right in his life. I'm sure. And he's bitter. This thing with Trisha is a major disappointment."

"And we all have them. Pain is a part of life, a part of God's love toward us."

"Absolutely."

"I love you, Susan. I can never get over the fact that you are my beautiful wife, that you left your home in Pennsylvania to move out here with me. And I'm not much."

Susan gazed across the lawn, watched the children playing, then turned to him. "You know I always love you. Even on my grouchy days, I never doubt my decision. Marriage is very fulfilling, even if not perfect. Nothing is perfect. I get my days of homesickness, sometimes even regret that I did this, but it all adds up to the contented feeling of knowing I am where God wants me to be."

Isaac blinked back tears, deeply touched.

"You're wonderful, Susan."

"I'm not, and you know it. I'm ordinary, and right this moment, fat and uncomfortable and ready to have this little one."

Isaac grinned. "I can't wait."

The sheriff came to talk to Titus later that morning, asking questions, quite stiff and stern, with piercing blue eyes that scared him.

He felt judged, condemned. Could he actually go to jail for this?

The sheriff told him both men were hurt, though not badly. He looked pointedly at Titus and said it could have been much worse. Titus was lucky the men had only gotten knocked over but not actually trampled. Titus realized, with a surprising sense of relief, that the bump he felt must not have been the wheel going over one of the men after all. The sheriff said he'd let him off with a warning. Yes, these men were asking for it, and now they knew who they were dealing with, but Titus better not make a habit of being that reckless.

"I thought the Amish wouldn't do this sort of thing," the sheriff commented, lifting eyebrows, his piercing eyes taking Titus by surprise.

"I'm not as Amish as some," Titus remarked.

"You must have known your horse."

"I did."

The sheriff gave him a tight smile and his eyes twinkled as he turned on his heel and left.

"Whew!" Isaac breathed.

He turned to Titus. "You won't do that again."

"I will if they try anything."

"You know it could turn nasty, if they take you to court."

"So now you're on their side. You may as well be, everyone else is out to get me."

And he walked away, leaving Isaac unsure of having said or done one thing right.

He sincerely regretted leaving him alone so much of the time, as if the logging business meant more to him than his own children. Remorse was an uncomfortable piece of luggage to drag around, he thought, but in this case, it was the harvest of sowing the seeds of self-ishness, the times he did not give up his own will for his son.

He prayed for forgiveness, prayed for the soul of his son, who was still enmeshed in the bitter struggle of accepting Jesus as his Savior.

A checkup at the surgeon's office confirmed that his face was doing great, the healing going faster than the doctor had hoped. Another few months and he'd look even better. Titus was encouraged, although he felt no need to look good for Trisha anymore. He took Sharon to the youth's gatherings, but mostly he sat on the sidelines to watch her enjoy her social life, trying not to show the hurt of seeing Trisha radiant with newfound happiness.

The only saving grace was the fact he had never asked her, so he could keep his pride intact, at least in theory. In practice, he often felt as if his pride was glued together with glue that wasn't as efficient as it should have been. He found himself watching some of the other girls, wondering if he could fall in love again.

Thoughts of leaving the community, of leaving the only culture he had ever known, entered his mind repeatedly. What if he had to escape the restrictions of Amish life in order to reach his full potential?

He weighed his possibilities, the hurt he would inflict on his parents, versus living a life of freedom, of making his own choices, being who he wanted to be, without worrying about pleasing anyone else.

Would it be so hard to leave?

This thought flavored his days. It provided a welcome respite from the dull monotony, coupled with ongoing heartache and disappointment. It was new, it was exciting, the prospect of change replacing the thrill of asking Trisha that had lingered for so long.

He imagined where he would go, what he would do, the vehicle he would buy.

He certainly wouldn't hang out in Wyoming. There was so much more to see. He would be free of all restrictions, all restraints. Free to find out who he really was, which might not look anything like who he was expected to be.

THEN, THAT SUMMER, there was talk of wildfires cropping up here and there. Nothing unusual, although one of them proved especially troublesome.

Weather conditions were perfect for a major fire, the men agreed, standing around after church services with sober faces. The drought had been long, the wind unrelenting, and all it would take was one hurled cigarette butt, or a sloppy camper who was not aware of the explosive potential of the bone-dry grass, the underbrush and tumble-weed like tinder.

Titus listened to the wind, searched the cloudless sky, and hoped for rain, knowing the vast amount of forest that could be destroyed by licking flames. He picked up a paper at the small quick shop every morning, listened to the old ranchers' predictions, and wondered.

SUSAN WAS DELIVERED of another little boy, arriving early, weighing in at only six pounds and four ounces. With a thatch of dark hair, a mighty wail, and a red, wrinkled face, he looked like a little old man and was promptly named David after Susan's father, who was still bravely battling his pancreatic cancer.

David Arlen. Susan was so proud, happiness beaming from her face as she dressed him in too-large clothing, swaddled him in soft blankets, rocked and nursed and loved this tiny newborn who resembled her father.

Isaac was glad she had regained her strength quickly when he brought the sobering news of the Stillwater fire now raging out of control. Titus smelled the smoke drifting across half the state and felt mildly alarmed. He thought if he was no longer Amish, he would fight forest fires. The challenge and excitement welled up in him. He wondered what it would take.

Then the news came. The community just next to Oak Bluffs was under siege, families facing evacuation.

Isaac was incredulous, telling Susan he didn't think forest fires would ever get so bad as to touch their surrounding communities.

Susan, still pale and a bit puffy, her mood often on the side of irritation, snorted audibly.

"You know, that really upsets me. Why do we as Amish people think we're above reproach? Like God would stop natural disasters because we're better than average."

"That's not what I meant."

"Then say what you mean."

Isaac chose to ignore that bit of carping, then changed the subject.

"Isn't that where those folks . . . what were their names?"

"Who are you talking about?" Susan asked, pushing away the second cupcake she so wanted to eat.

"Those people at the hospital. With the sick daughter."

"Oh, that was Samuel . . ."

"No, Simon and Betty Bontrager," Titus said.

"You remember," Isaac observed.

"I do. The daughter's name was Rachel."

Isaac and Susan exchanged a look, then she sighed, looking at the cluttered table, the mess Thayer had made from his booster seat, and said it would be nice to have help in the kitchen. At that moment the baby sent up a lusty wail, which Susan remedied immediately, leaving Isaac and Titus looking at the disastrous kitchen, then each other.

Isaac grinned. "You go first."

"We never do dishes. Where's Sharon?"

"She's staying at Rebecca's house. Come on, Titus. We can do this. You want to be a real man, I'll teach you."

"Yeah. Right."

But they cleared the table, and Isaac put the plug in the sink, ran hot water, and pumped the dish soap dispenser. Titus was on his hands and knees and swiping at soggy peas and sticky macaroni stuck to the floor. Thayer stood watching, his face smeared with food residue. He narrowed his eyes and tried to climb on Titus's back.

"Hey, get off of me. You're covered in food."

Titus reached back and hauled him forward, holding him tight and swabbing at his face while Thayer screeched and fought.

Susan yelled, "The same rag you used on the floor? Whatever, Titus."

"Better than being covered in macaroni and cheese."

He dried the dishes his father washed. The thought of telling him about leaving the logging business, getting out of Wyoming, rose up in him, followed by the knowing he could not do it yet. It would hurt his father too much.

Isaac stood with a dish towel, waiting until Titus had a pot cleaned to his satisfaction.

"You're the slowest dishwasher in the world."

"Think so? I guarantee my dishes are clean."

"You know, Titus, there was a time when you wouldn't have done this. Straight to your room after supper."

"Not always. Sometimes I went to the barn."

Isaac looked at Titus. Really looked into his eyes. "You're growing in a lot of ways, Titus. I appreciate that. I'm proud of who you've become. And another thing. This Trisha deal . . . I have prayed for you, and you've handled it pretty good."

Titus felt as if his heart would burst right out of his chest.

He wanted to laugh and cry simultaneously.

What he did do was shake his head, tell his father it wasn't easy.

"I guess not. You were pretty serious about her. Well, the only thing I can tell you is God must not have chosen her for you. It simply isn't meant to be."

"God has nothing to do with it."

"God has everything to do with it. Let go of your own control, Titus. Fall into the arms of Jesus. Let Him take care of you and watch how things start to unfold."

"You sound like some evangelist."

"I am one. Inside. I love Jesus."

"That's childish."

"Titus, listen. It's time you let go. Give your heart to Jesus. Seriously. Why do you think I'm so happy and love to see people, always glad to see my friends, anyone on God's earth? That is the commandment He gave us, to love one another."

"Good for you."

"And let me tell you, somewhere, sometime, He has a very special girl waiting just for you."

"I wish I could find a girl like Kay."

"Kay? Why?"

"She's so easy to talk to. Like, I could go up and say, 'Hey, you want to go for ice cream?' and you know she'd say yes. And we'd talk all night. Easy."

"Trisha isn't like that?"

"No. Trisha has a lot of pride."

"And so do you, son. Sorry."

Isaac hung up the dishrag, grabbed the bottom of the faucet, and pressed the button, sending a spray of water to rinse the sink. He turned, clapped a hand on Titus's shoulder, said, "I love you, man."

And Titus felt a quick wave of unwanted emotion, followed by the conviction he could never tell his father the thing he was planning to do.

He couldn't do it. It would be worse than asking Trisha.

He marveled at the revelation of his father's heart. He had never spoken to him like that. Men didn't. He wondered how his father came to be so sure about Jesus.

Isaac wasn't perfect. He groused around the barn when he felt overwhelmed with all that manure hauling and he was never too happy about lost bridles and mislaid currycombs. And sometimes Susan got under his skin. He yelled at Kayla. Sometimes he swore at work, when he got his chainsaw tight. He said rude things, like that Abram Yoder was fat and lazy, no wonder he couldn't make a decent living.

Was that allowed by his Jesus?

Titus felt he had been dealt a miserable hand by the Big Man in the sky. Dead mother, lost Trisha, smacked in the face by a tree, no friends to speak of, plodding to work every day, doing the same old thing. There had to be something better somewhere.

But still. His father's life hadn't been perfect either, but he seemed to know a contentment that Titus knew he himself lacked. Was that just his personality, or did it have more to do with his faith?

CHAPTER 16

Titus's face hurt. He sat on the edge of his bed, his face in his hands, his elbows propped on his knees. He groaned. Four o'clock in the morning, and in no mood to face the day.

What was this life? The girl he loved was smitten with someone else, his face felt like there was a brick sewn inside it, the air was so thick and heavy that just breathing felt gross.

He sniffed, then sniffed again. Definitely worse than usual. A spit of adrenaline shot through him. He dressed quickly, brushed his teeth, and put tentative fingers to the throbbing in his cheek before dragging a comb through his thick hair.

He met his father standing by the coffee maker, a scowl on his face.

"Smoke worse?" he growled.

"Definitely no better."

"The way the wind's carrying it?"

"I don't know. Honestly, Titus, it's unsettling. With September around the corner, you know the wind will be picking up. No rain in sight. You want coffee? We'll pick up breakfast and lunch. Your mother didn't sleep much."

Titus nodded, poured a cup, heard the thin wail of his tiny half-brother David. He felt a stab of pity for Susan, having her sleep disturbed repeatedly by a thin, wrinkled little guy with a roiling stomach, throwing up and screeching like a hoot owl. Why they kept on having babies was beyond him.

Isaac went to the bedroom and spoke in a low voice. Susan appeared in a pink bathrobe, her hair disheveled, her face puffy with weariness, the baby still screeching. She sank into the glider rocker and Titus left, went outside the way he did when she needed to feed an infant. It was the respectful thing to do. Susan told him he didn't need to, that she had a cloth to cover with, but he felt awkward.

Outside, he lifted his face, sniffed again.

They rode to work and stopped at the usual quick shop where all the talk was about the fires. Ranchers, retired farmers, the women behind the counter—everyone seemed shrunken with worry, lines drawn on foreheads, scowls creating deep vertical fissures in weathered faces with skin like old leather.

"It's comin' down those foothills," old Henry Sprinkle ground out, his voice pushed through a throat riddled by years of cigarette smoke. "Less than fifty miles to go."

"They're workin' on it, Henry. Don't get your pants in a twist." This from the rotund Barb, sliding breakfast sandwiches toward Isaac, nodding to Titus.

"Good morning, Barb," Titus said, smiling at her.

"You're just a sweetheart, Titus. Come here. I wanna check out that face."

He obeyed, and she bent over the counter, peered through scratched bifocals, clucked and shook her head.

"You're a lucky boy. The Man upstairs had His hand on you."

He smiled, said thanks for his sandwich, then waited for his father, who was conversing with a group of men seated around a table. As usual, he was holding forth with his own highly esteemed opinion of what was going to be, the direction of the wind, the probability of rain, which group of firefighters would be available.

Titus sat in a booth and unwrapped his sandwich. Sometimes, he wanted to slap his father around. Get his attention. He didn't know a thing about any of this. No one did.

"Hey, Titus, what do you think?"

Old Clement pushed his chair sideways, his stomach hanging over his belt as if he'd brought his bed pillow under his shirt.

Titus chewed, swallowed.

"About what?"

"The fires."

Titus shrugged. "Nobody can predict what's going to happen."

Isaac opened his mouth, closed it again.

"Not even you, Dad."

The men laughed uproariously, slapped Isaac's arm, settled back to enjoy their coffee, chuckling.

"Ain't that the truth?" they chortled.

Isaac was quiet much of the day, but Titus didn't mind. It didn't hurt him to be called out, all that empty-headed talk to impress these simple old ranchers and farmers. He could talk all day, and those men would hang on to every word.

Nothing wrong with being a fact checker.

SUSAN'S FACE WAS sober. There had been a message on the line. The Oak Bluffs community was forced to evacuate, and the way it looked now, there were at least three Amish homes directly in line of the raging fire.

"You're kidding me," Isaac said, sinking into a kitchen chair.

"No. Some of the men from here are going to help move them. I think you should both go."

"And leave you alone?"

"I have Sharon. The fire isn't close to us. Not yet . . ."

A few phone calls were made and they were on their way the following morning with six other men. The closer they drove toward the community of Oak Bluffs, the more it seemed as if the sun shone through a weird curtain, as if a sheer black fabric was drawn across it. And the wind. The unrelenting wail, the buffeting against the westbound vehicle. How could anything withstand its force?

Titus noticed the beauty of the western landscape, saw the cliffs like orange walls, golden eagles circling warm updrafts, dry creek beds filled with tumbleweed, sagebrush leaning in the wind.

A herd of mule deer spooked, ran on delicate legs, disappeared around a stand of Douglas spruce.

He gasped as he saw the billowing white cloud of smoke, melded into the sky as if to camouflage the fact it was a fire-breathing dragon. There was an advancing army of flames, licking up the dried-out underbrush and dying trees, the smoke creating a sickening veil of reality.

Homes were like sitting ducks, unable to defend their existence. It all seemed unfair, terribly pitiful, the fact these pioneers had relocated from familiar areas, only to be consumed by forces of nature, having no control over their circumstances.

And everyone would, of course, still believe God was loving.

Belongings were being hauled away as they drove to the first home, a Levi Troyer family. They were a young family, white-faced with alarm, the wife patient as she directed the men, small children playing in the dust.

They were ready to go, but they were told to head to the Bontragers' place. Their plans had been stalled when the truck didn't show up that morning. So Titus and Isaac and the other men drove on, watching out the windows at the line of black smoke moving into gray, then white.

They drove through a line of trees, brown pastures like deserts, windmills pumping the needed water in stock tanks, fences and dusty roads snaking through the level land. A stillness inside the vehicle spoke of the raw dread, the calamity ready to unfold as they drove up to a set of new buildings, a huge barn, a two-story house built with the best log siding, wide porches, decorative split rail fencing.

Would this actually all be consumed?

They found Simon pacing, watching the sky. He was trembling. His wife came quickly, her face softened with relief. They were greeted warmly, thanked effusively, invited to come sit on the porch, the truck would surely be here soon.

There were children, a few boys younger than Titus, all friendly, introducing themselves as Willie and Dannie. The cattle and horses were already shipped to areas safely away from the advancing fire, but the household goods would still need to go.

Titus watched as a few school-aged girls appeared, then another, older girl who was not Rachel.

He wasn't aware of watching for Rachel, but was glad to see her come through the door. She was so thin and pale, her eyes too large and dark in the small face. He was surprised to see her ignore the men on the porch and walk straight across the dry grass to him.

"I remember you," she said. "You're Titus."

"Yes. From the hospital."

"How are you?"

"Doing okay. You?"

"That's good. I guess I'm doing alright. I never really know. Cancer is a weird disease." She smiled at him. "Not the most pressing issue right now."

She nodded her head in the direction of the smoke.

"Pretty scary."

"Do you have a place to go?" Titus asked.

"Dat says we do."

They talked about the absence of the truck, watched the smoke, heard the drone of airplanes, and were cheered when they heard the shifting of gears, a large eighteen-wheeler appearing from the line of trees.

"Here we go," Titus said.

Dannie and Willie were already on their way. Rachel searched Titus's face, told him it didn't look too bad. He reached up to touch his face, said it was healing, but still caused him pain at times.

He looked down at her upturned face, the skin like porcelain and as smooth as velvet, no color in her cheeks, her eyes large and the color of a sunlit pool. They were no color, really, and he wondered if leukemia changed eye color. He had never seen eyes like this.

Why did he feel powerful in her presence, lose all sense of shyness, shed inhibitions like outerwear?

"We'll help here, then move on to the next place, but first I would be happy to have your address. Would you write back if I wrote to you?" He could hardly believe the words coming out of his mouth.

"Of course I would. I would love to receive a letter from you. There's a reason we met at the hospital, and now this coincidence. You got smacked in the face, and I have cancer. That's plenty of reason to write letters."

"Your home might not be here." Immediately he felt badly for saying it out loud, but it was true. "I mean, if I send a letter here, it might not get to you."

"We'll be back. Oh, you could come help rebuild. Then I could see you again, right?"

Titus looked into her strange and beautiful eyes and thought her speech was like a spring breeze, so sweet and honest it stirred his soul. There was no guessing, no self-loathing of his own ability to say the proper thing, dress in his absolute best, or worry about his appearance at all. She liked him exactly the way he was. She wanted to see him again.

He nodded, his own eyes filled with the light of thousands of stars, and it was barely midday.

"You might think me forthright, Titus, but I may not have much time. Does that make it hard for you?"

"You won't die. I don't believe it."

"Good. Then I have another soldier in my army against leukemia."

When she turned away, he wanted to pluck at her dress sleeve, keep her from leaving. He resented the presence of every other person surrounding them. He breathed a sigh of resignation and watched her go, so painfully thin her modest dress hung on her small frame as if it were on a clothes rack. An unnamed feeling rose in his chest. Not pity, not the heart-thumping breathlessness of the proximity to Trisha, only a tenderness, a caring he knew he had never experienced until now.

To help the family evacuate was like a glimpse into her personal life—the furniture, the boxes packed and ready to go. The parents grimaced as they lifted worried eyes to the roiling smoke repeatedly.

Nothing could compare with the sense of awe, the sense of helplessness in the face of the approaching flames, destroying everything in their path. Water would be like spitting in its face. Shovels, chemicals, manpower, airplanes, man doing his level best, and still the perimeters of the fire moved on.

Titus found the loading of household goods strenuous. He coughed repeatedly, his breathing constricted. He watched the sky and was shocked to find the smoke increasing as the fire neared.

Men hustled now, faster. Perspiration poured as they heaved sofas and dressers, mattresses and kitchen appliances. Titus worked alongside, his face reddened with the heat and exertion, spoke little, listening to his father talk nonstop as he heaved furniture effortlessly.

When the family stood in a group to thank them, Rachel crooked a finger at him, a smile on her pale face. She pressed a slip of paper in his hand, her fingers cold to the touch, smiled up at him with those tawny eyes and said, "Now you have to write. Include your address, and I'll write back."

"Stay safe, Rachel," he said softly, and she nodded, giving him one last look before moving away.

Two more families were helped and sent on their way before everyone piled back into the van, sweating and thirsty, in need of food and a cold drink. Titus was present, but felt elevated, lifted above the men's conversation. The immediate danger of being consumed by the wildfire was eclipsed by the talk he'd had with Rachel.

He felt as if it were an honor to know her name.

Rachel. A beautiful name. So brave in the face of the dreaded cancer. It was odd, really, how he'd landed in the hospital and met her parents. But what was so perfectly normal and wonderful about the whole thing was how she made him feel whole, the best version of himself, and he barely knew her.

Life was strange indeed.

Three homes out of the seventeen Amish homesteads were burned to the ground, dissolved into a silt of gray ash and timbers reduced to charcoal, twisted piles of charred metal roofing. The landscape was apocalyptic.

It was named the Stillwater Fire, its origins somewhere close to the lonely outpost of Stillwater at the base of the Bighorns. It was finally contained in October with the blessed help of a twenty-hour deluge from the north, a cold rain bringing the necessary beginning of a hard-fought victory, leaving scattered families mourning the loss of beloved homes.

No one was injured. "Just material possessions," people said, but the loss was still tremendous for those whose homes had wound up in the fire's path.

The rebuilding began in earnest. Buses filled with relatives and acquaintances traveled to the west, curious easterners who found this a good excuse to travel, to experience the long, lonely stretches through North Dakota and into Wyoming. They marveled at the vast amount of land available for homesteaders, even in this modern age. But it was not for them, most said. Not for them. How would you make a decent living, settled on the plains like that? There was nothing there. Many of them were comfortably entrenched in good businesses back East, coffers lined well.

Isaac said they'd take a few weeks off, get Jason to take them up there every day. They'd come home at night, for Susan's sake; she was worn to a frazzle with the colicky David, diagnosed with a severe case of infant acid reflux.

Titus wondered again why they would want more children. Five was way plenty, but they always seemed thrilled to herald the arrival of another one.

Titus was eager to go to the Oak Bluffs settlement, eager to work on Simon Bontrager's buildings. They had lost everything they had not carried away, which was sobering. It was a genuine shock to start over again, after all the hard work put into the ranch only five years ago.

He thought they must be wondering, too, about all this love of God talk, sending the leukemia and now the fire. Who could go through all that and still believe in a loving God?

He hadn't written to Rachel, not knowing where she was staying until their home was rebuilt. But he had thought of her daily.

He worked on the massive barn, enjoying every minute of being on the trusses as they were set. He wielded a nail gun with the best of them, met his father's twinkling eyes and knew he'd done well.

Always, he watched for Rachel.

Finally, on the third day, he glimpsed her, her dress flapping in the stiff gale, the October weather as fickle as a young colt. She was watching the men put the roof on the barn, a small figure appearing forlorn, pale and thin. A protective feeling rose in him, the need to take her away from the curse of the fire.

The desire to talk to her was overwhelming, but he reasoned that climbing down the ladder and sprinting in her direction might be a bit too forward. He forced himself to wait until an appropriate time for a break.

When he did descend the ladder, one of her brothers approached him with a slip of paper. He looked at it, a question in his eyes.

"Rachel wants you to have this."

"Oh. Well, thanks."

In neat handwriting, the words made him dizzy with happiness.

"Would you accompany me to pick up a few things in town?"

Her brother watched, then smiled when Titus said yes.

"Driver's waiting."

"I'm not very spruced up."

"It's fine. You can wash up in the lean-to."

A temporary shelter had been erected for cooking and washing up, so Titus did the best he could with what was available. He thought of the painstaking care he had taken when he was thinking of Trisha, the desperation of decision based on just the right shirt, his hair arranged to perfection. And here he was in his work clothes. He let his dad know he was leaving and was met with raised eyebrows and then a smile as Isaac put two and two together. Titus couldn't help a little grin himself as he turned to meet Rachel.

She smiled at him sheepishly. "Is this stupid?" she asked.

"You mean, asking me to accompany you?"

"Yes."

"Certainly not."

The driver was a retired rancher with a penchant for chewing tobacco, talking nonstop around the juicy brown wad in his cheek, spitting delicately into a plastic root beer bottle, holding it in one hand as he held onto the steering wheel with the other, drifting off the road a few times, the tires spitting gravel before he was back on the road.

Titus sat in the front seat, commenting occasionally, while the driver kept up a running description of ranch life in general. Rachel was quiet, which left Titus feeling awkward.

Relieved to arrive at the drugstore, a small place squeezed between a western wear store and a sewing shop, he hopped out quickly and went to open the door for her. She swung her legs over and stood immediately, then swayed, grabbed quickly for the door, and closed her eyes.

Titus reached for her arm. "You OK?"

"I'm fine. It happens when I get up quickly."

"Why don't you stay in the car and I'll pick up the prescription?"

"No, I'll be okay."

He accompanied her into the pharmacy and was relieved to see she had recovered quickly and was quite capable on her own. The friendly pharmacist chatted with her. Titus could barely take his eyes off Rachel, the delicate texture of her skin, the hair shot through with streaks of blond.

"You all have a nice day now," the pharmacist called out as they turned to leave.

"We will," she answered.

"He seems to know you," Titus observed.

"Well, I've certainly been in here enough. I don't love taking so many medicines, but they must be helping because I'm still alive."

He wasn't sure how to respond, so he said nothing as they reentered the vehicle and she directed the driver to her next stop. When Titus saw the supermarket sign, he dreaded going through the maze of aisles with the dizzying array of food and produce. He detested shopping for food, had too many memories of blindly following his father as a young boy, intimidated by the hard stares of shoppers unaccustomed to the Amish dress. He felt like a freak, an oddity, like the calf with two heads he'd viewed through glass at the western museum. He wanted to yell, kick at the gawking locals, but knew that would not be the proper thing to do, according to his father, who smiled, waved, said hello, while he stood unnoticed, a tagalong in a battered straw hat.

"You don't have to help me, Titus. Most men don't like to shop," Rachel said, in the low, hoarse voice he had come to appreciate.

"I'll help. I don't mind."

"That's very kind of you."

She had no idea. When the doors opened ahead of them, his chest tightened. He took a deep breath, told himself it was ridiculous to feel scared of a grocery store.

She seemed to know where the items were kept. Coffee. Milk. She ticked them off her list, one by one, keeping up a lively conversation. He found her delightful, the way she described their temporary living conditions, devoid of self-pity.

"Hey, Titus!"

He turned, amazed to find Barb and Eilene from the quick shop bustling over, her eyes gleaming with happiness at sight of him.

"How are you, Barb? Eilene?"

"Great. We're having a day off. Never thought we'd see you here. This your girlfriend?"

"A friend. Rachel, this is Barb and Eilene from a place we stop on the way to work. Almost every morning."

"Yeah. We love Titus. Always nice, puts money in the tip jar." Barb winked at Titus. "It's good to meet you, Rachel."

Rachel smiled, said it was nice meeting them both.

They moved on down the aisle, and Titus felt a sense of pride. This time, he was his father. He was Isaac, greeted by acquaintances tickled to see him, hurrying over to talk to him. His chest expanded, he breathed deeply, lifted his head, and lengthened his steps.

"They really like you," Rachel observed.

"They're great, both of them. They make the best sandwiches in the West. Sausages hot off the grill, dripping grease and melted cheese, a thick layer of fluffy eggs with hot sauce. It's unreal."

Rachel laughed, a pure sound of honest enjoyment.

Why was she so easy to be with? He simply could not figure this one out. If he had been with Trisha in a grocery store, to meet someone like Barb would have been terrifying. His feet would have felt large and clumsy, his hair uncombed, his shirttail never tucked in his trousers quite properly. He'd be afraid of opening his mouth, frightened of saying or doing the wrong thing, or the right thing at the wrong time, or not saying enough, or the worst fear of all, saying too much.

Here was little Rachel, having gone through too much, still weak, unsure of her future, the top of her head barely reaching his shoulder, her voice gravelly, her skin without the rosy tone of a healthy person.

And Titus felt larger, expanded, confident.

She had asked him to accompany her, a bold move, and now he had the next few hours to anticipate. They'd go somewhere to eat, which meant they'd sit together at a table, an intimacy that would have scared the daylights out of him with Trisha.

He pushed the grocery cart, amazed at this new turn of events.

Chapter 17

Seated in an upholstered booth, the wooden boards on the walls adorned with western paraphernalia, the scent of charcoal heat and sizzling beef swirling through the atmosphere, Titus had never felt happier.

Rachel shrugged out of her coat and laid it on the seat beside her, the green dress highlighting the green flecks in her eyes. She simply folded her hands on the table in front of her, found his eyes on hers, and stayed.

Their eyes rested in each other's, receiving the knowledge there was something between them. Whatever it was, it was right and solid and honest.

Words seemed frivolous, unnecessary.

She took a small breath.

"Well, Titus," she said, smiling a small, secretive smile.

And he answered the smile with one of his own.

"Well, Rachel. Here we are."

"Yes. Here we are. I'm glad I met you."

He was overcome with a longing to hold her hand, to convey the message of his own happiness at their unlikely meeting. He didn't stop to think, but simply reached out and loosened one of her hands from the other, then held it with his own, a small, white hand lost in the large, brown calloused one.

Hands that could have been the hands of his father, covered with callouses, strong and assured. But they were his own hands, and here with Rachel, his chest swelled with the truth of who he was.

Her protector. He was capable. He was enough.

"Can I ask you something?" he questioned.

"Yes."

"Are you well enough to start dating?"

She drew in a quick breath.

"Oh yes. Yes. Are you sure, though? Leukemia is . . . it's a lot to take on."

"I know. I mean, I'm sure I don't know all of it, everything you're going through. But I want to know."

"The doctors say I'm coming in on the home stretch, but you never really know with cancer. It could come back even stronger."

"I'll be by your side. We'll be in this together."

"Thank you. I accept that."

"I can hardly wait to get to know you," he said, his voice breathless with the ongoing thrill of being seated here with her. It was the easiest thing he'd ever done, asking her. He hadn't had one intimidating thought.

Their meal was great, but food wasn't important. They spoke to the waitress, they sipped their drinks, but it was all secondary. Nothing mattered except the fact they were together, and he had asked her to be his girlfriend.

She asked more questions about his face and he described the accident.

She told him God had orchestrated the whole thing. Her leukemia, his battered face. When he said nothing, she felt a chill, a shadow across the room. Confusion clouded her vision.

"Did I say something wrong?"

"No. Not at all. I just have a problem with that sort of thing."

"What sort of thing?"

Her eyes were concerned, her brows drawn down.

"Oh, nothing. Just stuff. Never mind."

She decided to let it rest. She knew there was something amiss, but she was mature beyond her years, having been through trials of physical suffering, and she knew this wasn't the time to push the topic. The trepidation was replaced by the joy of knowing they would have many weekends together, and as the relationship grew, she would come to understand his inner workings.

"You'll have to travel to our area, since you have no home yet. But I'll get a driver and come get you."

"Six hours? It's three hours one way, isn't it?"

"Something like that."

She laughed, teased him with her eyes. She said that wouldn't be very much for him, but he assured her it was not a long time at all. He wanted to say more, but thought it was a bit soon.

THAT FOLLOWING WEEK, he told Susan they would have a guest on Saturday evening and Sunday. She was a bit apprehensive, wanting to know who, and why. When he told her, she smiled slowly at first, then genuinely, finally laughing out loud, her eyes shining with unshed tears.

"Oh, Titus," was all she said.

But she sat at the kitchen table with another cup of peppermint tea, having had to give up her beloved coffee for little David and his finicky belly. Well, here was a good reason to spruce up the house and change the bedding in the guest room. She'd be able to use the pretty lavender sachets on the pillows, open the new decorative box of Kleenex, use her towels she'd bought at Rockvale Square in Lancaster.

She remembered Rachel only vaguely, but could picture the parents. As she reflected, her excitement turned to worry. Was this just a way to forget Trisha? He and Trisha had never actually dated, as far as she knew, but still, she was sure he hadn't recovered from the heartbreak he'd felt. It was too soon to dive into a new relationship, wasn't it? He was just plunging into this recklessly in an attempt to mask his wounds. And what about her health? What if she couldn't have children? Didn't chemotherapy sometimes sterilize young people?

She went to the bookshelf, got down the *Merck Manual*, and flipped pages. She couldn't find the topic before resorting to the index. Her eyes scanned the pages. Her mind raced.

Well, no information there. She asked Isaac, and he told her he wouldn't worry about anything like that, which just made her mad. Men were such big duds. They didn't think farther than the end of their nose. Here was his son, bringing home a girl with leukemia, and Isaac wasn't even thinking about potential complications. At least she was smart enough to be prepared.

All that week, she cleaned, redecorated, eyed the walls of the guest bedroom and thought them too sterile. The poor girl had spent enough time in a dreadful hospital room, and who knew what her lodging had been like since their house burned down. She put the Double Wedding Ring quilt on the bed after she'd snapped and tugged the sheets in place, then thought it looked suggestive, as in, "Are you going to marry our son?" She took it off, folded it, and put it back in the cedar chest with the rest of the quilts. She was on her way up to the attic to look for some pictures to spruce up the walls when she heard Kayla yelling for her.

"Yes, Kayla. I'll be down."

And then David was screaming and she reversed her steps to go back downstairs. She cooed and unwrapped him, changed his diaper, cuddled and calmed him before plopping into the rocker recliner to feed him. Thayer looked up from his Legos, a smile so much like Isaac's on his cherubic face.

"What are you building, Sweetie?"

"A cabin for my people. A fire wrecked their house."

"I see. You feeling better, Kayla?"

"No."

"Ach my. I'll make you some tea as soon as David's fed."

She thought how thinly mothers were spread out. A grown son bringing home a girlfriend, a sick daughter home from school, a colicky newborn . . . no wonder she ate so many high-calorie snacks. The quick bursts of energy they provided were a lifesaver, plus there was a certain comfort in the cookies and pies she baked.

But she had to go on a diet. Any diet. She thought of her sister Rose. Surely she wouldn't end up looking like her. She plucked at the sleeve of her dress, thinking of the snug fit, lifted the pleats around her hips, and hoped she would never wear clothes that were much too small.

Then there was the problem of baking something Rachel would like. Did she eat pastries? Did leukemia patients have to eat certain foods?

She threw on a coat and went to the phone to call Rose.

Rose shrieked, exclaimed, congratulated until Susan held the phone away from her ear.

"What do you make if Kay has friends at the house?"

"They're hardly ever here. You know how they get around in cars now. They go to Starbucks or someplace. Teenagers will eat anything."

"This girl had leukemia."

"You're kidding me."

Then the fuss really began, driving home more worries until Susan regretted making the phone call. She told Rose she had to go, that Kayla was alone in the house with the little ones and wasn't feeling well.

So much for sisters.

She decided on pumpkin bars with cream cheese icing, thinking it was October and pumpkin was fitting. She also made fresh chicken salad and homemade rolls, a batch of red beet eggs, and chocolate chip bars.

Isaac came in from driving horses and ate almost a third of the pumpkin bars, creating the unsettling feeling she wouldn't have enough.

Titus whistled and grinned his way through the day. He seemed so at ease. She asked him if Rachel was really arriving that evening.

"Of course. I'm going to pick her up with Jason and the work truck."

"Well, shouldn't you be ready? What time are you leaving?"

"In an hour. At one."

"Did you shower? What are you wearing?"

"No. I did not get my shower. And very likely I will be wearing clothes."

Isaac laughed, his face lifted to the ceiling. There was a dab of cream cheese frosting on his beard, and she told him immediately. He looked down, swiped at it with his fingers, and wiped it on his trousers.

She gave him a look, handed him a paper towel.

"What's that for?" he joked, and she walked by and slapped his shoulder. He ducked, said ow, and she held her head high and sniffed.

Titus could hardly wait for a relationship like that. So much ease, hardly ever a serious offense taken, and on the rare occasion it did happen, the storm blew over almost before it began.

He felt as if he had a good foundation to stand on, a good example to follow in his parents' footsteps.

HE GREETED HER parents and promised to take care of Rachel. Living in the makeshift trailer, their faces haggard with the weariness of strenuous days, their life in shambles around them, Titus felt genuinely concerned for them. The whole family had been through so much, first with Rachel and now this.

Rachel seemed a bit shy, tentative at first, but when she saw the ease in Titus, she seemed to relax.

Her mother checked and rechecked her luggage, counted the pills in her pillbox, then turned to Titus.

"I trust you won't take her to the singing. I am really sorry to require that, but I'm sure you understand."

"I do. I wasn't planning on it."

"Thank you. I apologize."

Rachel smiled. "Mom, I can take care of myself. I am stronger than I was."

"I know you are. But you still need to be careful."

They exchanged a look of so much caring, Titus felt an outsider. But he knew the relationship she had with her parents was a good thing. He'd struggled for too many years with his own parents. He was aware of her fragile immune system, the need to not be around too many people lest she catch something her body couldn't fight off. But really, he was glad for a reason to stay at home rather than going to the signing. He wanted every precious hour with just her. They would have so much to share, so much to find out about each other.

The three hours to his home seemed only minutes. He found the time with her was like an undeserved gift, the way she could keep up a lively conversation, including Jason, who was like a favorite uncle. By the time they reached the homestead, he felt as if he had indeed found a special friend.

It was only when they slowed, turned, and headed up the long drive, the imposing house in the glow of the evening sun, that he noticed the silence, the drawing into herself.

"Here we are," he announced, looking over at her.

Her eyes were large in her pale face, her mouth open in awe.

"Wow!" she breathed. "Really? You expect me to believe this is where you live? Come on, Titus."

"I'm sorry."

"No, really. This is not where you actually live."

"Yes. My dad is a pretty well-known logger."

"But I don't get it. It isn't even Amish," she said forthrightly.

"It's just big. With log siding. And some stone."

"It's whopping big."

Jason Luhrs laughed amiably. "So is Isaac."

"I'm not used to these kind of houses. I'm only a country girl from Oak Bluffs." But she was smiling as he helped her down. She took a deep breath to steady herself and nodded at Titus, who led the way to the front door.

The air was definitely cold, and becoming even colder by the hour. The front porch was blasted with a stiff gale as he opened the door and stepped back, touching her elbow to guide her through. He couldn't help grinning to himself.

Susan was warm and welcoming, followed by Isaac, who had been well schooled by Susan in the way of meeting brand-new girlfriends, his voice strangely hushed and rough with emotion. Sharon, shy and petite, lisped her soft hello, then stood back, watching.

"Yes, I'm Rachel. It's good to see you again."

Sharon asked about her health, and Rachel was honest, saying she had her last chemotherapy treatment, but she needed time to know if she was in remission. It had been quite an experience, but she'd felt the presence of Jesus so many times. Isaac's face lit up and his eyes sparkled. His voice grew steadily as he asked her question after question, both about cancer and about her faith.

Titus was mortified. He caught Susan's eye and signaled for help with an exaggerated eye roll. She understood immediately.

"You must be starved, Rachel. I made a veggie stromboli that will be ready in five minutes. Would you like to freshen up? The bathroom is on the left, through the living room."

"Oh, thank you. Perfect."

Titus was proud of his stepmother, her warm welcome and impeccable manners. But that father of his. All that enthusiasm about Jesus. It was embarrassing. Why couldn't he keep that voice down for two minutes?

Susan sidled up to Titus. "Is there anything she can't eat?"

"I don't think so."

"No restrictions?"

"I didn't notice any when we ate at a restaurant."

Rachel appeared, so pale, so delicate in her blue dress, the color accentuating the dark circles under those amazing eyes. Even her lips were pale, and no color graced her cheeks, the toll leukemia had taken on her vibrant health suddenly apparent. Titus felt a tenderness grow and blossom, felt the need to protect her from any discomfort.

He touched her back. She turned to look at him, a question in her eyes.

"You sure you're not too tired to sit at the table? We can bring your food to the recliner, and you can put your feet up."

She hesitated. She watched Susan open the oven door, retrieve a pan bearing a huge stromboli, the crust browned and puffy.

She leaned into him.

"If you don't mind, I'll take the recliner. I appreciate it," she whispered.

Titus led her to the chair, waited till she was comfortable, then explained to his family, who immediately brought a light throw, pillows, and a bed tray to rest on the arms of the recliner.

She sighed gratefully, and Titus felt a deep contentment.

He noticed Rachel picking at her food, cutting off mini pieces of stromboli, occasionally lifting a small section to her mouth. Alarmed, he could not take his eyes off her, but said nothing. She told him one of the side effects of chemotherapy was a loss of appetite, it wasn't the stromboli. "Please tell your mother it's delicious," she said, clearly embarrassed. He took her plate away and explained to Susan, who became flustered, keeping a thousand questions tucked away.

Over the course of the evening, Rachel told them more about her disease. It had been caught in the early stages, a chronic leukemia, which left unchecked would have developed into acute leukemia, often requiring a bone marrow transplant and having a much slimmer chance of full recovery. She was doing well now, but over the next two years she would be watched closely to see if the cancer would return. She spoke of hospital stays, the friendships she found in the staff, other cancer patients, caring doctors.

"The fear of infection is the hardest thing now. Fear actually lives with you, like an actual being, a ghost haunting your waking hours, giving you insomnia and nightmares," she said, in her soft, hoarse voice.

Isaac quickly spoke up.

"Susan is my second wife, Rachel. My first wife, Naomi, developed cancer after we were married. Nothing is promised. Nothing. We can't calculate our own footsteps, keeping ourselves free of suffering or heartache. All we can do is trust in God's goodness and do our best to follow His guidance in our lives."

Rachel nodded, a smile lighting her pale face.

"Yes."

Titus had the distinct sensation of being left out, being the outside looking in on a scene he couldn't comprehend.

His father went on and on, an appreciative audience the only thing he needed to become fired up. Embarrassed, Titus squirmed uncomfortably.

Susan served ice cream with chocolate syrup and changed the subject in the way only a mother can, tactfully getting her husband to quiet down without being too apparent.

After everyone was put to bed, Isaac and Susan retired themselves, creating a warm cocoon of privacy for Titus and Rachel, the time he had looked forward to all evening. He was not disappointed.

In her soft, hoarse voice, she shared more about her illness, the fear of its power, like a lurking beast in the marrow of her bones, waiting to unleash its deadly growth.

"It's when we're helpless, and know we are powerless, we place our trust in doctors, until they aren't sure of the best treatment. And then when every fiber of your being is in misery, your mouth infested with horrible sores, your hair falling out of your head in clumps, and you truly believe you are dying, that you strain toward God. It's like leaning in, leaning in to the real Jesus. The Bible story books with the portraits of a kind, bearded man in a white robe, with sandals and a shining light around him . . . that's all nice, but sometimes it's not until you're desperate that you realize He is real. He's right there beside your hospital bed, and you can just feel His enormous love."

Titus was quiet, long moments slipping past before he sighed.

"I just don't get it, Rachel."

"I know. And I'm so sorry for bringing it up."

"You know how I feel?"

"I do."

"The thing is, how can you say . . ."

He hesitated, the word "Jesus" stuck on his tongue.

"How can you say He loves you if it's His fault you're suffering in the first place?"

"It's all love, Titus. The pain is His love to us, making us grow into better human beings. Every single circumstance in our life is another step, another push to make us better, even if we refuse to see it, to see past our own selves."

"When He takes away a mother, kills her with cancer, that's love?"

"Yes."

"But it's not fair. Shouldn't love be fair?"

"Titus, you suffered, yes. But that has not diminished your potential to be the kindhearted person you are now. I can see how you are with your little siblings. Kayla? Is it Thayer?"

He nodded.

"You love them. You work hard for your father, which shows character. And more love. You have come through bitterness, but I believe you know and feel more than you're willing to admit."

The grandfather clock between the wide swath of windows ticked on, the large pendulum swinging back and forth behind the glass. A log fell in the fireplace, a volley of sparks shooting up the chimney. In the downstairs bedroom, Isaac coughed.

Titus cleared his throat.

"How can you be so positive?"

"I just told you. I had nothing else to lean on, so I gathered the fringes of my new faith, and it just kept multiplying. It's a great comfort when we're on the verge of a black abyss and know we might fall headlong, your body ravaged and weakened, lying in that bed with too bright lights, poison dripping into your veins to battle the monster in your bone marrow, clicks and ticking pounding into your head until you honestly believe you will go insane."

"Wow. I guess being smacked in the face by a tree is nothing."

"It is something, of course." She paused. "Can I touch your face? See what it feels like?"

He swallowed, bent toward the recliner from his chair, took her hand and guided it to the spot where the titanium plate was attached to the remains of his cheekbone. He felt the tips of her fingers exploring the hard surface, then sliding lower to touch the scar on his chin.

"You are patched up good and proper," she said, laughing softly. Then she said, without reserve, "You have a handsome face."

She laughed again. "When I saw you first, you were without bandages, your face puffy and swollen." She hesitated. "But I could hardly wait to see you after healing took place. I never doubted we'd meet someday, somehow."

"You were so sure?"

"I was."

And quite suddenly, Titus realized he was missing out on something he could not name. To come out on the other side of suffering as intense as she described, the bright light of her faith illuminating her spirit, was nothing short of amazing. People actually came through terrible circumstances, suffering beyond anything he could imagine, polished and gleaming from the inside.

She lay on that chair, so painfully thin she looked lost beneath the soft blanket, her face sharp with too much weight loss. But those wonderful eyes were alight with an inner glow, watching him, a sweet smile playing across her mouth. He was certain of some power greater than both of them watching over the room with the soft yellow light, the flickering firelight, the darkness through the windows lit from the faraway crescent moon hanging above the dark, jagged line of Douglas fir. There was a lifting of an unseen weight from his whole being. The feeling was so light, so smooth, it was like liquid in his spine, honey colored and glowing as it moved along his back, releasing tension and fear, melting bitterness as it prepared the way for something beyond his grasp.

CHAPTER 18

THE FOLLOWING WEEK HIS FEET BARELY TOUCHED THE EARTH. HE skimmed above reality, his head in the clouds, humming beneath his breath. Until he rolled the skidder, taking the turn too sharp on a flat surface. As usual, his father came crashing through the underbrush like some cranky grizzly, yelled, and hopped and waved his arms, while Titus calmly crawled out the side door, which was now the top, sat on the suspended tire, and told him to calm down.

Skidders were made to roll, with safety features built in for that purpose. No one tried to deliberately dump one over, but it was usually no big deal, not unless you were logging with Isaac Miller, the loudest person on earth.

"You know, Titus, you better get your head on straight. Mooning around all week, it's driving me nuts."

Titus sat on the tire, his heels propped against the closed door, and grinned down at his father.

"It's all good. We'll get it set up."

Which only served the purpose of sending him even closer to the edge.

From down at the loading area, the trucker and Jason heard the ruckus and drove to the spot, climbed out of the ATV, and burst out laughing. Titus saw Isaac wrestle with his fury. He managed to keep quiet, but turned on his heel and ground out, "I'm going to get the Cat."

Titus hopped down, shook his head.

"That was a dumb one. Should have watched where I was going."

"Well, don't tell the old man. He's hopping mad."

"He'll get over it."

By the time the skidder was back in running order, production for the day was cut in half, Isaac was frustrated, and nothing seemed to be going his way. He stood watching the clouds, his brow furrowed.

A thick layer of clouds had swallowed the weak sun, a boiling mass of pewter-colored storm clouds churning across the Bighorns, turning the forest dark and ominous. The wind picked up, bending treetops, hissing among fir trees.

Isaac stood, his feet planted solidly on uneven soil, his flannel shirt torn at the stretched seams, his huge arms crossed on his massive chest. His face showed the ravages of his work ethic, the constant push to exceed yesterday's limit, always aiming to raise the bar. His face was craggy, the surgery scars visible in the harsh light, but he was still a handsome man.

Titus reached up to touch his own face. What were the chances of his injury being so much like his father's? Would he follow his father in everything? Sometimes, he felt the boil of adrenaline in his veins. Felt as if he were indestructible, nothing too difficult, his heavy saw biting into timber with a satisfying accuracy, the thrill of yet another tree crashing through branches, snapping them like twigs.

It was in his blood now. When he'd started, he was thin, weak, a sapling. He'd felt the lump in his throat when a tree shivered before it fell, like the throes of death. Small brown leaves shaking their goodbye before the tree crashed to the forest floor, a sadness so deep he could not explain it welling up in his chest.

And here he was, loving it as much as his father did. He pushed away the thought of Rachel's disease, hoping he was not being blind to what could happen in the future. He could not change his feelings for her. The course had been set, and now he would run it.

He wondered at the great difference between Rachel and Trisha.

Sometimes, he still felt a limp kind of grief, the mourning for the times when he could go for days simply looking forward to seeing

Trisha at the singing. But with Rachel, there was a calming, steady joy, a looking forward to being her protector, her hero. Which he knew he was, and the whole earth sang with him. He heard it from the birds in the trees, in the wind sighing its primal song among pine needles.

He was in love with a sweet girl.

That night, they were glad to arrive home, the rectangles of light from the house a welcoming beacon. Temperatures dropping, the wind picking up, leaves and debris skittering across the yard, the cows' lowing uncomfortably in the pasture—all signs of a proper western storm.

Susan greeted them from the warmth of the kitchen, steam rising from the sink as she bent over it, plying the potato masher. Isaac plopped his lunch bucket on the counter, an arm across her back, then bent to kiss her cheek. She stopped, touched his chest with the easy familiarity of marriage, said, "Howdy doody."

They both grinned like idiots.

Titus thought, "Mushy," but looked forward to his own days of marriage. Isaac and Susan were far from perfect. In fact, some days he wondered if a union such as this was what you'd call a "good" marriage. Days when Susan was overwhelmed and Isaac as thoughtless as a stump. Or days when she missed her family and he was still as thoughtless as a stump.

"Mashed potatoes and stuffed pork chops, fresh bread," she announced. Isaac gave her a big smile and a thumbs-up, then yelled for Thayer to come sit on his lap. Thayer brought one of his many Matchbox cars and was lifted into a massive bear hug where he was kissed and cuddled till he yelled in protest. Kayla looked up from her coloring book, then went back to coloring.

"Hey, Kayla."

She looked up at Titus. "Want to color?"

"Sure. Which coloring book?"

"You pick."

He folded his tall frame into a small wooden chair, flipped through a coloring book until he found a horse, and began the process of making it brown. Kayla smiled at him, told him he barely fit in the chair.

He heard the wind hitting the side of the house, felt the pressure as it slammed against windows, shaking the glass in its teeth.

"Snow or rain?" he called out to Isaac.

"Probably both."

Titus nodded.

Sharon helped serve the meal, and they all sat, bowed their heads in silent grace, then looked around the table at the food and each other.

The lamplight spread a soft glow across the warm kitchen, the dishes catching the light, creating a gleam, the white tablecloth and shining utensils all thanks to Susan's housekeeping. The pork chops were stuffed with fragrant bread filling, the gravy thick and rich, perfect with the buttery mashed potatoes.

Conversation flowed freely. Sometimes Isaac and Susan both talked at once, neither of them listening to the other's words, but if they found this companionable, who was he to critique it? Sharon caught his eye, gave him a wink and a grin.

This was home, Titus thought. A place unlike any other. You could voice your opinion, take another one to examine, discard it or agree with it, you could scratch where it itched, or belch comfortably if necessity called for it. You could shed a tear, or laugh uproariously, tease someone and take teasing in return, say what you felt like saying, and if there were repercussions, you swallowed them without serious offense.

Susan was happy, she said, because her housecleaning was finished completely, having just done the basement. She was ready to host church services in two weeks, so this time there would be no last-minute panic.

Isaac said he didn't know why she spent so much time housecleaning twice a year.

Susan seemed to rise taller in her chair.

"I come from Lancaster County, where everyone does it. We're proud of our cleanliness."

"It isn't necessary, in my book," Isaac continued.

"It is in mine."

And that was that. Susan was meticulous about everything. His bedding was washed every week, hung on the line to dry in the stiff

Wyoming gale, the upstairs bathroom as clean as a whistle every Friday evening, his room dusted, swept, clothes put away, books placed back on the shelf, pens put away.

She liked housekeeping, she said. It was satisfying in an honest, rewarding way, the menial tasks of washing, cleaning, baking, and cooking.

The windows rattled with the bits of ice hurled against them by the force of the wind. Isaac looked up from his second helping of mashed potatoes, his eyes going to the dark windows.

"Jason said it'll be a doozy tonight, and he's right."

"Guess we better batten down the hatches in the barn," Titus said.

"Yeah. Want to come, Thayer?"

When they opened the door to step outside, the wind took their breath away, so Isaac carried Thayer, his face hidden against his shoulder, as they struggled to the barn. The wind caught the door and flung it out of their hands as they burst inside, breathless. But inside it was warm and still, the air heavy with the smell of grain and hay, slightly acidic from the trampled manure in the horse stalls.

As Titus brushed one of the powerful black Friesian-Standardbred cross horses, he started thinking about the night he and Sharon had encountered the troublemakers on the road. "Nobody ever have another run-in with that diesel pickup?" he asked Isaac.

"Haven't heard anything."

Isaac considered, then burst out in a raucous laugh.

"Guess they didn't plan on meeting up with a guy with a love life gone haywire driving that black monster, mad as a hornet."

Titus grinned, shook his head. "I sure was. I don't think I was ever as energized with pure anger. Made me mad, these dimwits driving around at night, thinking these dumb Amish are sitting ducks."

"Well, Titus, never be afraid of being human."

"What's that mean?"

"Just that. We aren't flawless saints. You should've called the sheriff as soon as you could to have someone go check on those idiots. But

I was actually proud of you for giving them a good scare, although I realize a lot of parents wouldn't be. Not in our culture."

Titus grinned. "We're loggers."

"I love you, man," Isaac said, giving him the old shoulder clap. Titus winced, wondering how many men gritted their teeth whenever he drew back for the old clap on the shoulder.

There was a new comradeship between them now, a man-to-man spirit of accomplishment, a hurdle cleared. Years of anger, of pain and genuine sorrow, had sent Isaac to his knees many times, but Titus did not need to know this just yet.

In the morning, the world outside was gray, low clouds like a blanket covering the Bighorn Mountains, the sun cloaked in the silent, strange cloud cover spitting hail and wind. Isaac yelled up the stairs, told Titus he could sleep in, no use going out in this stuff. Titus burrowed under the flannel sheets and comforter with a deep sigh of contentment.

At ten, there was voice mail on the machine from Simon Bontrager. Isaac listened to the steady voice of Rachel's father informing them of his daughter being taken to the hospital in Sheridan with double pneumonia.

Her condition was serious enough to be in isolation, but there was no immediate danger to her life. They would keep them informed, and as soon as she was in a room, they'd supply a phone number.

For a long time, Isaac sat in his office, the wood paneled walls covered with mule deer and whit tail horns, swimming in the tears springing from his compassionate soul.

Was this relationship fair to Titus? The boy had lost his mother to cancer. Was he going to have to lose his girlfriend, too?

Titus was hunched over a plate of scrambled eggs and bacon, his hair tousled, a hole in his clean white sock, appearing strangely vulnerable with the snarl of hair on the back of his head. Like a little boy.

"Voice mail for you, from Rachel's dad."

Titus looked up, alarmed.

"Is she okay?"

"You better go listen."

His chair was shoved back and he moved to the mudroom, the plate of scrambled eggs growing cold on the table.

With a heavy weight in his chest, he listened to the calm voice.

When it was over, he hit the seven, replaced the receiver, and sat staring at the wall, his thoughts spinning in a thousand directions. He felt lost, completely at sea, drowning with the weight of doubt. He should have known. The whole world was out to get him. His luck always ran out, leaving him to deal with whatever the devil could throw at him. He sat, seeing nothing, wallowing in the marshy swamp of self-pity, unable to free himself from the quicksand of his own making. Rain and ice sluiced against the windowpane, wind howled and moaned around the eaves, but he saw and heard nothing.

She might die alone in that hospital. Probably would. Panic ripped at the seams of his consciousness, tore away the bit of comprehensive thinking he had left. He could not weep, could not feel anything except the stone in his chest and erratic pounding of his heart.

Why? Why him? Why had he even met her?

He didn't know how long he sat there. He only knew he wanted to flee when he heard the outer door open.

He did not look up when his father's tall form filled the door.

Without speaking, his father sat with him. A mouse ran out from beneath the desk, dashed behind the waste can, then scurried along the wall till it reached the file cabinet. A loose shingle flapped on the roof.

"Titus."

"Shut up, Dat. For once in your life, just shut your mouth. You don't know anything. You don't know why or how or if she's going to get better. And I don't know if I can stand one word about your loving God." He rose to his feet, kicked the office chair, breathed hard with clenched fists.

"Titus."

"I don't want to hear it."

"Okay."

Titus slammed the door so hard one of the set of horns fell off the wall, rolled, and rocked to a standstill.

Isaac was heartsick. His spirit felt injured, raw with the pain of his son's words. Immediately, his thoughts went to Jesus, to the cross, to the foundation of his faith, so he closed his eyes, whispered, "Thy will be done. Help Titus. Keep knocking, Lord. Let me know if you have a job for me to do."

Then he felt his courage bolstered, reached into the drawer for the stack of monthly bills, and set to work, thanking God for the blessing of available funds. He wrote a sizable check for the fund set up for the three families from Oak Bluff and hummed his favorite hymn low under his breath.

Susan looked up in alarm as Titus burst through the mudroom door, kicked off his boots, and slammed upstairs. She held baby David too tightly, anxiety creasing the lines on her forehead.

"Titus?"

When no answer was forthcoming, she leaped to her feet, laid David in his crib, and went to find Isaac, bending her head to the fury of wind and ice. She found him quietly seated in his office, doing bookwork.

He answered her questions, said yes, this was a major setback for Titus.

"He doesn't have the cushion of his faith to fall back on."

Susan shook her head. "No, he doesn't. How can we ever bring him to the light?"

"We can't. It's not our job. Only the true power of the Holy Spirit can do the actual work."

There was a space of silence, where they sat, each to their own thoughts.

"The thing is, Susan, our children grow up in the church. They hear this explained every two weeks, but do they really get it? Did you? Did I?"

"No."

"And no for me. But we know right from wrong, we gather bits and pieces. It's a beginning, eventually. The milk of the Word. But I'm not sure Titus has even that."

Susan nodded. "What concerns me most is, he doesn't seem to believe in God at all. He wants to push away any thought of spiritual reasoning."

"He believes. Titus rebels because of his mother's death. Now Trisha is lumped into that, and we can only hope Rachel doesn't become one more blow."

"We can't run ahead of that boy fixing everything for him. It's like we anxiously remove obstacles so he doesn't have to suffer more. And it seems as if God places His own hurdles as fast as we remove them."

"Smart, Susan. I've never thought of that before. It's true."

FOR TWO DAYS, they checked their voice mail. Two days and nights of knowing nothing. The storm turned into a weeping deluge of rain and then the heavy gray clouds were broken by the rays of brilliant light behind them, turning red, then orange, and finally the clouds were scattered by the setting sun, creating a vista of golden October light, every tree and hedge, every blade of grass covered in a shimmering coat of ice.

The men did not leave the homestead, and Titus seldom left his room, creating an air of crackling anxiety wherever he went.

Without realizing, the whole family tiptoed around him, except for David, who bellowed with indignation whenever he felt hungry, or too full, or if he was bored.

On the evening of the second day, finally the name came up on the caller ID, leaving Isaac with bated breath as he listened to Simon's voice.

She was out of the woods. His voice bordered on weeping as he told them to come for a short visit. She was asking for Titus. The doctors were hopeful.

He found Titus in the barn, idly polishing a stirrup. He looked up when Isaac entered.

"There's a voice mail."

The stirrup was dropped and he was gone. Isaac resisted following him, but watched as the door to the office opened and Titus went to the house.

They couldn't make it that evening, but hired a driver for the following afternoon. Susan opted to stay, on account of the baby, so Isaac accompanied Titus, who begrudgingly accepted his offer to go.

SHE WAS SLEEPING, a pale wraith of a girl, dark circles under her eyes, lost in the blue hospital gown, attached to monitors and IV poles. Titus immediately felt his throat tighten. Isaac stood back, bewildered.

Both parents rose to their feet, faces lined with weariness, defeat hovering in their eyes.

"Come on in. She'll be awake when she knows you're here."

Titus had never felt more awkward or bereft of language. He walked quietly to the side of her bed, his hands at his side. Isaac didn't think he was aware of anyone else in the room, the way his eyes stayed on her face, with an expression so tender it hurt his throat.

"Rachel," her mother called softly.

Her heavy eyelids moved, She turned her head and saw him. Slowly, a smile spread across her face, and she reached out a hand toward him.

"Titus."

"Hello, Rachel."

"I'm so happy to see you."

"No oxygen?"

"Not anymore."

"That's good. You gave us a proper scare."

She shrugged. The gown fell sideways, revealing her prominent collarbone, her eyes large in her thin face.

"I'll be back to normal soon."

"I would love to stay."

She turned her head to her parents and Isaac.

"Do you want a break? Can he stay?"

Her mother looked doubtful. Her father looked at Isaac.

"Is it proper?" he asked.

"He can always step outside if need be."

"I wouldn't. The hospital might not allow it," her mother broke in. "I'll stay. Simon has to find us a better place to live until our house is built. It's why she got sick, the drafty little shack we live in."

Her voice was edged with the saltiness of a concerned mother, ready to fly into the face of adversity.

There was nothing for Titus to do but listen to his superiors. Mercifully, they all stepped out, saying they'd have coffee and a sandwich at the cafeteria, and he moved closer to her immediately. Her eyes found his and stayed.

"Titus."

"Rachel."

"I'm not sure it's fair to ask you to keep up this friendship. I'm telling you this to allow you time to think. I'm not well. They think I'm in remission, yes, but it could be two years until I am considered free. After that, there is no promise of the cancer never returning. You're taking a risk, you know. While I was so sick, I knew I had to be honest with you. I don't want to, but it's a sacrifice I have to make."

She hesitated.

"And here is the hardest part."

She looked at him, then her eyes fell away, her heavy lids falling over her unusual eyes. Her thin white fingers plucked at the white bedding. She shifted her weight, moved her feet beneath the covers.

"This might not seem proper, but you must know this."

Her eyes stayed hidden, but a tear appeared on the outside corner of her eyelash, trembled, and fell on the porcelain cheek.

"I . . . I may not be able to have children."

For a long moment Titus could not bring himself to speak. He shifted his weight from one foot to the other.

Finally, he said hoarsely, "No chance at all?"

"We can't know for sure."

Again, he could not find words of reassurance. To see her in this condition, to know this might be for the rest of his life if they married—a wife who had a compromised immune system, repeated hospital stays, drained finances, and no children to grace their house with childish lisps, perfect versions of themselves to love.

Rachel continued in small, quick sentences, grabbing for breath in between.

"You know the old saying: 'If you love something, set it free.'" She gave a small laugh. "It's what I'm attempting to do."

He considered her words. He moved away, put his hands behind his back, gazed out the fifth-floor window onto the rooftop below, the wind rustling the few leaves clinging to bare branches. Vehicles moved slowly, stopped at red lights, moved on after they turned green. Pedestrians strolled in the sun, scarves and hats keeping the October chill at bay. A dachshund on a leash scuttled along on his short legs.

He could not rein in his thoughts. The great disappointment steamrolled all his hopes flat, leaving his mind and spirit swept clean. Nothing was there to fill it up. He had never felt so empty in all his life. He was devoid of sympathy for her, devoid of one single emotion.

He watched the dachshund lift a leg, his owner waiting patiently. She was wearing a pink stocking cap, a long black coat covering jeans. And he thought of Trisha. Healthy, vibrant Trisha. As strong as he was, likely. Riding horses, the wind in her hair, laughing, her cheeks glowing with wholeness, the stamina to ride for miles.

Oh, Trisha, he groaned inwardly.

"Titus?"

He turned, but said nothing.

"Here is my biggest fear," she said. "I may as well add this one to the rest of the baggage I'm asking you to carry. Don't mistake sympathy for the real thing. Don't pity me and mistake it for love. I want us to be together, but only in total honesty."

"I don't know, Rachel," was all he could manage.

CHAPTER 19

Titus broke off the friendship about a month later. He told her he needed time to find out who he was, but more important, to understand why he could not fully believe in God the way other people did.

Her health had improved and her family was now living in the new house, safe from the ravages of the cold and snow. He had come on this Saturday evening to make known his decision.

As long as he lived, he would never forget the bravery in her eyes, the beginning of a delicate blush of color on her cheeks. He sat in the passenger seat being driven from her home with the uneasy knowledge of committing some unreasonable crime.

Trisha had taken up space in his mind again. She lived in his dreams and in his waking hours. He bought new shirts again, cut his hair with extreme precision, drove Sharon to the singing, and saw Trisha, alive and radiant at the singing table, just the way he'd pictured her. He took a long, fulfilling look. He watched her fill a glass of water, her arms tanned, round and supple, her dress and cape fitting her curves. He thought he might be able to win her away from Abram. Who was he? Some skinny loser. He felt himself filling up with resolve, like a balloon filled with helium, and devised a way to talk to Trisha. He started by joining a circle of conversation that included Duane and Millie and then gradually cut them out so that he was only speaking with her. It had been surprisingly easy, but he came away from that singing with the certainty he had committed another dastardly crime.

Every weekend, he spoke to her. She gave him a flat-eyed stare in the beginning, but as time went on, she warmed to his advances, even giggled and blushed sometimes.

Oak Bluffs? Simon Bontragers? Had he ever met Rachel?

When spring breezes broke through the ice and snow of winter, his thoughts were consumed, on fire with Trisha. The old obsession was back, alive and well. He stayed within conventional boundaries, never flirted too apparently, but was becoming quite suave in the way of getting her to notice him. In other words, he was having the time of his life, all while making life miserable for Abram.

Guilt became his daily adversity, the disquieting sense of having done something wrong. He tried covering it up with doing good deeds, like helping Susan in the garden without her asking, driving the pony with Kayla in the cart beside him, among many other acts of righteousness, but he always fell asleep with the uneasiness of having displeasure hanging over his head.

He couldn't be sure he was making much progress with Trisha, the way she hung on to Abram, but he would bide his time.

Sometimes he missed Rachel in a vague way, but he consoled himself by thinking they hadn't known each other all that long. He wished her well, hoped she really was still in remission.

He was not enjoying his logging that spring, either.

For some unknown reason, the mud and the whining of saws got on his nerves, made him jumpy, touchy. He swore at his father, made a crude gesture at Jason. He pushed all the wrong buttons for both men, until one day Jason told Isaac if he didn't straighten that kid out he was leaving, and he could look for another driver.

Isaac and Susan were having their own worries about Titus, the way he seemed to become steadily more arrogant, in your face. He'd taken to going away on Saturday evenings without telling either of his parents what he was up to, and got into endless arguments with Sharon.

Isaac put his head in his hands, said he was tired of praying.

Susan saw the dejected slump of his shoulders, her big powerful man reduced to this aging, discouraged bulk who seemed stripped of his usual power, his zest for living. A tender pity welled up in her, and she sat beside him on the couch, put her head on his back, her arms around him, and murmured words of encouragement. He took her into his arms and told her she was the best woman a man could ask for, and this was the truth.

Susan's father improved, was pronounced cancer free, was told he was one of the most fortunate ones, catching the disease in its early stages. Susan sang songs of praise all that week after learning the good news.

Rose called, screeched and shouted, sighed and exclaimed. Kay had had her first date. Oh, he was *hesslich* (very) cute. All the other girls would have taken him, but who did he pick? Her Kay. Kay was pretty, and she had such a good attitude, such a fun-loving personality. They were for real the cutest couple.

Susan duly congratulated her sister, laughed and exclaimed with her, and did not judge. Sisterhood was very different with two thousand miles between them, and love was a constant buffer for any ill thoughts.

"If you had a phone I'd send a picture, but you guys are so old-fashioned, living in the boonies," she crowed.

"Oh, come on, Rose. We're just fine without all that."

Kate was not doing well, her hope of Levi's return morphing into the reality that was sure to come. Her love turned into a terrible resentment, a thirst for revenge as she worked her long hours, her oldest daughter responsible for the care of her siblings.

This was hard for Susan. She could hear the bitterness, her voice caustic with hatred, an alarming turn of events. Who could have known this was possible?

Sweet Kate, so patient in the face of the worst barriers on her journey through life. Who could possibly judge her? She was, after all, merely a human being, in flesh and blood, prone to exhaustion and self-pity. Lonely, her responsibilities Herculean, surely the family and friends around her could lend an understanding ear. ·

There were days when the family drama wiped the slate of worries about Titus clean. He, too, was only human, and who could possibly place blame? Rachel, however, was a saint. To Susan's way of thinking, she had done it exactly right. She had set him free, allowing him time to figure everything out, which he was doing, whether he was aware of it or not.

The heart of summer increased the aura of unhappiness in Titus, so testy some days it was all Isaac could do to keep him on the job. On one particularly miserable day, after coming close to pinching Jason between a tree and the skidder, Isaac lost every ounce of patience, yelled and hopped, threatened to fire him, throwing every caution to the wind. He didn't care if he lost everything he'd gained in five years. He was done. Done tiptoeing around Titus, treating him like a fine china treasure, done worrying, praying, losing sleep, his wide-open eyes trained on the ceiling.

When Titus stalked off after giving him a venomous glare, he realized with frightening clarity that he didn't care. All Isaac remembered afterward was the garbled thinking, a mish-mash of thoughts, and a deep longing for help.

Take him, Lord. I'm done.

He felt like a failure as he told Susan, watching her face for signs of alarm, but she only nodded her head, then shook it sideways, saying perhaps now was the time for tough love.

Titus pouted for days, tried to harness his family to his cumbersome sledge of control, and was confused when no one seemed to care.

The discomfort of his unnamed weight grew as the summer wore on. He found a thick cloud of depression pressing him into his pillow upon awakening, his morning ritual doing little to dispel it. Wake up, brush teeth, wash face, comb hair, go downstairs.

What was the point?

He was on thin ice, he thought. Shaky ground. But he couldn't see why. He still went to church every two weeks, sat in with the row of young men, dressed in the same Sunday attire as everyone else, hoped he'd blend in without causing attention. He knew one thing, as he camouflaged the misery of his mind—his heart didn't come close to the goodness of his peers.

Then one day, out of nowhere, the thought of having committed the unpardonable sin struck him with the slicing of a sword.

He didn't know what that sin was, but he was absolutely certain that sometime in his life, he had done it. He broke out in a cold sweat. His chainsaw shook in his hand. He felt as if he were going on a dark journey, devoid of light. The importance of keeping this certain sin to himself overrode the desire to beg his father to explain what was happening to him. He distracted himself with a stack of old Zane Grey novels, then moved on to other westerns.

He trained colts for a neighboring ranch on Saturdays, went to the singings, and lost all hope of Trisha when she became engaged to Abram. She was married that summer, a ceremony he chose not to attend.

He thought of going to Lancaster to find a new girl to think about, but didn't want the responsibility of bringing her to Wyoming. Then he gave up on girls completely, told himself they were all stupid. He lived with the burr of his own guilt riding shotgun in his heart.

He'd reached a compromise of sorts with his father, working long, hard hours but remaining separated, a wall of hurt and unwanted negativity between them. He asked him one day about the unpardonable sin, hoping it was in a nonchalant manner, not in the burning, anxious way he felt in his heart.

"That's a tough one, Titus. Every single sin you can think of is washed away, so I'm not sure there is one. For someone sorry for their sins, the blood of Jesus covers anything. Sometimes I wonder if the only unforgivable sin is simply not believing in the power of the blood."

That was jarring. He didn't know if he really believed that.

He gave his father a wild-eyed look, then bent to the job of de-limbing a fallen log.

How could anyone ever believe all that Bible stuff for real? Did you have to know for sure, or did you merely go through life hoping it had happened in case you weren't good enough to get to Heaven by yourself, which, according to the ministers, no one was?

And still his load of guilt increased.

He remembered, then, the liquid gold sensation in his spine, back when he was with Rachel. That was something akin to peace, which he certainly had lost and wanted back, but had no idea how to acquire it.

He was increasingly curious about her, wondering what had become of her, but without any sense of urgency. Just a vague thought.

Then Sharon began dating a young man who lived only two miles away, an acquaintance from school, but one four years her senior. He'd been in eighth grade when she was in fourth, a spindly child with eyes like forget-me-nots and a stepmother from Pennsylvania. He had always been kind to her, throwing the ball too high so the first baseman couldn't reach and she'd be safe. Once, he'd given her a roll of Smarties candy when she scraped a knee. Danny Mast.

Isaac and Susan were thrilled, of course. The parents became best friends, enjoying neighborhood picnics together. It was perfect. But then, Sharon was blessed, had always been.

The good girl. He was the troublemaker.

He took to going on long hunts, hunting for any wild animal in season. Dressed in camouflage, he missed Darlene. She'd written a few times, with glowing reports of the husband, her life as a wife in the community, the acceptance so wonderful.

He thought of her solid form scrambling over rocks and down ravines, the great shot she'd been, tagging elk and mule deer along with the best of them. He wondered sometimes if he would have actually gone out into the great wide world and left his Amish heritage if she hadn't taken charge.

They were rough years. Rough for Amish standards.

As he sat on a grassy hillside, a forest behind him, binoculars to his eyes, he thought perhaps one of the few happy times in his life was the days spent with Rachel. But then, he couldn't blame himself, could he?

There was a herd of whitetails. A buck, that back one.

Adrenaline pumped in his veins, the old thrill of the hunt. Darlene would have a fit. They weren't two hundred yards away.

Whitetail season wasn't in yet, so he could only watch as they moved away with all the grace of a dancer.

He realized how much he still loved nature, how the rugged beauty around him spoke volumes. If all else failed, when the turmoil in his chest became too uncomfortable to tolerate, there was always the wide open sky, the jutting Bighorns vying for position, the endless array of fractured ravines, golden cliffs with the deep green pines, decorating it all like fine fabric.

He had no dreams of a young woman to share his life, no prospects of asking someone in all of Wyoming to be his friend and partner. He threw himself into his work, argued with his father on many occasions, then pouted for a day or so until it all blew over. Duane and Millie were married and had a little boy. Titus went to visit, answered Duane's dozens of probing questions, and was still uncertain about his place in the larger picture of life.

THE SUMMER AFTER Sharon was married, he decided the emptiness in him was the absence of faith. His doubts about God were turning him into a bitter, anxious, and reclusive human being, with nothing to keep him anchored to the Amish lifestyle. He asked to join the church, without Susan or Isaac knowing anything about it.

He was as unsure of God as he had ever been, but was positive there was an important element of his well-being missing. So he went to talk to the only one he imagined would care enough to help him out, Ezra Glick, one of the middle-aged ministers whose origins were from Holmes County, Ohio.

No longer a young, scared teenager, but a man in his own right, he simply rode his black horse over to his small, well-kept ranch and fired questions he knew were difficult to answer.

It was a warm summer evening, the chirping of birds in the Douglas firs creating a sense of peace.

Ezra was a short man, Titus towering over him, but he was wide of shoulder, sturdy and weathered, his blue eyes crinkling with good humor and kindness. Children played in the golden evening light, their sounds reminding him of his own home.

They spoke of logging, the weather, and cows.

Finally, Ezra gave him a piercing look.

"So, what is the real reason for your visit?"

Titus sat on a lawn chair, his elbows resting on his knees, his head bowed. For a long moment, he could not find the words he needed to explain himself. Finally, he took a long, cleansing breath, slowly shook his head, then lifted his face and slid back in his chair.

"I think the best way to describe it is, I have this sense of something being unexplainably wrong."

Ezra tugged at his graying beard, then leaned back and crossed his hands over his stomach, elbows propped on the arms of his chair. Titus noticed the crisscrossing blue veins bulging on the backs of his hands.

"Wrong?" he queried.

"Yeah. Like, something is off. Zig-zagging when it should be straight."

Ezra nodded.

"Well, Titus, you have a bit of age now. Older than most when they join."

"I realize that."

"But you finally feel that you're ready to trust Christ?"

Titus hesitated, then asked, "Does He exist for sure?"

Ezra sat up, his blue eyes alight, his voice edged with disbelief.

"Really, Titus?"

"Yes. Really. How does anyone know any of the stuff you preach is even true?"

His heartbeat increased, his nostrils dilated, his breathing became labored. When he spoke, his voice was laced with bitterness, edged with the power of his doubts. He became agitated, squirmed in his chair, picked at the cuticles of his thumb.

Quietly, Ezra spoke. "We don't."

"What do you mean by that?"

"We don't know."

Ezra watched the young man opposite, saw the tension in the thick shoulders, the lines of bitterness circling the fine, chiseled mouth.

His eyes crackled with sarcasm, his tone mocking, his handsome face twisted into a venomous version of what could have been. Ezra felt a shiver of real fear in the pit of his stomach and sent a quick plea for God's help.

"So, you just get up and preach this nonsense and admit you don't know whether you know it or not."

"Exactly."

"What? Come on."

"Our faith in God, in His Son, is far above that."

"Explain, please."

"Do you read your Bible?"

"Sometimes. Plus, we hear that stuff over and over every two weeks. It gets old."

To Titus's surprise, Ezra chuckled.

"Well, Titus, you have one thing going for you, and that's your complete honesty. You sure don't beat around the bush."

Titus made no comment.

"However, if you feel an emptiness inside, and you know you need something, then I think, in spite of everything, you're on the right track. If you want to begin instruction, we'll do all we can to help you."

"I thought a person is supposed to be born again first, and that bit of language takes me for a loop every time. What is it even supposed to mean?"

"Well, Nicodemus . . ."

"Don't mention that guy. What was he doing being a member of the Sanhedrin if he didn't know anything?"

And Ezra squinted his eyes, surprised by Titus's knowledge. He knew he was a smart boy. Too smart, in fact, to accept things at face value.

Ezra inhaled, exhaled slowly, called out a child's name, beckoning the girl over. When she came to stand beside him, he reached out to put his arm around her, and asked her to see if Mom had some iced tea in the fridge.

"Thirsty, Titus?"

"Don't change the subject."

"Alright, if you want me to continue, I will." He spoke then of the wealthy ruler's quest for truth, and the need for him to see the changing heart, the true transformation from the inside after accepting Christ.

"I don't get it. That part is too hard."

"You know what, Titus? You don't have to get it. Not right now. Not anytime soon. The important part is the fact you've come to see me, knowing there's an emptiness inside. That's taking one big step on a journey that will continue for the rest of your life."

Titus watched as the child brought a tray containing two tall glasses of tea, ice cubes clinking against the frosted glass.

He smiled at her as he took one, and she smiled back, in only the way a small child will do.

"Thanks, Karen," her father said.

They drank their tea in silence. Ezra sighed.

"My mother died when I was a child," Titus offered quietly.

"I know. That happens."

"But it happened to me."

"Are you any different than any of the thousands of children who have lost their mother in the past, and no doubt the thousands who will lose them in the future? It is sad, and no doubt, even more so than I can imagine, but life isn't all about you. What about your Dad, and Sharon? They were no different."

"Yes, they were. Sharon was . . . was very young, and my dad didn't love my mother the way I did. It was hard for me."

"I'm sure it was. But I find it hard to believe about your father."

"You don't know him."

"Titus, why do I feel the need to defend myself with every sentence?"

"I don't know. Guess it's your job."

"No, you're blaming me for things that don't apply to me at all."

"What? Come on."

"Yes. Troubled people blame others, creating a bubble of righteousness that is as deceiving as a venomous snake. Of course your father loved his first wife. I watched him suffer through the cancer with her. He gave his life for her if ever a man did. She had the best doctors, the best hospitals. He stopped at nothing. He sat in church soaking his handkerchief, this big, loud man reduced to a waterfall of tears. Don't accuse your father of not caring, as it simply isn't true."

"If he suffered, he recovered awful fast. He married that next year, and he shouldn't have."

"It was longer than that, Titus."

"He shouldn't have married again."

"But he did."

Confused, Titus searched Ezra's face, found the blue eyes piercing, the kindness still there, but an edge of truth that frightened him, somehow. Instantly, the old rebellion leaped into action.

"Mom died, okay? How could he love anyone else? Then, I lost Trisha, the only girl I ever wanted."

His voice rang like cold, hard steel, but he felt the beginning of a shudder, a shakiness inside, blinked, set his mouth in a firm line.

"Yes. Yes, you did. So that was your father's fault, too?"

"He started it. If he wouldn't be so loud and confident and full of himself, I would have had the nerve to ask Trisha. He takes away every ounce of my own confidence, makes me feel small and insignificant, like a horrible little worm."

He was sobbing now, his big frame shuddering as the dry, animal sounds came from his throat.

The words came between bouts of raw pain, the unleashing of years of pent-up emotion, kept in check by a large helping of pride and refusal to accept any responsibility. The story of Rachel capped a pouring of inner demons unlike anything Ezra had ever experienced.

The sun slid behind the jagged line of firs, creating a twilight of beauty and calm. The children went to the house, the twittering of the birds increased as they called their fledglings to the nests.

Finally, Ezra spoke.

"Titus, I care very much about you, but I feel a bit unqualified here. As you spoke, I felt the presence of the Holy Spirit, and I believe you would profit very much from a few sessions with a good, Christian counselor. This can be kept between you and me, and you may begin instruction class in the church whenever you're ready."

He sighed deeply.

"I believe in you, Titus. And I believe your feet were already traveling in the right direction, with Rachel's friendship. Your story contained ups and downs, but mostly you were in a good place when you were in her presence. Am I right?"

Titus wiped his face, sniffed, pocketed his crumpled everyday handkerchief. That broke Ezra's heart, the sight of the masculine red piece of cloth used for tough jobs like wiping blood from a logger's nicks and cuts, attaching it to protruding logs on trailers, not normally applied to a young man's tears.

He lifted red-rimmed eyes, swallowed, nodded.

"You broke up on account of her health."

"Pretty low, isn't it?" he croaked.

"Not necessarily. Just scared."

"Same thing."

Titus pondered this acknowledgement, then shook his head.

"So this . . . this boulder on my chest can be removed, maybe, if I, you know, sort of try out my wings?" he asked.

Ezra felt the overwhelming desire to yell hallelujah, but through his tears, he said softly, "Something like that."

CHAPTER 20

He began instruction class a few months later after speaking to a man situated in Oak Bluffs. The thought of Rachel was distant, but as the weeks went by, remembering the time with her became a sort of morning light, when dawn breaks through the night sky and illuminates objects you know were there in the dark. As the dawn turned to brighter light, images were revealed to him, images startling in their clarity.

Isaac and Susan were beyond grateful for his willingness to show he needed spiritual guidance, his father encouraging him with gruff words, words garbled by emotion. Susan told him of her happiness with tears being wiped delicately.

At one point the maelstrom of emotional baggage was too much, and he told his father he needed a week off, a week of camping and backpacking in the wilderness. Alone. Isaac's brow furrowed, disapproval clouded his vision, but he agreed, knowing he was in a better place than a year ago. Susan was distraught, Kayla jealous, saying she would go with him, but was quickly reminded of school.

On an overcast morning, he was dropped off at a national forest that stretched before him for hundreds of miles. He assured his father he'd meet other campers, hikers, hunters, he'd be absolutely fine. And Isaac said he didn't doubt it, but not to worry them, to be at this exact spot a week from this hour.

He shouldered his heavy pack, grinned, waved, and walked off, a spring in his step, exhilaration replacing the weeks of painful unpacking of past grievances, making neat bundles of every negative emotion, labeling them, acknowledging the work as he hurled them over imaginary cliffs into the water below.

The first day he walked until his legs practically gave way. The pack rubbed the space between his trouser belt and his hip, creating a chafed area so painful he was forced to make camp before dark.

Storm clouds moved in as he unsnapped his small tent and pellets of rain hammered his face as he quickly started a fire, crashing through underbrush to retrieve sizable chunks of firewood. He could feel the temperature dropping, the cold snapping against his cheeks, and welcomed the challenge. He beckoned the elements to throw everything out here, he felt ready to put all his survival skills to the test.

For a moment, he wished he had Wolf, the companion of his youth, another hurdle he'd had to label and hurl over the cliff. Why had he blamed his father for so much? How could he have done that?

Unexpectedly, joy shot through his veins, creating an unreasonable euphoria, a quickening of every glad thought he'd ever had. He stood with his hands to the fire, his face to the scudding clouds, the raindrops like jewels, piling blessings on his head.

God was still far away, a dot on the horizon, but He was there. He was in the low, wet clouds, hiding the mountain, in the damp leaves and underbrush, in the gray twilight, even if the image of Him was distant.

He found himself thinking of Him, a thought about Ezra and the quiet, wise, kind, and helpful men in Oak Bluffs. Another thought about Rachel, but that wasn't up to him.

He thought how he was an ugly fledgling eagle, perched on the edge of the rough pile of sticks and sharp twigs, lifting his wings to feel the strength, feel the weight of the bone and muscle, wonder if it was the right time to experience the air beneath the weight.

And he thought he might need help, God, if it's okay.

He laughed out loud as he burned his oatmeal over the too-hot fire. He was scraping the remains into the bushes when he thought if he kept this up, he'd run out of food. He ate a granola bar and thought of Susan's pot roast and mashed potatoes, went to the tent, and rolled himself in his sleeping bag. He listened to the rain on the tent and fell into a deep and restful slumber.

The rain had stopped by morning, the air gray and misty. All around him, the silence was complete, except for the faraway call of a lone bird. The firepit was black, soaked firewood useless, so he ate another granola bar, drank his share of water, and set to work packing his gear. He stepped out on the trail, invigorated, lean and hungry, the strength in his legs and shoulders rejuvenated.

All day, the sun remained hidden, low clouds blanketing its warm yellow light, trees dripping moisture as he walked. He skirted the edge of a cliff, found treetops surrounding a small body of water below, was tempted to make his way down, but decided against it. He climbed steadily upward, was winded by lunchtime, then sat against the base of a massive cottonwood to rest, glad to be rid of the cumbersome pack.

He walked on, reaching the summit of a long, tall ridge adjacent to the mountain, then walked downhill, the descent surprisingly hard to navigate. A hawk screeched a warning as he approached, and crows flapped their black wings, darting through trees like shadowy spirits.

The ground beneath his feet was spongy, wet with the previous rain, so he wasn't surprised when he saw a shimmering of water between trees.

Good. A perfect place to stay for the night. He'd filter lake water into his bottle, catch a few trout to cook for supper. He felt proud of his fishing skills, something he'd taught himself with Wolf by his side on the creek bank. He was six years old when he caught his first brook trout. His father hadn't known he was by the creek and he was scolded proudly, the brook trout disintegrating in value.

But those thoughts had to go, the kind, wise counselor advised. The pride in the trout could stay, but he knew his father was merely afraid of his tumbling into the creek.

He was elated at having found this perfect spot, smiling as he dropped his pack and scouted for dry firewood. He'd done it hundreds of times, scrabbling in hollow logs or beneath fallen trees for slivers of dry wood that would catch fire easily, so he felt confident of a hot meal, a comfortable fire.

He caught two trout in less than a half hour, cleaned them, and set the camping pan on the coals. He became aware of voices, of footsteps coming from the opposite direction he had come. He stiffened, straightened from his crouched position. He had no real fear, only a need to meet the person who was navigating the same trail.

It was a young boy, wearing a gray stocking cap and a denim coat, and was followed by a girl, also wearing a beanie . . . and a skirt. He never imagined anyone of the Amish faith, thought perhaps some Hutterite or Mennonite. As they drew closer, he thought he'd seen this young man somewhere, hadn't he?

A sting shot through him as the young man's eyes lit up in recognition.

"Titus Miller!" he shouted.

She stepped out from behind her brother and time stood still. He saw her, but could not comprehend the change in her face. Tanned, laughing, her eyes alight with the gladness mirrored in his own.

On they came, dropping their packs, hands extended.

"I can't believe it," was all he could think to say.

"Titus Miller," Dannie said again.

"It's me alright. Seriously, what are the chances?" He laughed.

Rachel became shy, then, seeing Titus after all this time, the aura of him as she remembered, but even better, unshaven, his eyes clear and liquid with the happiness coming from within.

Dannie told Titus they were on the trail as a personal challenge to Rachel. She was the one who had come up with the idea, a test to her strength. There had been months of exercising, walking, bike riding, lifting weights, her diet steadily monitored, plus monthly doctor visits for bloodwork, scans. And still the big question was unanswered.

"Here."

Titus became flustered and rolled a log over for her to be seated. She put up a hand, said she was perfectly comfortable on the ground, folded her frame into a cross-legged position, and smiled up at him.

He took in the glowing cheeks and sparkling eyes, and knew he was not worthy of beholding this budding of regained health.

He could never hope to have her, after copping out like the worst coward, thinking only of himself, knowing nothing of self-sacrifice or a faith in God.

They caught more fish, cleaned and fried them, sprinkled them liberally with salt. They boiled ramen noodles and then had granola with powdered milk for dessert. It was an absolute feast. He watched Rachel lift portions of steaming trout to her mouth, chewing with appreciation and asking for more. He felt only shame and remorse.

Why had he done that, left her stranded when she needed him most?

Dannie played the harmonica with the night sky surrounding them, the fire leaping and crackling to the yipping of faraway coyotes. They talked of rebuilding after the fire, of Rachel's journey to better health, the joys of hiking in true wilderness. Often, he found Rachel's eyes searching his face, but when he met her eyes, she always looked away, back to the flames.

When Dannie yawned and stretched, she made no move to join him, although her tent had been snapped, maneuvered, and pegged into place beside his. When he dove headlong through the opening, grunted, and rolled and rustled into his sleeping bag, they laughed out loud, then became silent, an awkward quiet like a stone between them.

"Titus, I . . ." she began.

Titus shook his head. "Don't."

"What?"

"I don't want you to talk about us."

Her eyes lowered. "I just wanted to ask if you found someone." Still as honest and straightforward as ever, he thought.

"It doesn't matter."

"It does matter to me."

"Why?"

She shrugged.

"I guess I have unrealistic expectations after all this time."

Titus stared into the fire, afraid to question her, afraid of his own assumption.

He took a deep breath. Dannie muttered to himself inside his tent.

"You still trying to find a comfortable position?" he called.

"Ain't no such thing," he shot back.

"That's right. You're in the wilderness now."

The spell was broken then, and they made small talk, intentionally skirting the issue of what might have been. An almost full moon climbed the night sky, the sprinkling of stars like grains of salt inside a gigantic black bowl. Water rippled quietly, marten and beaver gliding stealthily through the night, creating an otherworldly illusion.

She began again.

"Tell me about your life after we parted ways," she said softly.

"All of it?"

"Every bit."

So he did, beginning with the distinct knowledge he'd done something wrong, ending with the answer to his misery. He included the honesty about Trisha, the regret he had carried too long.

"And you never wondered about me?"

"Yes, of course I did." He paused. "My mother died of cancer, and I felt I couldn't go through that again."

For a long moment, she said nothing. Slowly, she looked around, found a thin twig, then poked at the fire, watching the flames shoot upward. Her lips moved, and he thought he saw the tiniest shaking of her head, as if she planned on saying something, then changed her mind.

"Rachel, I am a true coward. I may as well grow a comb and a wattle, then go around pecking in the dirt."

She looked up, gave a small laugh.

"And where does that piece of profound knowledge come from? You must have dredged it up from the bottom of some murky lake."

"A real man would have stood by your side, sick or healthy. The only thing I have is regret."

"That's a start.

He looked at her. "You can't mean that."

"But I do. I can also guarantee you, ninety percent of young men would do the same."

"But you deserve someone from the ten percent, someone who knows what sacrifice is, someone who is genuinely good from the inside."

"If you would have stayed, Titus, you would not have made it. Then it would have been far worse."

"How can you be so sure?"

"That you wouldn't have stayed in the long run? I was sick too often, too many frightening episodes. Immune systems are hard to understand. They have a mind of their own. I worked hard to regain strength, am still working hard, and what do I have? I don't know. I am in remission, but the big question mark in the sky is still there, fluorescent pink and pulsating in my head. Will I be cured? Will I live to an old age? No one knows."

Quickly, Titus said he could be killed next week, hit in the head by a falling tree. No one was promised a long and healthy life. That was why he should have stayed.

"Sounds as if you had to get this Trisha out of your head first, anyway."

"I'm embarrassed. Rachel, I'm so sorry."

"No. You had a good solid reason to . . . to do what you did."

As the night wore on, their speech became even more heartfelt, living one another's struggles and heartaches of the past year. Rachel had fallen to the lowest depths after contracting a stomach virus that put her in the hospital for a week, wanting to end it all somehow.

She said suffering was a way of life eventually, but nothing you could get used to, as miserable after a few years as you were in the beginning. After a length of time, you wondered if the struggle was worth the effort.

He asked if she still felt that way.

"No, of course not, Titus," she said, her eyes on his in the firelight.

Slowly, he got up, put a few more logs in the fire, then lowered himself beside her.

"We can talk better this way," he said, looking down at her.

"Don't come too close. I haven't bathed or changed clothes for four days. Only washed my face with cold water and brushed my teeth without toothpaste."

But she was laughing.

"So, what shall we do about us?" he asked.

"Get together, I guess."

"Did you just say that?"

"I did. We are together again. We were never apart in spirit. The image of your face was in my dreams, in my waking hours, on the walls of the hospital and in the darkest night. I believe God brought us together and I bargained with Him, although my mother said you shouldn't do that. I told God that if I become healthy, and He led us together again, well, then, obviously, it's meant to be."

"But I don't deserve this, Rachel. You know that. I deserted you in your greatest hour of need."

"I won't let you do it again. Really, I pushed you away. It was the hardest thing I have ever done, but I don't think it was wrong. Now tell me, did you really think of me sometimes?"

"I did. It's just that I was so busy untangling myself from the net of the wrongs I thought were done to me in the past, untangling myself from bitterness . . . and well, you know." He waved a hand. "It's just all like a mist. You have to let it evaporate, let it go."

He tried to get closer, wanting to hold her for only a bit, but she scooted away.

"Hu-uh. No, Titus. Nope."

They laughed together, but the happiness was deep and genuine, the future stretching before them, lit by a million stars.

They did not finish their hike together, but promised to be in touch at the end of the week. Titus walked on air, his feet carrying him away from her, the memory of those golden-green eyes misty with sleep, her hair tousled, shot through with blond streaks, her strong supple arms and legs, the way she squatted by the lake's edge to work the pump on her water bottle, safely filtering it, dropping in an iodine tablet, looking up at him, her eyes dancing.

He felt like a king, a prophet of old, an Indian chief bedecked in ceremonial garb. He snapped off twigs, flung them through thinning trees, he whooped and sang, spotted a grizzly on the side of a steep hill, digging in soft earth for grubs.

He didn't need food, didn't need a drink of water. Over and over, her tanned face, the skin glowing from being outdoors, her blunt way of speaking her mind without waiting for the proper time to say only half as much, the way most girls would. Perhaps she had learned life was too short for all that.

He thought of marriage, marriage without children, her leukemia returning . . . what would happen? And he realized with startling clarity: he did not need to know. Faith is not knowing, but a substance of believing the unknown. Nothing was promised, here on earth, but everything was blessed, all of it ordained by God, even pain and heartache.

Even pain.

Boy, that kind of took you for a loop, kind of took your breath away. What was there to fear? If God—and out here in the wilderness, God was very real—was merciful and allowed him to roll around in the sludge of his own self-pity until he saw who he really was, well then, all of life contained no real anxiety. You just had to keep your eyes centered straight on that invisible Power out there.

He whistled, flung another branch, watched it sail across a clear cut.

He sat on the bank of a bubbling creek that reminded him of her eyes and sang praises to the tune of "Red River Valley" that made no sense. He didn't care if the words were garbled with a lump in his throat. He carved "Rachel + Titus" in a pine tree, then apologized to the tree and patted it gently before moving on, taking off his stocking cap and slapping it against a huddle of brown leaves, scattering them over the trail. He imagined they were rice, or whatever it was English people threw at a newly married couple, imagined Rachel in her chaste bridal dress.

He wondered where they'd live. Would she give up her family at Oak Bluffs to accommodate his logging job? He knew suddenly how very much he wanted to stay with his father, how much he loved his job.

Well, this would be discussed, and the greatest part was she would not be afraid to speak her mind.

THE LAST NIGHT on the trail was absolute misery, with a wet snow carpeting the ground, his tent leaking, his rations completely gone. Too cold and played out to fish, he got up, shivered into every piece of clothing he brought, buckled on his wet pack, and stomped down the trail, his teeth chattering before he had a chance to work up a sweat, wondering, hoping Rachel and Dannie got out okay.

When he finally arrived at the logging site, the work truck had never been a more welcome sight, his father's big bulk pacing the perimeter, too anxious to sit still. When he spied Titus he whooped and yelled, came crashing down the hillside, almost knocking him over with the force of his hug.

He stood back, gripping his shoulders, took in the week's worth of stubble, the grime, the ripe smell, backed away and held his nose, Jason Luhrs bent over double laughing.

And Titus grinned, slapped at his father, and laughed out loud. Then he said if he didn't get something to eat soon, he'd have to crawl to the truck.

Home had never been sweeter. Susan's cooking was appreciated more than ever, and Thayer listened wide-eyed to his stories. He told his parents about Rachel and was met with Isaac's resounding "No!" and Susan's tears.

Prayers were answered, they said. Real prayers with real answers. And Titus nodded, his eyes soft with love and thanks.

SHE WAS DRESSED in a color that matched her eyes, waiting for him on the porch, her arms wrapped around her waist to stay warm. He could not walk fast enough, could not hold her hand long enough. She smiled and blushed. They said hello to her parents, chatted about ordinary things, before making their way to the basement where a huge stone fireplace was exuding a cheery warmth, a circular couch and coffee table providing a haven for them both.

They drank in the sight of each other, could hardly comprehend the fact they were here together, that she really was healthy.

She'd finished the hike with flying colors, the first place winner of her self-imposed grueling race, Dannie cheering her on.

And yes, she had carved their names in a pine tree. With a heart.

When he took her in his arms, he knew he had come home. He had retired from a long journey rife with misconception, stumbled over hurdles placed in his path by no one but his own stubborn will. To feel the warmth of this lovely girl, who had been victorious over much more than he could imagine, was a gift of mammoth proportions.

When he bent to place his lips on hers, she drew back, placed a finger on his perfect mouth.

"If it's okay, Titus, could we wait till marriage? I may be old-fashioned and stuffy, frightfully Victorian, but for some reason, it seems like the right thing to do. My parents are, well, they're pretty conservative, and gave me a real lecture. After all they have been through, the least I can do is respect their wishes."

Titus was taken aback and felt the shadow of the old rebellion, but quickly realized this was the beginning of giving his life to the one he loved. If God could give his only Son to save him, he could surely make this one small sacrifice.

That night, their hearts united, Titus knew without a doubt he had found his soulmate. Amazed at her forgiveness, for the fact he had deserted her, he found he was amazed at God's forgiveness as well. He could go to church now, and every sermon, every Scripture would be alive, ripe with meaning, feeding his soul until he could know his Lord and Savior personally.

She had wanted to die many times, she said, but always felt like she had some purpose, some reason to fight on. And he told her that surely that was God giving her the strength to keep fighting, and that perhaps his salvaging was one of the reasons. He'd been saved from a selfish life devoid of God's goodness, and God had used her selflessness to teach him.

She smiled deeply into his eyes and promised him that if the Lord allowed it, she'd always be there for him.

He smiled to himself, thinking how he probably wouldn't need to propose, she'd very likely beat him to it.

He could hardly wait for the rest of his life to begin.

THE END

ABOUT THE AUTHOR

LINDA BYLER WAS RAISED IN AN AMISH FAMILY AND IS AN ACTIVE member of the Amish church today. Growing up, Linda loved to read and write. In fact, she still does. Linda is well known within the Amish community as a columnist for a weekly Amish newspaper. She writes all her novels by hand in notebooks.

Linda is the author of several series of novels, all set among the Amish communities of North America: Lizzie Searches for Love, Sadie's Montana, Lancaster Burning, Hester's Hunt for Home, the Dakota Series, The Long Road Home, New Directions, and the Buggy Spoke Series for younger readers. Linda has also written several Christmas romances set among the Amish: *Mary's Christmas Goodbye, The Christmas Visitor, The Little Amish Matchmaker, Becky Meets Her Match, A Dog for Christmas, A Horse for Elsie, The More the Merrier, A Christmas Engagement,* and *Love Conquers All.* Linda has coauthored *Lizzie's Amish Cookbook: Favorite Recipes from Three Generations of Amish Cooks!, Amish Christmas Cookbook,* and *Amish Soups & Casseroles.*

OTHER BOOKS BY
LINDA BYLER

LIZZIE SEARCHES FOR LOVE SERIES

BOOK ONE   BOOK TWO   BOOK THREE

TRILOGY   COOKBOOK

SADIE'S MONTANA SERIES

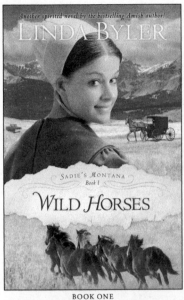

BOOK ONE

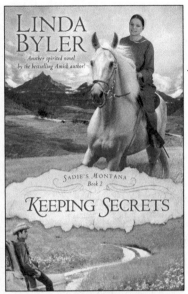

BOOK TWO

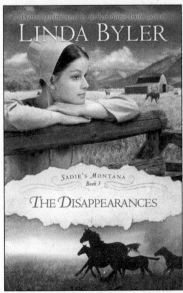

BOOK THREE

TRILOGY

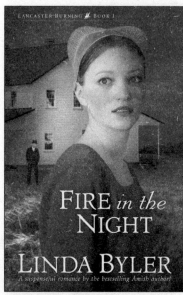

BOOK ONE

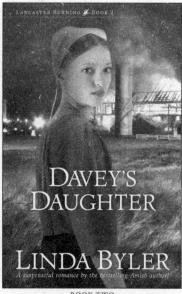

BOOK TWO

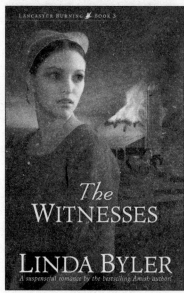

BOOK THREE

TRILOGY

HESTER'S HUNT FOR HOME SERIES

BOOK ONE

BOOK TWO

BOOK THREE

TRILOGY

The Dakota Series

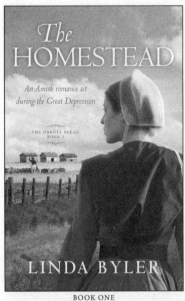

BOOK ONE

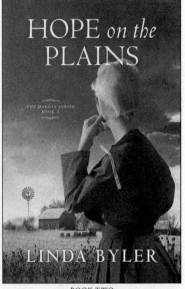

BOOK TWO

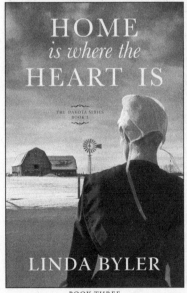

BOOK THREE

TRILOGY

Long Road Home Series

BOOK ONE

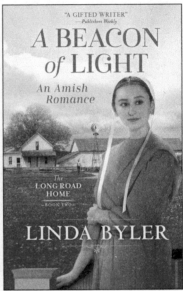

BOOK TWO

BOOK THREE

NEW DIRECTIONS SERIES

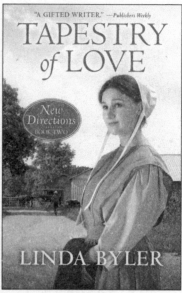

BOOK ONE

BOOK TWO

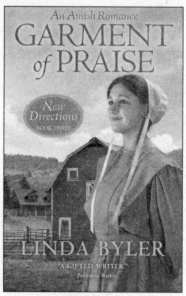

BOOK THREE

BUGGY SPOKE SERIES FOR YOUNG READERS

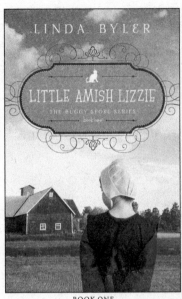

BOOK ONE

BOOK TWO

BOOK THREE

CHRISTMAS NOVELLAS

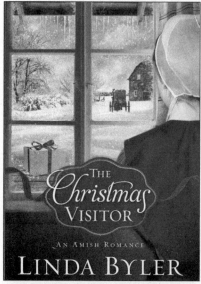

THE CHRISTMAS VISITOR

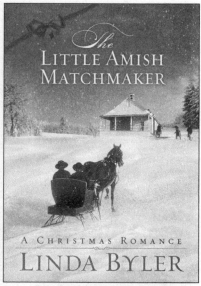

THE LITTLE AMISH MATCHMAKER

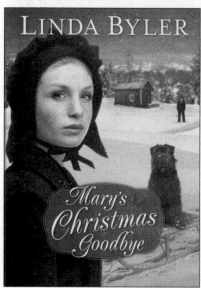

MARY'S CHRISTMAS GOODBYE

BECKY MEETS HER MATCH

A DOG FOR CHRISTMAS

A HORSE FOR ELSIE

THE MORE THE MERRIER

A CHRISTMAS ENGAGEMENT

LOVE CONQUERS ALL

Christmas Collections

AMISH CHRISTMAS ROMANCE COLLECTION

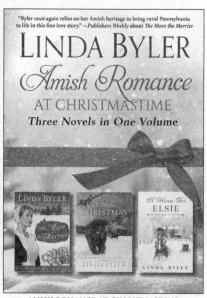

AMISH ROMANCE AT CHRISTMASTIME

STANDALONE NOVELS

THE HEALING

A SECOND CHANCE

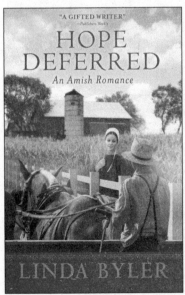

HOPE DEFERRED

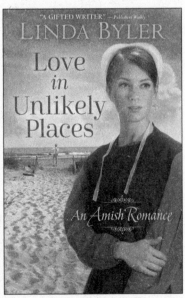

LOVE IN UNLIKELY PLACES